Stella Duffy was born in the UK and grew up in New Zealand. She now lives in London where she is an actor and comedian. She has published four short stories and is the author of a play, *The Hand*, for Gay Sweatshop, a one woman show, *The Tedious Predictability of Falling in Love*, and a novel, *Calendar Girl*, which is also published by Serpent's Tail.

Other Mask Noir titles

Alex Abella	*The Killing of the Saints*
Susan Wittig Albert	*Thyme of Death*
Gopal Baratham	*Moonrise, Sunset*
Nicholas Blincoe	*Acid Casuals*
Pieke Biermann	*Violetta*
Jerome Charyn	*Maria's Girls*
Didier Daeninckx	*Murder in Memoriam* *A Very Profitable War*
John Dale	*Dark Angel*
Stella Duffy	*Calendar Girl*
Graeme Gordon	*Bayswater Bodycount*
Maxim Jakubowski (ed)	*London Noir*
Elsa Lewin	*I, Anna*
Walter Mosley	*Black Betty* *Devil in a Blue Dress* *A Red Death* *White Butterfly*
Julian Rathbone	*Accidents Will Happen* *Sand Blind*
Derek Raymond	*The Crust on Its Uppers* *A State of Denmark*
Sam Reaves	*Fear Will Do It* *A Long Cold Fall*
Manuel Vazquez Montalban	*The Angst-Ridden Executive* *Murder in the Central Committee* *An Olympic Death* *Southern Seas*
David Veronese	*Jana*

WAVEWALKER

Stella Duffy

Library of Congress Catalog Card Number: 95–72967

A full catalogue record for this book can be obtained from
the British Library on request

The right of Stella Duffy to be acknowledged as the author
of this work has been asserted by her in accordance with
the Copyright, Designs and Patents Act 1988

Copyright © 1996 Stella Duffy

First published in 1996 by Serpent's Tail, 4 Blackstock Mews,
London N4, and 180 Varick Street, 10th floor, New York, NY
10014

Typeset in 10pt ITC Century Book by Intype Ltd., London
Printed in Great Britain by Cox & Wyman Ltd., Reading,
Berkshire

For my mother Peg, with love and gratitude.

Thanks to:

Shelley always, Yvonne of course, Doug Nunn, Tracy
Burns, Judy Burns and Hilary Burns for a North Californian imagination – with special thanks to Tracy for the
belt buckles and to Doug for Mendocino mendacity, The
Amsterdam Hotel, San Francisco – Caron Pascoe and
Isobel Middleton for compassionate reading, Vee for first
teaching me how to talk to women, Luke Sorba for the
non censoring, Rebecca Ellis for the icecream and most
especially Laurence O'Toole for editing a big lump of stuff
into readability.

CHAPTER 1

He looked down at the syringe in his hand. It was shaking. Both his hand and the syringe were shaking. Anita stirred in the bed, more worried by her dreams than by the man leaning over her. The only light was from the little oil lamp and it cast his shadow huge against the opposite wall. He grabbed her shoulder and turned her to face him.

"Anita?"

"Mmm? What? I'm asleep . . . What do you want?"

"I need to talk to you."

"Go to bed. We'll talk in the morning. I don't want to talk about this any more."

"You have to."

Anita sat up in bed.

"For God's sake, be quiet, you'll wake John."

"No, I won't."

"You will if you carry on with this shouting."

"Believe me, I won't."

"Look, there is nothing to discuss. Everything is settled, just as we said at dinner tonight. We will finalize all the details in the morning before you leave."

"I don't think you really want to do this."

"You're wrong. I know what I want to do, and I don't need you to tell me. Not any more. If you don't go, I'll wake John and tell him to get you out of here."

"You won't."

"That's it. I told you this morning that you will never

again tell me what to do. I want you to go! John ...
John?"

Anita rolled John over to her and opened her mouth to
scream when she felt the heavy, dead weight of her husband as it fell against her body. She would have
screamed, she was ready to scream, she'd opened her
mouth to scream, but the man was kissing her as he
pushed in the syringe and then the only sound was the
rushing of blood in her ears and then there was no sound
at all.

He burnt their bodies and the farmhouse for safety – and
a certain degree of malice, during the two days he'd
stayed with them, Anita had, despite his protestations,
refused to give him an extra blanket for his chilly room.

He'd known what he planned to do when he arrived, it
had just taken a couple of days to be sure it was really
necessary. It was.

What he didn't know was that every night Anita's daughter went to sleep crying for her mummy. The child that
lived with her aunt and visited Anita and John once a
month. Or had, until their deaths. But, despite her tears,
she knew him. She knew who he was.

wavewalker

I am walking between them. Walking between her and him. Holding him back and bringing her forward. Walking with silent steps that leave only prints in the sand, washed away by the next wave. There will be a time when the wave does not wash my print away. When I choose to make a mark that will be seen. I am both hunter and fisherwoman and bide my time until the moment. I will know when the time comes.

So will he.

CHAPTER 2

In 1970 Maxwell North was twenty-seven and dissatisfied. A promising career in any of several medical fields awaited him, but he couldn't quite bring himself to care enough to make the commitment any one of them would require. He'd been in full-time education from the age of four until he graduated from Harvard Medical School at twenty-three, he'd followed that with two years in a city hospital, another year studying specialist psychiatric methods (contributing two highly respected papers to the field), six months at an inner city rehabilitation centre dealing mainly with alcoholism and finally a year in his father's practice in a wealthy Boston suburb – where there were plenty of alcoholics and valium addicts available to use as guinea pigs. And he still had to make a decision. Several long and frustrating arguments with his father had created not so much a resolution as deadlock.

"How can I decide what it is I want to do. I'm only just starting to break into this field, and it's huge – I've got more choices than most people I know . . ."

"That ought to make it easier."

"But it doesn't, I'm twenty-seven. I've only discovered where my interests lie in the past couple of years."

"At your age I was married and your sister was two years old."

"Yes, I know Father, but the truth is that you didn't have all the options open to me, you were only ever going to go into general practice."

"Well, it's certainly been good enough to provide for this family, not to mention putting you and your sister through school!"

"I know. I'm not saying for a moment that you haven't done well, for yourself and for all of us, I just don't know if that's what I want – I don't want to settle down yet, general practice is good and stable and I think maybe I could do . . . "

"Better?"

"No. Just more. Maybe I could really achieve something . . ."

"Then go into research, you know I'm prepared to back you."

"But I want to research with people, I want a new type of clinic, I don't even know where to begin!"

"Maxwell, this conversation is, as always, going nowhere. Now listen to my proposal. Either go into general practice, I'm prepared to make you a partner, or help you set up your own practice, whichever you wish, or – if you really feel that you have 'more to do', then go into research, I'm sure I have some contacts who can help get you started. But I am not prepared to have this discussion any longer. Make a decision and let me know in the morning. Now if you'll excuse me, your mother has been waiting for over an hour and I'm not going to hold her up any longer. We will be dining out tonight, you can let me know your decision at breakfast. Goodnight."

"Goodnight, Sir."

Peter North strode out of the room, leaving his son staring after him.

"Yes Sir, no Sir, three bags full Sir, I'm twenty-seven but I'll do as you say Sir, after all, you hold the keys to the bank."

For as long as he could remember, Max's decisions had

been dictated by his father. While his older sister Diana had been allowed to do pretty much as she chose, within the bounds of taste decreed in the Ivy League code of ethics, he had been expected to follow exactly the same route as all the other men in his family. Good degree from Harvard Medical School followed by a career in medicine and, until the past couple of years, that hadn't been too hard. Max had been happy to accept the advantages his family had been able to offer and had looked forward to becoming a younger version of his father – a well-respected, solid citizen, settling down with a nice girl very like his own sister and breeding more little Norths to carry on the family tradition and inherit the family wealth. And then last year he'd met Anita. She'd come into his father's surgery with a sprained ankle acquired running away from the police at a demonstration. She was Dutch, young, pretty and stood for everything Maxwell and indeed, the entire North tradition, believed was corrupting the youth of America. She was even on the pill. He'd taken a brief medical history, strapped her ankle and, in a moment of uncharacteristic vigour, had asked her out to lunch. Anita had surprised herself by accepting. They became lovers. And it was through meeting Anita, very much a European free spirit, a "hippie", that Max had started to realize he had more choices than he'd previously thought. And with that new point of view came something he had never previously experienced – dissatisfaction. Twenty-seven was late for a teenage rebellion, but it was exactly what Max was having. Which is why, after this last argument resulting in his father's ultimatum, he didn't try to reason with him, one grown man to another, but finished a bottle of his father's best malt whiskey, packed a medium-sized hand-tooled leather suitcase, called Anita and booked two one-way tickets to Mexico. At twenty-seven, having never attended a peace rally or listened to Bob Dylan, Maxwell North ran away from home.

It wasn't exactly "On The Road". For a start they travelled first class and secondly, Max, having worked as a doctor for the past four years, had not only his own savings but also his extensive earning ability to fall back on. But for a boy with his background it was brave. In the first month they played – swimming, hiking, staying up late, eating and drinking. Max chose not to call his parents and face an argument, but sent home a postcard every three days. By the second month this had dwindled to once a week and by the third month to once a fortnight. After three months in Mexico, Anita was starting to get restless.

"This is fine for you Max, you have never had such an experience. But I get tired of teaching you all the time."

"Teaching me?"

"Yes, about books, thought, the world. I have come to America to learn more myself. I want to travel more, to see more. There are other people you should be talking to, not just me. We must move on. You should find work."

"But I'm learning how to relax!"

"Max, you're rich, you don't need to practise relaxing, you need to practise real life. A real job, meet some real people. Let's go to California."

"Oh right, where the real people are, huh? Hippies and drop-outs and draft-dodgers?"

"There are medical centres, community programmes. You should use your training, I thought you wanted to do research? Just because you came to your profession through your family, doesn't mean you should turn your back on it altogether. You like being a doctor don't you?"

"Yes. But I thought what I did, living off my family's

inherited wealth and all that, was immoral and would be wiped out entirely, come the revolution?"

"Don't worry, it will. But for now you can repay your debt to society by taking me to California. You might even find some lives to save and then you wouldn't need to feel so guilty."

"I don't feel guilty."

"Then you should."

"Really?"

"No, not really. Guilt is a wasted emotion. Loving me Max, is not. Come here and hold me."

The sex Anita and Max had was beyond Max's wildest dreams. He'd "made love" to a variety of other girls, friends of his sister, friends of the family, girls he'd studied with – nice, ordinary, middle-class girls – and with all of them it had been the same. Max took the lead, Max made love to them and they moaned in more or less the right places and were very polite once it was over. They may even have enjoyed themselves, but neither they nor Max were likely to be brave enough to talk about it and find out. With Anita however, Max discovered sex. And passion. And desire. And the satisfaction of that desire. Anita was not at all the kind of woman to lie back and wait until Max was finished. She demanded orgasm and pleasuring and she too took control. Their mutual body feasting was ardent and fierce. With Anita, Max learnt not only how to pleasure her, but also how to receive pleasure, to acknowledge that he had a right to pleasure. She taught him how to give in to her and allow himself to be taken. For a man brought up to be as in control as he was, the pleasure of yielding was something he'd never even known existed, let alone one he could hope to experience on a regular basis. For Max, brought up in the strict Boston overcoat of conformity and social regulations, sex with Anita was like running naked through Times Square with everyone applauding and cheering him on.

They made love on yet another sandy beach and then Anita turned to Max.

"Now, I'm tired of hitch-hiking, I think we should drive up to San Francisco – what sort of a car do you want to buy?"

CHAPTER 3

The day that Max and Anita drove into San Francisco was a shiny blue and yellow summer day and Max felt like his life was finally happening. He'd had his holiday and now this would be the real thing. Admittedly, San Francisco was all the clichés Max had expected it to be – but it was also more. More than just the drop-outs and druggies and draft-dodgers, it was also new and vibrant. And gentle. Brought up in the East Coast extremes of climate, he was used to the overwhelmingly hot summers and bitter cold winters. He didn't yet know what gentle, moderate summer warmth can do to a city – how it makes the public come out on the streets, how people go to bed much later on balmy nights, what it was like to lie awake at 3 a.m., covered only by thin cotton and listen to the sounds of music from open windows all along his street. Even San Francisco's winter charmed him eventually – the rain and mist muting sharp corners and colours, softening his environment just as it threatened to soften his character.

At first they just floated around the city, both discovering it for the first time. After a couple of weeks staying with Anita's friends – mostly foreign, mostly female – Anita decided it was time they found a place of their own and so, after several blazing telephone rows with his father, Max finally had backing to look for a home.

"All right. You want to buy a house? Then you get a job too. No money from this family is going to support you and that ... that girl, until you at least attempt to make some contribution yourself. You find a place, apply for a licence and set up a practice – then I'll decide just how much of this ludicrous endeavour I'm prepared to pay for!"

Max took to walking the hills and a month later, with a secret loan from both his mother and his sister, he put a deposit on a house on the edge of North Beach. It was halfway up a hill, cable cars rumbled by just a block away and on a clear day the view from the upstairs windows looked clean across the bay out to Alcatraz and Angel Island. The seven-bedroom, three-reception, turn-of-the-century house wasn't quite Pacific Heights but Max decided it would do for the time being and, as Anita pointed out, it wasn't as if they had to squat Alcatraz like the Indians either.

"We've already got so much more than they have Max. If they can make that barren plot into a home, then we can definitely make this work."

And it did need a lot of work, not least in making friends with the neighbours, but while the locals were suspicious of Max, his East Coast vowels not sitting especially well in their immigrant area, they quickly warmed to Anita, who had far more points of common ground with their new neighbours than he did. For the next two months while he was waiting for his records to be checked by the California State Medical Board, Max cleaned out the basement, turning it into a workshop and then stripped and painted woodwork, plastered old walls, replaced cracked windows and even started work on the garden, a paved courtyard with a thin strip of grass and two trees – a stunted lemon tree and a persimmon tree laden with early fruit. It was probably more physical labour than he'd ever encountered in his life. Anita supported them with two waitressing jobs and occasional work as a model at life-drawing classes. She'd been disappointed that Max hadn't found them a home over on Haight, but understood his reasoning that if they were to take money from his father, they'd have to at least have the house in a place his father would cope with.

"Anita, as far as he's concerned, it's bad enough that I'm choosing to live out here, with you, unmarried. We can at least live in a neighbourhood where he'll be able to bring himself to write the address on an envelope."

"Just as long as it's the envelope that sends the cheque, that's cool."

"I thought you hippies didn't care about money?"

"Don't be silly Max – it's the redistribution of wealth we care about. Not a case of not having money, more a case of who keeps the money. Didn't you read those books I gave you?"

"Not really. I couldn't get past the stuff about the rich being such bad guys. Didn't seem to ring true somehow . . ."

Max's confession led to a hose fight in the garden where he was watering the new wisteria and jasmine vines – a concession to Anita, as he'd refused to plant marijuana, she'd insisted he at least plant sweet-smelling flowers instead – and, when they were both dirty and wet, an hour or so of sex al fresco to steam them dry. Anita lay on top of him, her still wet hair clinging to his shoulders.

"See Max? I told you the best part about these huge old houses was that the neighbours never looked out of their back windows."

"Right hon, all except that old man who's been staring at your gorgeous behind for the past ten minutes."

Anita spun around and looked up, shouting at their new neighbour, an old Chinese man who probably couldn't understand a word anyway, even more so given that half her abuse was delivered in the northern Netherlands dialect favoured by her father in moments of anger. After that she and Max confined their lovemaking to the house – or nights when the San Francisco fog held back the moonlight.

The house was part of a plan Max and Anita had talked about over long nights in Mexico. A big place where friends could come to stay, Max would have a couple of rooms for his practice and Anita would use another for classes – she was an advanced yoga student herself and was hoping to learn massage in San Francisco.

"See honey, you will be able to be a doctor – a good doctor, help people physically and I will help them emotionally, holistically."

"But Anita, you haven't even been trained."

"What is training? How many years did it take you to learn to be a doctor?"

"Seven or eight."

"And how many of those years taught you what you really need to know?"

"All of them!"

"No honey, I mean really need to know. How to heal people, how to talk to the people who need you? Well?"

"I don't know, it was really just the last couple of years I suppose, actually working in the profession taught me more than most of what I learnt at school."

"Exactly. It's like any job. You learn by doing it. So will I. You'll see. People will come to us – the straight ones will trust you, the groovy ones will be interested in me – and we can both give them what they need."

"Even what they didn't know they needed, like you did with me?"

"Exactly. They'll come."

"To live with us?"

"Yes, we have to fill all these rooms you've spent so long cleaning and painting. Some will come just to see you or me. Others will want to live with us."

"But I want to live with you. Only you."

"So, yes. That may be what you want, but what you need is to live with other people – to make a new family to replace the one that is giving you such a hard time."

"A new family?"

"Certainly. You have the old family that you were born into and you love them because you must. And we will make a new family that you will love because you want to. You won't have to fight them. We'll make a good house that is warm and loving and they'll come. Just wait."

And come they did. Within a few short months Max began to very much like his life. He had his medical practice and was developing a good reputation in the district, he had his life with Anita where the sex was always great and the friendship warm, he even had the beginnings of a good response from his father who, while disapproving of everything his son was doing, was at least relieved that he was now a doctor – "Making use of all those family dollars invested in him." But best of all, he had what Anita called "their family" – the people who had come to ask about Anita's classes or maybe to him with a medical problem, but who had stayed, often at first just for dinner or a weekend and then, if they fitted, were what Anita referred to as "family people", she would invite them to stay for good. People contributed what they could, money if they were working, possessions and time if not. Max's income was steady and Anita always seemed to be able to lay her hands on enough food to fill the table whether it was for just her and Max or for another fifteen people. They developed a routine and after a while Max saw his new life take shape around him.

Anita had been making their decisions since Max met her, and he'd been happy to go along with it, trusting her judgment, and whoever she judged worthy of a room in their home, he was prepared to take on too. By the early spring of 1971 Max and Anita had seven new house-mates. And they did like Anita, were "interested in her" as she'd said they would be. Interested in her and reassured by Max. They felt safe with him – here was a fairly young man, very straight, very traditional, who was prepared to try a new kind of life. He made it easier for them to do so too, all living in the same house, all eating the same food. They listened to Max, who had somehow achieved a version of the traditional East Coast patriarch without ever having to set up a single college fund. In a way, his silence and Anita's constant decision-making on their behalf, gave him the status and not her. Made it seem as if she was working for him, for his ideas. His natural reticence was interpreted as taking time for thought, so that when he did speak out he was always listened to. Anita wasn't sure how it had happened, but after the first year of their relationship, the dynamic had very much changed and by bringing other people into their home she had actually brought this about. By set-ting Max up in his own large home, with his work and other people around him, she had unwittingly given him everything he'd been trained for from birth – status as "doctor", as healer, a position as the father, the head of their family. By accident Max became the "head of the family". By accident Anita brought about the birth of a traditional patriarch in her untraditional home. In July of that year she also gave birth to their daughter. The family was complete. Max became the father both figurative and literal and as his status grew, his family grew, all listening to him. All listening to every word he said. Maxwell North, father's boy and mixed up East Coast "rebel" had become Max, patriarch of a new type of "hippie commune". And he liked it. Very much.

CHAPTER 4

Saz Martin ran into the entrance of her South London council block and pushed the lift button. As usual, both up and down arrows lit up and she turned on the heel of her brand new Reeboks and began the five-storey running climb to her flat. She double-locked the door behind her, shed her sweaty running clothes and forced herself under a cold shower. Two minutes later the bathroom door opened and a sleepy voice called, "Coffee? Or is that too poisonous for the woman who insists on waking me at the crack of dawn, just to ensure her breakfast will be ready when she gets back from her five-mile run?"

"Almost seven miles actually. And that's not fair. I woke you at six in the morning because I couldn't bear to leave without caressing your gorgeous body once again."

"Naturally."

"If you couldn't get back to sleep and if you then felt obliged to make my breakfast – possibly as a form of repayment given that you've spent the past week in my flat – "

"I thought . . ."

"Not that I'm complaining," Saz continued to shout as the shampoo bubbles filled her ears. "In any case, your sense of Catholic guilt is hardly my responsibility."

"Do Presbyterian Asians have a sense of Catholic guilt?"

"I don't know my Bengali baby, you tell me."

She poked her head out from behind the red plastic shower curtain. "Pass me the towel."

"Is that politically sound?"

"Wanting a towel? No idea."

"Calling me your Bengali baby."

"Not sure. Probably not. Let's see, 'my' implies ownership . . . "

"Very un-PC."

"And 'baby' implies the diminutive, which at – what are you? Five foot nine?"

"Nine and a half."

"Certainly not diminutive then. Not sure about Bengali – purely descriptive I would have thought. You were born in Calcutta after all."

"Yeah, and brought up in Dunoon."

"Haggis honey, then?"

"You're hopeless!"

"Hopelessly in love or hopelessly politically unsound?"

"Both I expect."

"Well, I'll just have to trust you not to call the dyke police, won't I? Now, could I have that towel, or do you want me to pull you into the shower with me?"

Twenty-five minutes later Saz and Molly Steele, her new love of three months, emerged from the shower.

"Aaah! Saz! It's eight o'clock – I'm going to be late again!"

"Just tell them your girlfriend had an urgent problem and you had to give her a hand."

"Consultant paediatricians at Great Ormond Street tend not to understand the finer complexities of lesbian innuendo, babe."

"More fool them. You get dressed, I'll make the coffee."

Half an hour later Saz had her flat to herself and was musing on the tedious predictability of falling in love – yet again – while making the bed. She'd met Molly by accident, literally. Her sister's daughter had been run over and was transferred to Great Ormond Street when her local suburban hospital had discovered that the latest health cuts meant that the intensive care required for a seven-year-old girl with a fractured pelvis, two broken legs and all the other "minor" injuries associated with a car going 40 m.p.h. round the corner from her school, just wasn't available. However, once transferred to the London hospital it was Amy's parents who weren't available. At seven months pregnant, with three other small children and a twenty-mile drive to the hospital, Cassie and Tony couldn't make it to visit Amy more than once every two days. Which was where Aunty Saz came in, a flexible work schedule and open visiting hours meant that Amy was kept happy and, once Saz had met her niece's doctor, so was she. Molly was tall, friendly, intelligent and stunningly good-looking, her Asian mother and Scottish father having combined to give her flawless brown skin, jet black hair and perfectly almond-shaped pale green eyes. Saz was taken aback by her gorgeousness, but she was even more shocked when, having seen her almost every day at the hospital, she bumped into Molly at a club a few weeks later.

"Oh! Hi ... um, you're my niece's doctor ... Amy Wallace?"

"Yeah, right. Saz isn't it? I'm Molly."

"I know, Amy told me."

"You asked?"

"Just in passing."

"Right, she's a great little talker your niece."

"She is?"

"Yep. We have lots of chats. She's very fond of you."

"Mmm?"

"Though she, like your sister I might add, seems to think it would be nice if you were to settle down. Find a nice girl ... I believe that's the expression your mother used."

"I'll kill her!"

"No don't, you'd miss her terribly. And anyway, she's lovely. The whole family is. They're all very fond of you."

"Great. I think I need a drink. Do you fancy pushing through that crowd at the bar?"

"No."

"Oh, sorry, are you here with someone?"

"No, I don't fancy pushing through the crowd. I fancy you."

"Ah. And I thought I was upfront!"

"Well, I've found it doesn't pay to waste time."

"Right. So do you want a drink?"

"Answer's still no I'm afraid, I was just about to leave, I've got a very early start tomorrow, I mean today. Were you planning to come and see Amy later?"

"Yeah, about two."

"Good, I finish at three-thirty. Fancy meeting for a late lunch?"

"Sure, I'll be waiting at the bedside."

"I'll come and find you. Bye."

"Yeah ... oh, and Molly? I ... I fancy you too."

"I know."

"What ... how?"

"Your mum told me. See you tomorrow."

Saz and Molly had lunch, dinner and then, much later, breakfast. That was three months ago and things were still very rosy. They were having good sex, good talks and good times. Molly had already met most of Saz's family at the hospital and the two women were planning a late summer return trip to Molly's parents in Dunoon, via a couple of weeks at the Edinburgh Festival. Saz, after almost four years of self-imposed celibacy, was excited, enthralled and terrified. As she'd explained in a two-hour transatlantic phone call to her ex-girlfriend Caroline.

"Listen Carrie, it took me two years to get over you . . . "

"Perfectly understandable."

"And I don't want that again. God knows, I don't need another friend."

"You want a wife?"

"A fiancée will do."

"You can't afford the flash ring, Saz."

"No, but I can't afford the heartbreak either."

"Good luck. And when you find a lover that comes with a guarantee, let me know and I'll call the Serious Fraud Office for you."

Over three months later, while Saz still had no guarantee, she was starting to ease into believing in a future with Molly.

With the bed made, dishes done and flat tidied, Saz threw open her windows and took her coffee and letters out to the tiny balcony of her 1960s flat to enjoy what she could of the hazy spring sunshine. Looking down at the communal "garden" – an uneven rectangle of green, with a small dirt mound and a selection of rubbish from several of the more popular multinational takeaways in her local high street, she sighed and thought of Molly's rather more sophisticated home.

"London, I'm very fond of you, but you're a hell of a lot easier on the eye in Hampstead than Camberwell!"

She opened her mail – a red phone bill, a blue gas bill, two bank statements in varying shades of red and black, a postcard from Caroline in New York and another from her friends Helen and Judith in Naxos.

Hot, wet, delicious – and that's just us.

Hope love's young dream is still sleeping soundly!
H&J xxx

She took another sip of her strong coffee and opened
the last letter. Inside the A4 manilla envelope was an old
photo of a young man smiling directly at the camera,
a photocopied newspaper cutting and a small envelope.
Nothing else. Saz unfolded the cutting – "Eminent physician Maxwell North, arriving with his sculptress wife
Caron, at the Arts Ball." The picture showed a seriously
beautiful couple. He was obviously the same man as in
the photo, twenty years on, with shorter hair and no
smile. Still mystified, Saz took the cutting inside to
spread it out on the kitchen table, ripping the envelope
open as she walked.

"This is more like it!"

Inside the envelope were twenty crisp new fifty-pound
notes.

"Goody! That'll pay the phone bill!"

There was nothing more. No address, no letter, not
even a note to tell her where it came from. She checked
the big envelope and saw it had a WC1 postmark.

"No help there either. OK, I'll make some preliminary
enquiries about Mr and Mrs Beautiful North, pay the
phone bill and delight the bank with the rest. Manna
from WC1 – well done Saz, yet another morning's splen-
did work!"

She then turned the answerphone on, the telephone
off and went back to bed as she usually did, to sleep
soundly until one o'clock when she could enjoy the afternoon news in the glad knowledge that the horrifyingly
addictive morning television she so despised wouldn't
accidently catch her unawares and force her into a
wasted morning of minor soap stars and new breast-
feeding techniques.

CHAPTER 5

She didn't have to wait long for further information. By the time the alarm went off at 1 p.m., she had several messages, one from Molly which brought a smile to her lips and a good glow to certain other parts of her body.

"My right hand has a sense memory of your smooth hip imbedded in it. I can't seem to hold a pen properly – is there any known cure? I'll expect you for a consultation at my place tonight – I don't mind if we have to invest in some serious research. Enough of the doctor stuff – usual time, I'll be waiting for you. Bring beverage."

One from her bank manager which brought neither smile nor glow, and one other which made her even more excited than Molly's.

"Ms Martin, I hope you received the correspondence this morning. I would like to engage your services to investigate Dr North. This morning's cash payment is the first of many – as many as it takes. I will provide you with more material at the appropriate time. In the meantime I suggest you start gathering information on Dr North. He's a very interesting man."

Saz took the tape out of her answermachine and replaced it with a new one, she then played the answerphone tape again on her little portable tape recorder. The voice was that of a woman, indeterminate age and transatlantic. Either an American who'd lived in Britain – probably London – for a while or vice versa. Rounded vowels, rolled R's. Saz wrote NORTH and the date on an envelope, put the tape in it and placed the sealed envelope in the lockable drawer of her immaculately tidy writing desk. She then called Molly. While she was waiting for her to be paged, Saz looked through the article again. When Molly finally came to the phone Saz asked,

"Know anything about a Dr Maxwell North?"

"What's that got to do with my inability to hold a pen?"

"Nothing. Not much to do with my glorious, if somewhat over-rated, hip-bones either, but could have a lot to do with why I'm going to be late for dinner tonight."

"Oh?"

"Just answer the question Moll, Maxwell North – any ideas?"

"Upper class, rich, American . . . "

"Where from?"

"I don't know, Ivy League, East Coast, why?"

"Just a little project. How do I find out more about him?"

"Personally or professionally?"

"Both."

"His professional life is no problem, I can get you a career record from my old college, he's taught there a bit and they're always printing stuff about him in the college magazine."

"And personally?"

"That's more your department isn't it?"

"Mmm. When can you get the stuff for me?"

"If you get off the phone, I'll call the college librarian, she could probably fax a couple of biogs through by this evening."

"She'll get it for you just like that?"

"We have an understanding. Or should I say had?"

"The past tense wording 'had' sits easier with my ever-increasing belief in serial monogamy."

"Then 'had' it shall be."

"Great. You bring the biogs, I'll bring the wine."

"Wow Saz, your romantic charm stuns me."

"I try. One more thing, what sort of a doctor is he?"

"Psychiatrist. Sort of."

"What sort?"

Molly sighed and held the phone to her other ear, "Don't you know anything? You really should watch more daytime TV – he's famous."

"What for?"

"Loads of stuff – new techniques in group therapy, eliminating drug use – pretty controversial too, totally against shock therapy. Lots of things. Big research programme going on at the moment, he may even be going to take his work into the NHS – what's left of it. I mean after all, if . . . "

"Don't start on the NHS," Saz interrupted her, "I don't have time. Just tell me about North."

"Very big time. Famous for saving even more famous drug addicts. Written books about it."

"Being famous?"

Molly, slightly pissed off at having her usual diatribe about the shortcomings of the NHS cut short yet again, didn't feel like playing along.

"No. I've probably got some of his research findings at home if you really want to have a look."

"The biogs will do for a start. Oh . . . and don't tell your friendly librarian what you want them for."

"You're not the only clever one around here, Saz. I'd already decided I'd tell her I was applying for a job and I'd heard he might be on the interviewing panel. They get that all the time."

"And I thought you were hanging on my every word."

"I can listen and think at the same time, you know."

"So can I . . . I'm thinking of your long back, of running my index finger slowly down the gentle curve of your spine, just down to that little dip where it turns into your delicious bum . . . "

"Enough! I'm at work, woman!"

"You started it, and anyway, I've decided you should consider making love to me your life's work, slowly, delicately, with just a hint of passionate abandon . . . "

Saz hung up, blew an airborne kiss to Molly on the other side of the river and jumped into the shower for the second time that day. An hour later she was walking into Vogue House, dressed in her best nice young lady clothes, posing as an American TV researcher. Having successfully negotiated the terrors of reception (nineteen-year-old bimbette, head to toe in '70's retro-groove, thinner than strictly necessary – even in that business) she was in the library, poring through their files. Two hours later she had a looming headache and twenty-five photocopied sheets mentioning Maxwell North directly, in passing or in conjunction with his wife, and all in glowing terms such as "The handsome Dr North", "Maxwell North and his glamorous wife", "Lord So-and-so with his good friend Max North".

She left with a feeling of overkill. If nothing else, Maxwell North was well-loved by the society press. He seemed to have attended at least half of all the charity balls in London in the past five years, always looking immaculately well-groomed and often with his "glamorous" wife on his arm. Caron North was small, thin, blonde and pretty in that pale way the upper-class English so often have. In photos her prettiness was overshadowed by her husband's classic American good looks – tall, square-jawed, lots of hair and big, round, baby eyes. Saz loathed them both on sight.

That night, after a little light sex, dinner and more dessert-inspired fumbling, Saz and Molly sat semi-dressed on the balcony overlooking the heath. The late spring weather was unusually warm and Molly had insisted they take full advantage of it, dining half in the flat and half on the balcony. Saz was re-reading the fifth biography in the pile Molly had brought home for her.

"See, there's just something odd going on here – none of these seem to tell exactly the same story."

"It's probably the writers Saz, just making things up because it's easier than checking the facts. They always do that."

"Sometimes your cynicism astounds me. Anyway, I don't think it is laziness. This one is the very first article. Dated 1978. All the others, which were written between '81 and '92 say he first lived in Boston from 1966 to the early seventies, no specifics. Then he travelled for a while, came to Britain in 1973, studied more, married into her family dynasty and became the great man he is today."

"So?"

"Well, this first one says he left Harvard in '66, worked in Boston until 1970, travelled a bit, moved to San Francisco and then came to Britain. None of the others even mention San Francisco, yet that's where all his work started according to you."

"All I know is that he started the Process stuff in San Francisco. Anyway, from what I remember of his theories, one of the most important things is that the past doesn't matter. I know that when I saw him at a lecture once and this guy asked him about the start of his work, North practically bit his head off – in a very charming way of course, you must remember, Dr North is incredibly charming – but he made a big fuss about how the past isn't relevant and it's not where we've come from but where we're going, all the same old stuff really."

"So maybe he was lying about the past to these journalists?"

"That's hardly likely, it should be easy enough to check. Maybe he really doesn't think it matters. Or whoever wrote it just got the travelling years mixed up. What does it matter where he lived? I'd be more interested in the travelling stuff anyway, if I were you. God, I wish my parents had been rich enough to let me swan off round the world for a few years and 'find myself'! Do they say where he went?"

"Travelled the States mostly, and South America, South-east Asia."

"Draft-dodging?"

"Chronic asthma."

"Lucky him. Come on babe, let's go to bed, I'm not used to you having a working life – I didn't realize it leeched into dinner as well."

"That wasn't enough for you?"

"That, my darling, was just an appetizer – I want the main course."

"Eat more pasta then, there's some left on my plate. I'm sorry, I know I'm being boring about this ... I get really involved when I'm starting to find out about someone."

"Well, come and find out more about me – it's only been three months, I'm sure I must have some secrets you could unearth."

"Oh, all right, seeing as you're looking so good and so sexy and warm and soft and so very delicious ... "

Saz was silenced as Molly kissed her and pulled her to her feet, the two women walked back into the bedroom, laughing as they pulled off their clothes for the third time that night, easier this time as Saz hadn't bothered to do up the buttons on her shirt yet again. Now, in the dark of Molly's room, away from the prying eyes of those walking beneath the balcony and away from the clatter of plates and pasta their lovemaking was fierce. Saz ran her tongue around Molly's mouth, tasting the sweet garlic and cold wine mix, then down her neck to the line between her breasts, taste sensation turning to slight salt from the sweat they had created earlier, were recreating now. Their sex life was still full of the joys of first passion, only slightly muted by a beginner's working knowledge of each other's bodies. Molly had soon sussed how to make Saz come quickly and easily but was still fascinated by how else she could manage to tease and tempt her new lover into giving up the secrets of her flesh, secrets Saz didn't yet even know she possessed, secrets she was more than happy to look for and then surrender.

After they had made love, Saz left Molly sleeping soundly and went back out to the kitchen. She made herself a cup of sweet tea and spread all the papers out on the table, opened her notebook and began to compile a chronological list of North's life. As far as she could tell, Maxwell North had come from a very well-respected East Coast family, followed the traditional private school route to Harvard and then worked in a medical practice in Boston from 1966, moved to England in 1973, marrying the furnishing heiress Caron McKenna in 1978 when he was an eligible thirty-five and she a mere slip of a girl at twenty-one. He was always reported in glowing terms and had pioneered several new types of therapy, dealing primarily with personality disorders and various addictions. But what all of the articles and biographies had in common was that with the exception of the one written in 1978, all stated he had come to England in 1973. None of the others however, mentioned specifically what he was doing in the years 1970 to '73. Either he was travelling, as was reported in the 1978 article, or doing nothing worth mentioning in any of the others, and somehow, Saz just couldn't seem to believe that. "Oh no wonderboy, anybody who does so well for the rest of his career that he rates this much attention, can't possibly have gone quiet for almost four years. I think you probably were 'travelling' – and there's nothing wrong with that, especially not for a nice wealthy boy like you – so why not tell the journalists? Even Protestant work ethic allows a couple of years off for good behaviour – unless of course what you're not telling is that it wasn't good behaviour at all?"

Saz yawned and looked at Molly's old grandfather clock, surprised to see it was suddenly four in the morning.

"Bloody hell, time flies when you're digging through someone else's past. Fuck this, I think I've had enough of doctors for one night. Well, maybe not ALL doctors . . ."

And Saz went back to bed to wake Molly and inform her that they had a good few hours before she had to get up for her run and therefore Molly had every reason to be thankful. About fifteen minutes after she had been slowly but surely awakened, Molly expressed her gratitude with a long, shuddering yell that also disturbed her downstairs neighbour, who tossed in his sleep, muttering disparaging comments about the voracious appetites of the neighbourhood cats.

On the other side of London in South Kensington, Dr Maxwell North stretched uncomfortably in his sleep and reached out for a comforting hand, but of course his wife was not there. It was past five o'clock and Caron was upstairs in her small home studio, deciding which of the

razor sharp chisels she should use to cut into the fine
block of virgin ebony she had before her. She made her
choice and began the slow and painstaking job of
uncovering the figure she knew lay quiet beneath the
dark wood.

CHAPTER 6

Max liked his new life very much – too much. Within three months of the birth of his daughter Maxwell North was less of a patriarch and more of an overlord. The whole house was run according to his demands and the residents had no choice but to go along with him, either that or leave – not that anyone wanted to leave. Max was trusted completely. All the "family" loved him, believed in him. In September of 1971 Max was only twenty-eight but he already had the status of a man twice his age.

Since giving birth to their daughter Anita had much less time to organize the running of the house and Max was now helped by two "apprentices" – Paul and Michael. Paul was in his early thirties and had first come to the house with a drinking problem. But after a week of intensive, ten-hours-a-day therapy with Max, Paul was dry – and stayed that way. The debilitating alcoholism which had held him back for the past ten years was completely gone and Paul felt he owed Max his life. He probably did. Michael had been diagnosed as manic depressive as a teenager, had spent years in and out of therapy groups and psychiatric units, most of the time on tranquillizers and punctuating his more lucid moments with various attempts at suicide. Anita had met him at a psychic fair where he was screaming at a clairvoyant to help him speak to his dead grandmother. She brought him home and moved him in. He was quickly befriended by Max and gradually gave up both his tranquillizers and bouts of furious self-loathing. He too, attributed his "cure" directly to Max's influence. Everyone loved Max, everyone trusted Max – everyone that is, except Anita. Their easy-going relationship was becoming anything but.

"Max, it is stupid. You cannot teach these men to help you with your work – you're a doctor, you are trained. Paul grew up on a farm and Michael's only twenty-one and he's never had a proper job in his life!"

"You sound like my father, Anita. You're the one who told me that I could help people – why not them?"

"You are different. Your whole background led you to this – Michael can barely take care of himself, let alone take on the cases you want to give him."

"I'm giving him a little responsibility at a time – I'm training him."

"The House is not a medical school! Anyway, most of the people coming here aren't coming with medical problems, they're coming because they're unhappy, they have emotional problems, they need understanding . . . "

"And who better to understand them than someone who has been there himself?"

"Max, he's still there!"

"Not for long – I'm working with him."

"This is stupid. You aren't qualified to do any of this."

"Since when did qualifications matter, Anita?"

"Since you started messing around with people's minds!"

"I've never hurt anybody – I don't make them come to me. They like me, they trust me. They want to put their faith in me – where's the harm in that?"

"You're a doctor Max, an ordinary doctor – not a guru."

"No? They think I am. And if in the thought that I am the guru, there is the seed of that which cures them, why prevent it?"

"It's just words, and it's not honest."

"What's honesty? Paul believes I cured his addiction to alcohol. I know I didn't. All I did was talk to him for ten hours a day, when he wasn't yelling at me. I know he exhausted me and half the time I wanted to tell him just to pull himself together and I switched off because his interminable stories about his evil mother and wicked father bored me beyond belief, but at the end of it he believed I had helped him get straight. That's why he's dry now – he believes in me. Who am I to deny him that?"

"Why can't you tell him he cured himself?"

"He wouldn't believe it. Everybody wants a saviour. You were mine. Now I'm his."

"But I never let you believe that I was the reason you were happier. I made sure you knew you could do it all yourself. I gave you the opportunity to grow into yourself."

"What do you want, Anita? Thanks? OK – thank you. Can I get back to work now? I can't pander to your jealous fears all day – I have people waiting for me."

"I'm not jealous! I'm concerned."

"Sounds a lot like jealousy to me. Scared, hysterical, female jealousy."

"What?"

"You're tired, caring for a new baby, little Jasmine is taking it out of you."

"It's not just that, I'm worried . . . "

"Listen to me, it's perfectly normal. Your routine is disrupted – you're not so important any more, the House can function without you. That's OK – you don't need to control everything. That's why Paul and Michael are needed to help me now – to give you a break. Just enjoy the time with Jasmine. Take your own advice. Go with it. Relax."

Max picked up their screaming baby and laughed,

handing her to Anita and shutting the door behind him. Anita felt well and truly cornered – she had told Max how wonderful he was, she had encouraged him to take control, she had welcomed her pregnancy and had been happy to give up some of her other work to devote more time to Jasmine. She was stuck, trapped by her own creation.

In the next year things became even worse for Anita. Following a disagreement with Max over the handling of the group's finances, he hardly ever spoke to her about the House any more, insisting that she left all decision-making to himself, Paul and Michael. She felt isolated at home and missed having her work as a distraction. To the people in her neighbourhood she was now just another young mother and since Jasmine's birth getting around in the city was much harder, especially since Max almost always seemed to need the car and she had to travel by public transport or walk. The public transport never seemed to go where she wanted to go, and the hills, tiring enough for a girl from the lowlands, were hell with a baby to push around. She was lonely, frustrated and bored. Max, on the other hand, couldn't have been happier. He still had Anita as his lover and as she was so lonely he could spend time with her whenever he wanted, she would always welcome a distraction from the pressures of motherhood, but now he also had comrades. An only son, with a difficult relationship with his sister, his years at boarding school had not found him close men friends and his relationship with his father had never improved, but here he was living in one house which included five other men who believed in him absolutely, to whom he was father and big brother rolled into one. Max had grown into a very attractive man – physically and emotionally he was big, a strong man that both the women and men in the House felt they could depend on, could lean on. Max enjoyed and fostered their dependence, he played with them and was fully a part of their lives while also maintaining a degree of calm and aloofness that held him apart, allowing him to be both of the group and also completely in control of it. Partly it was because, while he would listen to the House members for hours, he very rarely told anyone other than Anita of his own thoughts and preoccupations, and partly it was that he always seemed to know the right things to say – on the few occasions when he chose to speak. Max created an aura around himself of strength and silence and understanding and, if this all-knowing strength was partly an illusion created by the House members' need to be fathered, then Max wasn't likely to tell them he was conning them, he enjoyed being in control far too much for that. If only Anita hadn't been so uncertain of his role, his life would have been perfect. After a lot of discussion with Paul and Michael, Max decided he would have to deal with the problem that was their relationship and Anita was asked to go through the Process.

She was startled to find that in the time she'd become a mother and had been more or less excluded from Max's work, what had started out as an idea for talking to people as therapy, a way of gentle discussion, had become a whole technique – and what's more everyone in the House had now done it and was certain she'd benefit from it. Michael and Paul put a concerted effort into persuading her to try it and the others in the House assured her that while she took a couple of days off to undergo the Process, they'd be more than capable of looking after Jasmine.

"It'll be great Anita – now that Jasmine isn't so

demanding of your time, you need to get back into the rhythm of the House. Into the same rhythm as all of us."

"Yeah, sure you're uncertain, but it isn't really that big a deal, and you'll feel great afterwards. Everyone always does."

"We'll look after her, it's about time the rest of us took on more childcare anyway."

"Go on Anita – surely you're not scared?"

"You've been feeling left out for a while now, this is just what you need."

"It'll make things easier for you and Max."

"We know we've become a little elitist – you need to feel part of things again. Please?"

"Please?"

"Please?"

Since he'd devised the Process in his work with Paul and later with Michael, Max had insisted that anyone wanting to "make the change" as he put it, had to ask for it to happen. The others living in the House had done so and now Anita was worn down both by them and by her own desires – to join in, be part of her own home again, be part of Max again. A week after it was first mentioned, she went to find Max in the back room that was now his study.

"I'm ready to do it Max."

"Do what?"

"What do you think?"

"I don't know. You tell me."

"Ah – I'm ready to do the Process."

"Are you? Sounds like you've just been persuaded to do it."

"Well . . . yes . . . in a way."

"Then you're not ready."

"No, I mean I've been persuaded that it's a good idea."

"Have you?"

"I think so."

"Not good enough."

"For God's sake Max, what do you want?"

Max stood up from his desk and looked out at the view beneath him, the city lights gleaming up and down the people-covered hills surrounding them. With his back to her he spoke.

"I don't want anything Anita, you've come to me."

"This is impossible!"

"Nothing's impossible remember?"

"Talk to me Max. I'm your lover, your partner, we are the parents of a child!"

"Yes Anita, I know that."

"You're making me crazy."

Max turned from the window and smiled at her.

"No. I'm not making you feel anything Anita. You are responsible for your own feelings. Now, what is it that you think you are allowing yourself to get so upset about?"

"Why didn't you tell me about the Process? Why did I have to find out about it from Michael? Why am I the last one?"

"You did know about it. You live here. How could you not know about it?"

"Not in any detail. Why didn't you tell me?"

"No reason. You just never asked before. You weren't doing the Process, so you didn't need to know about it."

"Well I'm asking now."

"Are you asking to be told about the Process or are you asking to do it? Because there's no way I can tell you about it, it isn't a lecture to be reported, if you want to know about it, you will have to go through it."

"OK."

"OK what?"

"Fuck it!"

Anita slammed Max's desk.

"Fuck you Max. Fuck you and the damn Process!"

Max came towards her from the window and held her tight, pressing her into his chest. She was trembling with rage and frustration and he kept his voice light and gentle, speaking quietly and calmly,

"Ask me Anita. You have to ask to do it."

"Max – oh God . . . I can't, this is stupid, I don't know . . . I mean . . . how?"

"Ask, Anita."

"Max, can I do the Process?"

Max kissed her forehead.

"Of course, my darling. We'll start on Monday."

CHAPTER 7

After sitting alone in the room for an hour, Anita decided she could stand it no longer. Max had left her in the "Process Room" as he now called the large first floor room and told her to just sit and wait – he would be a while. She waited, and she waited, and it was starting to drive her crazy.

The room had been whitewashed in the summer and instead of putting back the bookcases and desk, Max had moved them into his practice office and left only one armchair in their place. No books, no pictures and, as the room was at the side of the house, just a view of the wall of the next door house, a mere four feet away. That wall had also been painted white. Anita paced the room and, finally deciding that perhaps Max had actually forgotten about her, went to the door. It was locked. She tried calling but there was no response. After a couple of minutes she gave up and went back to her chair. The house was still and quiet, it almost sounded as if everyone had gone out for the day. Anita could do nothing but sit and wait. As she had no watch, she could only tell the passage of time by watching the sun move around the room, lighting up dust-moted beams as a kind of reverse sundial. Max had taken her to the study at nine in the morning, now the sun was just about gone from the room which meant it had to be well past twelve. She figured she'd been there for at least three hours when she realized a strange thing. Four years of living in the States and talking to English-speaking people meant that, unless she was writing to her parents or talking to her sister who now lived with her American husband in Idaho, she almost always thought in English – she even dreamt in English – but here she was, after three hours with only her own company and she was thinking in Dutch. And not merely the Dutch she'd learnt in school, but the very specific dialect of their region. And the now foreign words were bringing with them a whole raft of memories she'd gladly left behind when she left home at sixteen. Her father's authoritarianism, her mother's unquestioning religious belief, how she broke her little finger skating when she was twelve, her little brother's funeral, the fights with her sister Julia, failing her French exam when she was fifteen, fighting with her mother about going to church ... her little brother's funeral.

Anita's brother had died when he was six and she was eight. It was Christmas Eve when his perfectly normal bout of childhood flu had suddenly developed complications, the flu became pneumonia and Francis died. She had been the oldest child. There was herself, then Francis and then Julia the baby, barely four years old. Anita not only lost her brother, she also lost her best friend and playmate. But worse than that, she lost her mother. Anita's mother had adored little Francis, a classic case of two sweet daughters but only one perfect son, and no matter what she did in future years, Anita could never live up to her mother's memories of Francis, the perfect boy. Her mother turned to the church in her grief, Anita's father took care of little Julia and at eight, Anita was left to grieve alone. Which she did – in a way. She dealt with her grief by pretending that Francis had never existed, at least in her own mind. Much as her mother talked about him, praised him, made an angel of her son,

Anita discarded her memories of their shared childhood until she was just left with the single image of her little brother's funeral. An image she'd never admitted for more than five minutes if she could help herself, even more so now since her own child had been born. An image she'd been too scared ever to look at for long. Too scared because she was aware enough to know that she might not be able to cope with the pain it would bring. But here she was, locked into Max's study, with nothing to do but think to herself and all she could see in her head was the double image of Francis lying in the hospital bed and Francis lying in his coffin. All she could see was the hot, fevered Francis and the cold, grey Francis. All she could see was her baby brother, dead.

When Max came into the room an hour later he found Anita curled up and sobbing in the corner. When he picked her up and held her to him she cried even more and, about half an hour later, when his comforting had quietened her and he tried to get her to tell him why she was so upset, Anita could hardly speak – at least not in English. Her words came out in a tumble of standard Dutch, regional dialect and heavily accented English. Max let her talk even though he barely understood even half of it, nodding encouragingly, making appropriate soothing noises and stroking her forehead.

When she woke up Anita was lying in their bed and Max was sitting beside her.

"Hello."

"Hi."

"Can you talk about it now?"

"I . . . just had no idea . . . I hadn't thought about him for so long . . . "

"You hadn't grieved, Anita."

"But it was years and years ago."

"It still made you cry."

"Does it happen to everyone?"

"Yes. Sometimes it's easier, sometimes it's much worse. Often it takes a lot longer. You were only there for three hours until it all came out. Michael took about ten. And that was on his second Process. It depends how deeply it's buried."

"I didn't think I had buried it. I told you all about Francis."

"Yes. You talked about him. I know what he looked like, what he enjoyed doing, what your mother thought about him, how your sister missed him. You told me about him like you must have told a hundred other people, the day you told me you gave me a rehearsed speech. You must have been telling people about when your brother died for years, you're good at talking about it, but what about the feelings there? I had no idea at all what losing him did to you."

"No, I guess I didn't either. Is that it?"

"Pretty much."

"What? You lock me in a room, I cry and it's all over?"

"That's the very basic facts. I leave you with no external stimulus. You have only yourself to talk to. After some time you actually start to listen to yourself as well. And you tell yourself those things you've been ignoring for years. You actually listen to yourself."

"And then?"

"Well, now we can talk about it if you want. Or not. It's up to you. What matters is that you've acknowledged your truth. The thing you were hiding from. You may not feel it now, but in a couple of days you'll start to feel a change. A lightness."

"So what's your role?"

"Anita, most people aren't as together as you. I expect

now that you have listened to yourself, you'll be able to deal with it. Other people need to talk about it to someone else."

"You?"

"Sometimes. Or anyone could do the trick if they can listen. Or maybe it isn't just about telling the story, maybe they need to address any issues it brings up – you know, behavioural changes, that sort of thing. And there may be other things they haven't looked at yet. They might need to do the Process again in a few months' time to get more out."

"Will I?"

"That's up to you. You'll know if you need more."

"How?"

"You'll know. Trust me."

"Have the others?"

"Paul has. Michael's done it several times. I worry that he wants to do it too much. Perhaps he's becoming dependent on it."

"How many times?"

"Ten."

Anita shivered and pulled the bedclothes tighter around her.

"Ten? He's been through this pain ten times?"

"He wanted to."

"But Max, you're not a psychiatrist."

"No. And I'm glad I'm not. Do you know how long traditional medicine would take to get these results – to uncover these sorts of truths? Years and years. Most people haven't got that sort of time. Or money. And it's not just time, sometimes they use medication to get at the truth – this is only people, Anita. People listening to themselves. People telling themselves what's wrong with them. People changing themselves."

"But what if they get it wrong?"

"They don't. You didn't."

"Well, no. But I've only done it once. What else might I come up with? What if someone comes up with something you can't cope with?"

"It hasn't happened Anita."

"But it might."

"It won't. How can anyone, now living and thriving, or even just living and barely getting through ... how can anyone who is at least coping, come up with anything that they couldn't deal with? The brain does it of its own accord. Trust Anita. Trust yourself. This is such an amazing thing, this Process. You must become your own God. Everything else is irrelevant. You give yourself what you need. You tell yourself what you need to know. You just need to be quiet and listen. That's all. It's so simple and so easy and so good. This will do for people what Freud hoped to and never achieved. This will set people free."

"How can you be so sure Max?"

"Knowledge is its own guarantee. Don't argue any more. You're tired, you've had a very long day. Go to sleep for a couple of hours and I'll wake you when it's time to put Jasmine to bed, she'll be glad to see you and it will be good for you to be with her for a while."

Max leant over to kiss Anita.

"Goodnight my darling. I'm glad you've come to us."

"I've come to you Max – for you, for you and me. To try to make us work."

"Well, I'm glad anyway, now sleep."

Two weeks later Michael killed himself.

w a v e w a l k e r

I have a friend who knew him once.

I was told about the past. Told that which cannot be
told.
Which, even in the telling, is a hurting.

And now I know.
It is fate and karma and right that I know.
That I do what I will do.

Sometimes, beside a sandcastle, you also build a
channel to take the water away, to save that castle
from the sea.
But there is no channel deep enough to hold the sea back
always.

The seventh wave is coming.
The wave which holds the flood and he doesn't even
care.
Because he doesn't know.
Yet.

CHAPTER 8

Saz's next move was to check up on Maxwell North's practice. This was easily arranged. Dr North was so well-known that at least half the pop stars in London had at one time attended his clinics, he himself had appeared either alone or with his latest "clean" celebrity success on most of the daytime talk shows and Saz, rapidly brought up to date by Molly, was now, like most of the British Sunday Newspaper Reading Public, well aware that he held monthly open meetings – not at his Harley Street offices of course, he had to make the rich and famous feel they were paying for something – but at a public hall in Bloomsbury. Saz went to one the following week.

It was advertised as starting at 8 a.m. and finishing "when the Process is complete" – Saz figured she could always extricate herself from the "Process" early if she didn't feel up to getting completely completed. At the entrance to the hall she handed over her £100 for the day long course and in return was given a name tag and a registration card, all the usual name, address and date of birth questions and then a section which Saz recognized as the "California Quotient".

Have you ever been in therapy? (if so, what sort?)
Are you addicted to alcohol? tobacco? drugs? sex? approval? exercise?
Do you come from a dysfunctional family?

*Are you now, or have you ever been, in an abusive
relationship?*
and finally
Are you prepared to CHANGE? ? ?

There was a coda reminding the attendees that in
agreeing to do the course they had promised "Not to
divulge any Process techniques to those Outside!" Saz
figured North had to make his vast amounts of money
somehow. She answered all the questions honestly except
the one that asked for her name and address, giving her
name as Molly Steele and her address as that of the
mother of her ex-girlfriend, Caroline.

She put "Probably" in response to the Change question.

The morning began with a lecture from one of Dr North's
assistants – about his work, about his "philosophy" – "Be
open to the whole and the whole will come to you" and
in general about how he had changed her life, her husband's life, her mother's life, not to mention the hundreds
of pop stars, media celebrities and the top secret wives of
government ministers he had "saved", and now, if they
were all prepared to really take up the challenge, he
would change their lives too. It was a good speech. Saz
wondered if she was the only person there thinking it
was too good not to be a con. She looked around at the
two hundred or so other "changees". The group was much
as she had expected – thirties to mid-forties, middle class
and looking hungry, metaphorically and literally, they'd
been told breakfast would be provided, but already it
was quarter to nine and Saz couldn't exactly smell the
welcoming scent of warm croissants and a rich Colum-
bian brew. Then another of North's assistants came on
stage, introducing himself as Malcolm, one of the facilitators on the Process and told them the rules for the day.

"OK. This is the hard part. There is to be no smoking – not even outside the hall. No talking while in session other than that directed by Dr North or the facilitators. There will be breaks every three hours when you may go to the toilet. If you decide to leave at any time other than those set down you will not be allowed back in. Maxwell North is a medical doctor and can assure you that you do not need to go to the loo more than once every three hours, it will not hurt your bladder to hold on! If you do feel the urge it is bound to be a physiological reaction to the lecture or discussion. Stay with it, your body is only trying to give you an excuse not to confront your reality, it's what you've been doing all those years wasting life and money on smoking and drinking and overeating and taking drugs. Fight it, the results are well worthwhile. Also, there will be herbal teas and water provided but no food!"

There was a rumble of dismay through the room and Malcolm laughed.

"Yes, I know it's a strange idea, but for too many in the western world food is also a crutch – look around, some of you should be grateful for the chance to fast! OK – that's it, please listen to the facilitators at all times, go with the course, try to surrender to it – fighting for your cigarette or sandwich will waste your time and ours and won't do you any good in the long run. Anyone who thinks they can't go with these rules is urged to leave now, your registration fee will be happily returned to you. You have five minutes to sort out your things – please hand all your coats and bags and shoes over to Janet in the cloakroom, anyone who can't make the commitment and wants to leave can sort that out with Anne Marie at the registration desk and I will take the rest of you through to the back hall in four minutes' time. Welcome! We're glad to have you with us."

Bitterly regretting that she hadn't eaten after her run, Saz took a few identifying papers from her bag and then handed her things over to the smiling Janet in the cloakroom. Anne Marie wasn't smiling quite so much as she returned money to the eight people who had chosen to leave and she almost lost her smile completely when one middle-aged man started shouting about the false advertising of breakfast. Luckily, Anne Marie quickly summoned another grinning assistant to help shuffle him out of the door. Saz was pleased to see that Malcolm was managing to smile a lot at the other end of the room.

"Down here everyone please. This is where the day really starts. Are we all gathered? Good. Now, when we go in to the back hall, I'd ask you not to sit next to anyone you know, we want you to expand as much as possible today, so no old patterns – please."

"Not bloody likely to be expanding much with no food all day!" said a young woman to Saz's left. She'd spoken quietly but Malcolm was on to her, he pushed through the crowd and came right up to her face.

"Very funny – let's see, Julie is it?"

"Yes."

"Do you have a problem with food, Julie?"

"Only when I can't get enough!" replied Julie who was slightly overweight.

"I'd say you had a big problem with food and that these jokes of yours were a very common defence mechanism. Wouldn't you?"

The laughter Julie's remarks had caused completely stopped now and everyone was staring in fascinated horror as Julie's face turned bright red. She looked up at Malcolm who was a good seven or eight inches taller than her.

"I . . . I don't . . . "

"Come on Julie. I'm sure you do know or you wouldn't

have decided to come today. Aren't you one of those who stood up when I asked who had a problem with food or drugs?"

"Yes."

"Right. So do you or do you not have a problem with food?"

Julie looked miserably down at her feet. Saz couldn't believe that no one told him to piss off and leave the poor woman alone. She couldn't believe that she didn't do so either. But she just stood there along with the other one hundred and ninety people, as they had done in countless school assemblies, glad it wasn't them and terrified of drawing attention to themselves. Malcolm stood over Julie for what felt like ages until she finally nodded her head. Then he hugged her and turned to the rest of the group.

"Julie's done very well, she's been honest, dealt with a denial and started the ball rolling. Thanks Julie."

Julie looked up at him in shock.

"But the rest of you probably feel like shit for not stopping me bullying her don't you?"

A couple of people laughed, most nodded and a few said "Yes" out loud.

"Well, that's OK too – partly you were wrong to say nothing, partly you were right. Plenty of people will be challenged today. Maybe not all of you, but most of you will be directly challenged by either Dr North or a member of the facilitating group. It will do no one any good at all if we have to waste time explaining the methods – believe me, by the end of the day you'll see how things work. Anyone who wants to can still leave now . . . No? Right. You've chosen to be here, so Be Here! Stay attentive, stay in there. It will become clear."

With this last cryptic message Malcolm knocked on the

two big doors leading to the back hall and, with his arm still around Julie's shoulders led them into the room.

With everyone else, Saz gasped as she saw the huge table with coffee and juice, bread, cheeses and fruit laid out in front of them. Standing on the other side of the table was Maxwell North. In his Armani suit and silk tie he looked like he'd just stepped out of one of the magazine photos Saz had spent the last few days poring over.

"Surprise! Breakfast is served!"

Everyone laughed as Malcolm led Julie to the table first and Dr North explained.

"Over the years running these seminars, we've found that there are always some for whom the idea of change is just too much. So we set up a few hurdles at the starting post, that way we can ensure that those who are here really want to be. Enjoy your breakfast while Malcolm tells you what our plans are for the day."

Saz helped herself to a big mug of coffee and a sticky Danish pastry while Malcolm told them that everything he'd already said still stood, he just said it nicer this time. No talking, no smoking and no loo-going during the three-hour sessions. He then gave them half an hour to chat and breakfast and told them the first session would start at nine thirty on the dot. Saz wondered if it was wise to fit another diuretic coffee in before then and wisely opted for another Danish instead.

CHAPTER 9

By the time Saz got home that night she was totally drained. Ignoring the frenzied flashing of her answerphone, she set her alarm for six and went straight to bed. She slept soundly until the alarm woke her, then she rolled out of bed and listened to the messages while she got ready for her run. The first was from her sister.

"Hi groover, it's Cassie. We're having a party for Amy's cast-removing and we thought you and Molly might want to come. Our place, midday, next Saturday. Bye."

The next message was also from Cassie.

"Me again. Listen, you don't really have any choice, Tony's got to go away and Mum's already said she isn't prepared to take on twenty little girls which is very ungrandmotherly of her and anyway you and Molly should be there – it's your social duty because I lead such a decadent, middle-class, heterosexual lifestyle and my children and their friends need better role models. Come in the morning then you can look after the others while I take Amy and the baby in for the great unplastering. Thanks. Bye."

Another beep and then,

"Hi girl, it's me. Hope your day was successful and life-enhancing. I'm sure you're exhausted – they say North's courses are pretty draining, so call me when you wake up tomorrow and either you can come here for dinner or I'll bring food over to yours. Love you. Love your body. Want them both. Very much. A lot. Right now, but I don't mind waiting. The anticipation is kind of pleasurable too. Bye."

The tape bleeped several times and rewound. Saz turned the machine on again and went out for her run. She'd been running first thing in the morning for about four years now and still couldn't get over how fine the world looked at six in the morning with early sunshine and dew everywhere, while for the rest of the day – particularly in Camberwell – it was invariably grey and grimy and cold. She ran for almost an hour and arrived back at her flat just as it began to cloud over.

"Never fails!" she thought to herself as she ran past the pointless lift and began the climb to her flat. Her weather forecaster's reverie was stopped in its tracks when she got to her door. There on the doorstep was a small bunch of flowers. Saz picked it up and her hand started to shake when she saw that it was a bunch of weeds – dandelions, daisies, grasses, along with an even smaller bunch of lily of the valley.

"What the fuck?"

Saz ran back out to the entrance to her floor but the lift was stuck open as always and there was no one around. She went inside, put the flowers in water and sat down intending to call Molly, but she couldn't bring herself to pick up the phone and an hour after she'd run up the stairs, she stripped off her sweaty training clothes and went back to bed.

Molly arrived on the doorstep promptly at eight with a bottle of New Zealand Chardonnay and more Chinese food than either of them could hope to eat.

"You OK babe? You sounded a bit strange on the phone – I hope your life hasn't been changed so much you've decided you don't like Chinese?"

"No, you know I love it, but don't you ever go to the Indian takeaway?"

Molly sighed, "Saz darling, I'd have thought you might have guessed that I am about as likely to enjoy cold paratha and packet-flavoured tandoori from the shop down the road, as you would if you were to buy your mother's home cooked speciality from your local takeaway only to find it covered in flowing oil and sold at eight times the homemade price."

Saz pulled her into the flat and closed the door behind them.

"For your information the Indian – no, make that Asian – takeaway down the road is totally authentic and their bhaji have not the merest hint of excess oil. What's more, my mother's seedy cake can't be bought in any shop. Overpriced or otherwise."

Over special fried rice, spring rolls, fried seaweed, crispy vegetables and sweet and sour prawns Saz explained how the course had gone and all about the false start.

"So by ten o'clock we were all coffee and caked out and more than a bit confused."

"Classic technique really."

"Yeah? I thought water torture and sleep deprivation were classic techniques, this just seemed like a good joke. And the coffee was great."

Molly refilled Saz's glass.

"Well, it is unusual, these sorts of things are more likely to be exactly as your man Malcolm said in the beginning – really harsh and exacting, but, having told you all that guff about needing to give yourself totally to it and rid themselves of the people who weren't likely to do so, he then turned it around, gave you food and was nice to you!"

"Ever so nice."

"And manipulative. Not only did he make you complicit in a trick against the ones who left, he even gave you food to reinforce his role as provider and protector."

"I thought you said you like this guy's work?"

"Admiration is not the same as liking. From what I've read, he has great results – sometimes that's all that matters, particularly when you're dealing with drug dependency or chronic depression, but it doesn't stop me being cynical about his methods."

"Anyway, it worked. I'm pretty cynical too – I was there to spy on him after all – and it wasn't as if I couldn't see they'd made it easier for themselves by getting rid of any potential troublemakers right at the start, but it did work."

"OK, keep going. What happened next?"

"We divided up into small groups, each one with a facilitator – my group had Malcolm – and talked about why we were there."

"What did you say?"

"I told them I was at a crossroads in my work and needed help finding which way to go next!"

"Very clever – didn't you have to be more specific?"

"No, that was the odd thing about the whole day really. I'd expected people confessing details of their sordid lives and those long boring stories of sad childhoods, but it was all much more abstract – feelings rather than incidents."

Molly nodded and nibbled on a cold clump of rice.

"That is unusual. Most group work is based on the idea that by telling something to a group you can get validation for the event and therefore for the feelings it engendered."

"Thanks Mrs Freud."

"You don't want my two years of psych training as a backup? That's fine. I won't help at all."

"Of course I do stupid, but just listen first and then

tell me what you make of the whole thing. You think telling only feelings is strange? Believe me, it gets lots weirder than that."

Saz told Molly about the rest of the day. The two hours they'd spent lying on the floor wrapped tightly in warm blankets as Dr North guided them in "visualizing" the future – all of them as happy, wealthy, creative and slim individuals leading purposeful and exciting lives.

"And you can't imagine how odd that new age stuff sounds coming from a man with a Harley Street practice and fierce reputation among the upper echelons of British medicine!"

"Not that odd Saz – nothing better to get a pliant patient than treating them like a toddler."

"Shut up – you're supposed to be listening – give me the diagnosis later."

Following their afternoon nap, one whole hour in a darkened room with soft music and the by now familiar warm blankets, they broke into small groups again and talked more. They were told to talk about what they wanted and, more importantly, how they planned to achieve it. For Saz this was a little harder as she still had to take care not to give anything away about her real work.

"So I concentrated on us Moll, and it was great – I told a group of ten strangers all about us. Well, about our relationship – I was careful not to give them any details about you."

"Thanks. Very considerate. And?"

"Well, it did things. One bloke said he'd never have guessed I was 'that way inclined'."

"Yeah, yeah, yawn!"

"Kind of, but it did make him think, made him look at the others differently too. And one woman came out!"

"Really came out? For the first time?"

"Yeah. And she wasn't even in my group, she'd just overheard me talking and decided she'd better use the opportunity."

"What happened?"

"She asked if her group and mine could be joined up and so we did – very accommodating this lot – and she told everyone she was gay, that she'd always been gay and that we were the first people she'd told, she'd never said it out loud before and consequently she'd never been able to have a relationship. Never! I mean for God's sake, the woman must have been in her late forties and she'd always been so scared she'd never had any relationship of any kind. Not even with a bloke. That's just so awful!"

"And?"

"Well, North was in charge of her group so he kind of took over from Malcolm and he told her how wonderful she was and all that nice affirming stuff and then he got everyone to turn to the person beside them and say one secret. Some really big secret or desire that they'd never told anyone, but it had to be about you. Really personal. He made all the other groups do it too. We sat in a big circle and all of us did it. A whole room of people saying their one big secret to the person sitting next to them. I heard one woman say she wanted to climb Mt Everest, another who was sure she was psychic. Another even said she would give up everything – her husband, kids, job, the lot – just to go to the moon. I really think she meant it too."

Molly suddenly became very interested in the dregs in her wine glass.

"What did you say?"

"Ah. Well, OK. This is going to sound a bit strange but, you know how Cassie and I love the sea?"

"Well, I know you do, I didn't know she did too. Go on."

"When we were little girls we used to swim all the time

and we had this idea that we would swim the Channel together."

"The English Channel?"

"What other channels are there?"

"Bristol perhaps. Geography not your hot point huh?"

"No. And it's my story, so listen. When we were kids we wanted to be the first sisters to swim the Channel. But I still want to do it. And I'm going to see if she does too."

"Swim the Channel?"

"Yes. It's possible. Because that was the main thing about it, they ditched the rest of that section of the workshop and we just worked on planning how we could achieve our secrets."

"Even the woman who wanted to go to the moon?"

"Yeah. She's going to write to NASA and contact those companies that are planning to do a moon trip one day – all the aerospace type places."

"And wonderful Mr North said he'd pay?"

"Dr North actually, no. But he did give her ten quid to start her savings account."

"So when do you make the big swim?"

"Whenever, maybe never, but the idea is, that by telling the secret you can start to do it – or accept it's impossible if it's beyond you."

"So you're now totally convinced that North is a great bloke and there's no mystery at all?"

"God no, I did get lots out of it and actually really enjoyed the day but it's not as if I wasn't aware how manipulative it all was. Or how much money they made – you know, the food was good, but it wasn't worth a hundred quid, and the 'work', especially the secret telling stuff, made me feel great, but I'm sure I could have achieved that in half an hour with a good therapist. And anyway, something else happened."

"There's more?"

"Well, I didn't get home until one o'clock in the morning. It did go on a bit. After everyone had made up their 'Achieve My Secret' plan, it was time for more food and then we came back to end it. The finishing off was more visualization stuff and a kind of committing ceremony where everyone said how much effort they were going to put into achieving their next goal – the ones we'd visualized in the morning, or into getting their secret to happen. I mean, it takes ages for two hundred people to say what they're going to do with their lives. And then there was a sort of group huggy thing and that was it."

"That counts as something else?"

"No, wait. You're so impatient!"

"Yeah, well, it's a good story and you tell it really well, but there's a certain large chunk of me that would rather you were doing something else with your mouth."

Saz smiled and picked up Molly's hand, kissing it and cramming the fingers into her mouth, she licked the tips of each finger and smiled.

"Not that large a part babe, more sort of soft and pink and delicate . . . "

Molly grimaced and pulled her hand back.

"Oh please, if we're going to do it, can we just do it? Your saliva all over my right hand is not exactly a major turn on you know and I prefer to actually have sex than to have my anatomy described to me in terms that would make a primary school teacher blush."

"That's not what my other lovers have said."

"Maybe you've had too many school teachers?"

"OK, I'll be brief. When I got home after my run this morning I found this on the doorstep."

Saz took the lily of the valley out of the vase on the table.

"Flowers?"

"Kind of. In the lunch break I was talking to a couple of other women. One of them had been to a funeral yesterday and she was talking about how she thought all the flowers were a waste of money and so I told them about my grandmother's funeral and how she'd always hated bouquets. She used to say they were a waste of good dirt in the garden when you could be growing food. So when she died, rather than put flowers on her grave, I got a tiny sprig of lily of the valley, which was pretty much the only flower she did like, and went to her vege-table garden and picked a whole bunch of things – carrot tops, greenery from the beans, potato leaves – and made it all into a little bouquet. I threw it on her coffin when they were lowering it down."

"And this was on your doorstep?"

"Yeah, it was some lily of the valley with a bunch of weeds."

"So one of those women must have come back this morning and left the flowers for you?"

"Well, someone did. Worst thing is that I don't know who. There were the two women I was talking to, but one of them was Janet, one of North's assistants and then when I was telling the end of the story, both North and Malcolm came round the corner. I don't know if they'd heard the rest of it, but North did sort of tell Janet off for letting me talk about the past when I should have been 'focused on the present' as he put it."

"So it could have been any of them."

"Yeah. But it kind of implies that he, or someone from his lot, knows I'm investigating him. I didn't even give anybody this address."

"Maybe one of them is the one who's employing you?"

"I thought about that, but there were a few Anglo-Americans there and I didn't recognize the voice. So I feel pretty strange now. You know, I enjoyed the course when I expected to think it was shit. I even liked what North did, though I still don't think I'd trust him. But I really don't like this thing about the flowers. I don't feel very safe here now and I hate that."

"Well, that makes things easier for me."

"Huh?"

"You weren't the only one planning your future yesterday."

"What did you plan then?"

"Ah – "

"Well?"

Molly sat up from where she'd been lying with her head in Saz's lap, finished off the last dribble of wine in the bottle and then looked, not at Saz, but intently at her own reflection in the blank TV screen.

"I decided I wanted to ask you to move in with me."

"You what?"

"You know there's more room at my place and I know you love South London but my place does have the heath and that would be good for your running and we spend all our time together anyway and I really am getting tired of driving across London eighteen times a week and I know we've only been together for a few months but you wouldn't have to get rid of this place, you could get someone else to move in and cover the rent and . . . well, at least you don't have to walk up five floors of stairs at my place."

Molly finally ran out of words, took a deep breath and turned her head to look at Saz, who just smiled and answered her with, "No, I 'spose you don't."

Molly waited for more, twisting a long strand of black hair around her index finger.

"Well? What do you think? Do you want to do it?"

"Ah . . . God! Sorry, I'm a bit shocked that's all. Um . . .

yes. Yes, I'd love to move in with you. I mean, I think I'd love to."

"I think so too. Scary eh?"

"Yep. Still, can't be any worse than telling a hundred and eighty-nine people that you're going to swim the Channel within the next five years."

"I hope not."

"Me too."

"There's a good pool near my place. You can start training straight away. For the Channel I mean."

"Great. In that case I'd better remember to pack my swimming costume."

Saz and Molly went to bed after that, Saz very carefully checking that all the doors and windows were securely locked before she turned off the lights. Their lovemaking was tentative at first, both terrified of doing something wrong after making such a big decision and not yet routine enough to be achieved on automatic. Molly fell asleep in Saz's arms and Saz lay awake for a long time trying to work out how much Maxwell North had heard her say. When she finally slept it was only to dream of her grandmother and Cassie and North all trying to swim the Channel while she picked beanflowers from Molly's garden and Amy flew above her, most of her body encased in a pink plaster cast. When her alarm went at six she was glad to get up and run the confusion out of her system.

In her white light studio, Caron North smashed a heavy chisel down on a new slab of stone and smiled satisfied when it split cleanly down the centre. She picked up one half and ran her hand over it, catching her little finger on a sharp edge and tearing a wedge of skin. She let her blood run down the white marble and watched it find its own pattern in the grain. Later that day she outlined the rivulet of dried blood, etching it into the stone. It would be a good starting point for her new piece.

CHAPTER 10

Max had been taking Michael through the Process yet
again. At Michael's request. At Michael's demand. Not
that Max minded. Michael was his protégé – the sad,
broken child he planned to make whole as a result of his
work. The one that would prove him right. Michael was
his Case Study. Max, on the other hand, was Michael's
idol.

Michael's history of self-mutilation and childhood pain
was well-known to everyone in the House. He had had a
classic "disturbed" childhood – early parental divorce,
emotional abuse from his overly religious stepfather
coupled with almost no contact with his own father and
on top of that, a scared mother who had always allowed
the men in her life to dominate her and consequently left
Michael and his siblings to fend for themselves. Michael's
sister and brother were both settled now and, despite
having had exactly the same upbringing, were functioning well, employed and fairly happy. This led Max to
believe that it was perfectly possible for Michael to obtain
the same degree of "social stability". Michael agreed with
him, though Michael would have agreed with him whatever the diagnosis, and therefore both felt ready to allow
Michael to "Process" whenever he wanted to.

What Max didn't realize was that Michael was in love
with him and had been in love with him ever since Anita
first brought him home to the House. Michael believed
Max was the one and only, that he could cure all ills
and that if, as was plainly evident, Max was straight and

would never love him back, then he would use any other means possible to get close to him. For Michael this meant that the Process, with its in-built closeness to Max and its painful climax with attendant comfort from Max, was not the "difficult yet worthwhile" experience it was for the other members of the household. It was in fact a desirable way to get Max's attention. And the more pain Michael could put himself through, the more attention he would get.

The gay revolution had passed Michael by and at twenty-three he was both terrified of his homosexuality and completely in love with Maxwell North. Max realized Michael's fixation on him was a little extreme, but would have been shocked to admit to himself that it was love he was receiving from Michael. And even more shocked to admit that he liked receiving that love. He saw himself as the Master and Michael as his Disciple. Anita tried to alert him to what was going on, but Max, still elated by what he perceived as his "victory" in winning her over to the Process, was in no mood to learn any lessons from Anita.

"Max, you've got to accept it. He's in love with you. That's why he wants to do this all the time."

"Don't be silly, Anita. Michael wants to Process because he benefits from it. That's perfectly understandable — after all, you did."

"Yes."

"So why do you have such a problem with Michael?"

"He isn't OK, Max."

"This is helping him to become OK."

"He's glorifying in it. He thinks you find him special."

"I do."

"But not because you love him."

"Of course I love him. You taught me that, I never

thought it was possible to really love another man as a friend until you showed me it could be done."

"I don't mean like that Max. You're deliberately missing the point. He doesn't love you as a friend. He is in love with you."

"Rubbish. If anything, he's in love with the Process."

"Only as an extension of you. He sees everything to do with you as good."

"Isn't it?"

"God Max, not even you are that perfect."

"Anita – look at what we've achieved here. This really is close to perfect. And all of it started with you."

"I know. And believe me, sometimes I wonder if I should feel so good about it."

"Why? The House is amazing. Everything is growing, expanding. People are calling from all over the city to come to the weekend workshops. Our child is being brought up in an open house where she sees all kinds of people, all of whom love her. Her parents are respected, her mother is loved, her father is . . . "

"Adored? Venerated? Worshipped?"

Max laughed.

"It's amazing how many words you know for a foreigner."

"Don't mock me, Max."

"Come on Anita, where's your sense of humour? You're getting carried away again."

Anita shook her head.

"I don't think so. Michael idolizes you. He'd do anything you asked him to and I'm scared, because every time he does the Process he emerges even more attached to you. Sure it was good for me. And probably for all the rest of the House too. But I've only done it once and so has everyone else."

"Paul's done it twice."

"OK twice. But Michael? How many times is this now?"

"Eleven."

"It's crazy Max. He used to be addicted to amphet-amines and psychics, now it's the Process and you."

Max sat on the bed and took Anita's hands in his own.

"I really don't think it's such a big deal Anita. He has great results. When he first came to us all he could talk about was his awful childhood and all the oppression – now he hardly ever mentions it. He's really getting better."

"I wish I was as confident as you."

"It's my job to be confident Anita. It's my Process. I made it. I believe in it."

"Yes. I know."

"Great. So come here and show me how much you love me."

Max ignored Anita's warnings. Michael completed another lengthy Process and two days later while Anita and Max fucked and moaned and tortured each other with the exquisite pleasure of their barely sated hunger, Michael Yardley cut deep and lengthwise into his wrists with his own father's cut-throat razor. As always, Anita and Max fell asleep heavy with sweat and spent sex as soon as they had both come.

Anita woke up, wide awake at 4.45 a.m.

"Max. Quick. Something's wrong."

"What?"

"It's wrong. It feels wrong. Get up. Get up!"

Max rolled out of bed and turned on the bedside light, shouting at Anita almost immediately.

"Don't look. Close your eyes. Don't look!"

But it was too late. Anita had already seen Michael, sitting on the chair at the bottom of their bed. He was wrapped in the quilt Anita's grandmother had made for her when she was fifteen. The quilt he'd taken from where it was usually folded at their feet, the quilt which was drenched in Michael's blood.

Max lifted the body on to their bed.

"I'll call an ambulance."

"It's too late, Anita."

"I'll call the police then."

"No."

"I have to tell someone."

"No! You have to tell no one."

"What are you talking about?"

"You must tell no one Anita, do you hear me? No one needs to know about this. It will ruin things. We will tell no one."

"What about his family?"

"They don't love him anyway, you know that."

"But they have a right . . . "

"What rights do they have? After the way they treated him? They did this to him. They killed him."

"He did this himself Max. He killed himself. Look at him."

"No. They did. They did it."

Max stood beside the bed and held Michael's head in his hands.

"He told them you know."

"Told them what?"

"That he was homosexual."

"He did? When?"

"A couple of days ago. After his Process finished."

"Did you tell him to call them?"

"He wanted to."

"Did you tell him to do it?"

"He wanted to."

"For Christ's sake Max," Anita screamed at him. "Did you make him call them?"

"Yes."

"Fuck! You idiot. You stupid damn fool."

"He wanted to be honest."

"You wanted him to be honest." Anita got out of bed and turned on the bright overhead light. "And what did these reactionary Christian fascists have to say when the little boy who only wanted them to love him told them that he was a homosexual? Huh? What did they say?"

Max looked back blankly at her, stroking Michael's hair.

"Well? Did they say 'Darling we love you?' Did they Max? Did they say it was all OK and they were going to be a good loving family from now on? Or did they tell him to go to hell? Well, Max? Which one was it?"

Max just looked from Anita down to Michael's body in his arms.

"Right. They said for him to go to hell, huh? Or maybe they actually told him he was already in hell. And what did you tell him Max? What comfort could you give him?"

Max was crying now, trying to pick Michael up, trying to make a little boy bundle of the grown dead man.

"I didn't know what to do. I left him to deal with it himself and then tonight I went to talk to him and he wanted me. He was upset and wanted me to hold him. So I did. Like I do with everyone, just hold them until they stop crying. To comfort them. But he wanted to sleep with me Anita and I didn't know what to do. He wanted me to kiss him, to hold him – hold him properly."

"So what did you do Max?"

"I came to bed."

"You left him? You came here to fuck me and left him alone?"

"I told him it would be fine. I told him he was tired, he should sleep. I told him he should put it all away. I took him to his room. He was tired."

Anita looked at Max, Michael in his arms, hands shaking from fear and exhaustion and pain.

"God Max. What have you done to him?"

"I didn't do this."

"What do we do now?"

"I'll think of something. Leave it to me."

And Max carried Michael back to his own room, stumbling both with the dead weight and the dry sobs racking his body.

CHAPTER 11

By 6 p.m. the next day, everything had been taken care of. Max carried Michael back to his room, calmed himself down and formed a plan of action that would have made his father proud. He cleaned up both the bloody mess and the body, bagged all Michael's clothes and possessions and locked the dead boy securely in his room. He showered, woke Anita from where she'd fallen asleep on the floor of their bedroom and went downstairs to make French toast for all the household.

After breakfast he told the other members of the House that Michael had decided to leave after his last Process and that they would not be seeing him again. And, ignoring their questions, he sent them all out to the coast for the day, with plenty of cash and instructions not to be back before nightfall.

"It's about time you all had a House outing – without Anita or myself. No, listen please, I have my reasons."

"But what about Michael? Didn't he leave us a note or anything?"

"No. He left nothing. And I think, now that Michael has left us, we need to look at the group dynamic here and see where maybe we've gone a little wrong and how we can improve. I also think that perhaps it should start with all of you rather than coming from Anita or myself. Please – you don't need to discuss Michael, really you don't. You need to discuss us. Our household, our family. Let him go and let us get on. It's past. He's past. Paul will take care of everyone's needs today, won't you Paul?"

"Um – yeah, sure." Paul answered with rapidly growing assurance, aware that without Michael, he was now the "Number One" disciple.

"Good. So – go out, have a great day. We'll see you tonight and we'll have a House Meeting then."

When the House was empty of all but Anita, Jasmine and Michael's cold body, Max made a single well-placed telephone call. It was to an old varsity friend now lecturing in anatomy at the University of San Francisco. A lecturer who readily agreed to take the body off Max's hands. Fresh, healthy, young corpses are fairly unusual and make by far the best case studies for blossoming medical students, but they're very hard to come by and if his old Ivy League buddy could assure him that this kid had no family or friends who were going to make a fuss, then he was more than willing to help Max out of a tight spot. Max gave the required assurances and a van arrived to pick up the body in the early afternoon.

Max went upstairs to find Anita had let herself into Michael's room.

"Where's Jasmine?"

"Sleeping. They're here?"

"Downstairs in the hall. Are you ready for them to come in and get him?"

"Almost. Won't they want to see a death certificate or something?"

"No. It's all organized. They take him into the school over on Parnassus and Jerry will just give the body the papers of some other guy who came in last week or something like that. They go through about ten corpses a week in his classes. Usually they get the unclaimed ones from the city morgue, but you have to wait months for them to be turned in. Or occasionally people allow their dead relatives to be 'used in the interests of science'. But they're not exactly ideal for study."

"Not usually quite as fresh as this one, huh?"

"No."

"So, Max. You're doing a good deed after all, aren't you? You're the good guy yet again."

"I can't talk about this now, Anita. They're waiting to take the body."

"Michael."

"Yes. Him. Now come on."

"I still think you should call his family."

"I really don't think they'd care."

"It's not that. I know you, you just don't want the cops to find out. You don't want them to know what you've been doing here."

"I haven't done anything wrong."

"Right Max. So you keep saying. That's why you sent everyone out today and that's why you aren't reporting this death and that's why we both feel like shit."

Max sat on the bed beside her and gently put his arms around her, drawing her to him.

"Anita – our friend has died. That's why we both feel so bad. But we're going to sort it out and then we're going to get on with it. This is one setback. Our first problem. I will not let this ruin my work and I won't let you ruin it either."

He grabbed a fistful of her hair, no gentle calmness now, and turned her to look at him, pulling her close to his face.

"I've had enough of your accusations, Anita and your self-pity and your guilt. If you want to run and hide, feel free to do so, but Michael is dead. This is just another corpse. He's gone. His spirit is gone and no amount of you sitting there and stroking his hair is going to change that. This is just a cold piece of dead meat. So let's get on with it. Yes?" Max stood Anita up and half dragged, half carried her into their bedroom where he left her.

The two guys from the university came upstairs, wrapped Michael in a body bag and carried him away. Anita took her sleepy child and sat with her, looking down at their tiny garden, eyes blinded and swollen from an overwash of tears. By the time everyone else got home that night Max had cleared Michael's room completely. He'd contacted the family to tell them Michael had left with no forwarding address – they didn't want one anyway – and then he set up the central room for a House Meeting. When he heard the two cars drive up he ran upstairs to Anita.

"Come on, they're here. We're going to do this together. You and me. And we're going to be happy about it and it will all be fine."

"I don't think I can face them. I can't do this lie. You'll have to go down by yourself."

"You don't have any choice Anita. You're complicit already."

"But it wasn't my idea to lie about Michael. You wouldn't let me call the cops."

"It doesn't matter. By their standards you're just as guilty as me. Only I don't feel guilty and you do. That's why you can't cope and I can."

"You should feel guilty."

"No. There is no 'should' about it. As you've said so many times yourself, 'guilt is a useless emotion'. That is what we all believe isn't it? Haven't you told me time and again that all my guilt is merely a result of my middle-class repressed upbringing? Guess I learnt the lesson real well?"

"It doesn't count as middle-class guilt when you've just killed someone."

Max whirled around, grabbed Anita's shoulders and pulled her to her feet.

"I didn't kill him. He killed himself. He set himself free. I have no guilt."

"Yeah, yeah . . . "

"Come on Anita, you can't change the story now. What is it you always say? What's your mantra? Let me see . . . oh yeah – 'I choose not to involve myself in the patriarchal conspiracy of blame and regret that prevents me from attaining my true nature'. That's the one!"

"You're a bastard."

"Why? For quoting your own words back at you? Oh, I think not. Michael had a choice and he chose to run away. To attain his 'true nature', no doubt. I choose to keep going – and if you know what's good for you, so will you."

"Are you threatening me, Max?"

"Probably."

Max let her go and she fell away from him back against the bed.

"Now, get yourself together Anita and come downstairs – and make sure you wash your face first, you look like crap."

CHAPTER 12

By the time Anita came downstairs half an hour later, the House had already convened. Her seat beside Max was empty and Michael's seat on the other side of Max was now taken by Paul. The ten of them sat around the big oak table. Max at the head, with the huge arched windows behind him, the setting sunlight flooding in from behind making it hard to see his face properly, while clearly illuminating all the others, something he'd often used to his advantage in the past. Anita to his left, Paul masking Michael's absence to his right.

Anita sat down and they began. Max welcomed each one in turn and then, as always, they sat silently, eyes closed, hands on the table before them, little fingertips touching until Max told them they were "one" and could now begin the Group Process.

This Process had been invented by Max and Anita within the first few months they'd been in the House – though it hadn't been called a Process at the time. It was designed to allow everyone a chance to speak, while not letting those to whom speaking came naturally overtake the others. Each person was given three minutes, the others were not allowed to interrupt, having to listen silently while whoever was speaking said their piece. Everyone had to take a turn whether they had anything to say or not, either talking for their three minutes or staying silent under group scrutiny. Anita timed the minutes strictly, calling out when one, two and then three minutes had passed. Max believed the three-minute limit meant that people chose to speak about what really mattered to them, rather than just waffling and then throwing a "hot bone of an idea" in at the last sentence, disrupting the group. The next person would then speak for the duration of their own three minutes. No one was allowed to use their time to address the speech of another, or to defend themselves. Max would then, after speaking for his own three minutes, take twenty minutes to "facilitate" – to tell the others what they were really talking about, to draw all the thoughts together and to plan the agenda for what was to become the solid basis of the rest of the meeting over the next five hours. All meetings lasted five hours with one ten-minute break at the three-hour mark. The House had been having monthly meetings ever since it first started and occasional meetings in moments of crisis, but they always followed the same pattern. This evening, Paul began.

"To tell the truth, I'm glad Michael's gone. I hadn't felt comfortable with him for a long time. He seemed to always want to compete with me and I have only ever wanted to serve this group, you know that, to help create our whole. I've felt for some time now that Mike was not happy with the group and needed to be away. Which is fine. Perhaps we weren't working for him either. I'm glad he's gone and I don't expect to miss him at all. That's all I've got to say."

The group then waited in silence until Anita called the end of Paul's three minutes and turned to Rose sitting beside him. From the midwest and just turned seventeen, Rose had come to the House four months pregnant. She was now due to have her baby within the month and had been very close to Michael. She cried for the first two minutes of her time and then started to speak between her sobs, holding tightly to the bump in front of her, as if the unborn child was a buffer against the pain.

"I feel I should have given Michael more, but he was just being so supportive to me and Babe that I didn't know . . . I mean . . . that he didn't love us. Like I thought he did. I thought he loved us. Really. He wanted to be Babe's father, he told me that and I believed him . . . I thought he was so cool . . . I thought he's gonna stay and do it, you know, not like them all back home? And we could, you know, maybe we would move away together and . . . I'm not stupid . . . "

She stuttered and gave up a watery smile.

"Well, not very – I know that he didn't really want to live with me . . . I mean, not any girl . . . but he played along with my story, and it made me feel good. Made us feel good, me and Babe . . . and now I just . . . I don't know, I think maybe I should move on too, I'm not . . . "

Anita looked up from the stopwatch and said sharply, "That's enough Rose. Time. John?"

John had his arm around Rose and was staring at Max. He was a big man from Virginia who didn't speak much and maintained that he came to the House both to "hide from the wreck" that his marriage had been and to find a new way of being with people. A way that didn't involve families and traditions and the misery that his previous life had become. A way that didn't yet exist, but he was hoping to force into being by the very strength of his need. He kept his eyes on Max the whole time he spoke.

"I don't know either. Come on now, Rosie honey, dry those eyes."

He handed his handkerchief to Rose and was reprimanded by Max.

"That's conversation John."

"Shut up, Max. It's not conversation, it's humanity.

This little girl is crying and she needs some attention. She's a child and she's lost a friend. She's going to get some attention from me. I don't care that the rule is not to deal with someone else's pain. I actually don't care about the rules at all. I care about the people. So, Max – do you want to discuss it?"

"No John, I don't. Because to discuss it would be to break even more of the rules than you just did. You have about two minutes more."

"Yeah well. Somehow, I don't think two minutes is going to do it. Perhaps we ought to be looking at these rules and maybe getting rid of some of them. I think we ought to be looking at quite a few things. You know, I don't know that these rules have got us all that far actually, there's a whole lot of stuff going on that maybe we should be ... "

"Um, one minute John."

"Yeah Anita. Right. One minute more to see just how far I can push – ah, don't look so scared, it's not that big a deal. Anyway, I think I've said all I really wanted to. For now. Just a little experiment and it seems to have worked. Simple really – break a rule, stand back and stare in wonder when the whole world doesn't crumble before your very eyes. Almost satisfying. But maybe not quite satisfying enough, huh Max? We'll see."

John leant back in his chair holding Rose against his shoulder and smiling at Max over her head. Max just stared back at John and then waited for Anita as she timed the remaining minute. Doug and Jake then followed, each expressing dismay that Michael had left without talking to them but, both being young men who had come to the House looking for security rather than anything more challenging, they echoed Paul's sentiments that they'd rather just get on with things than rake over the past. While neither of them was allowed to say so, they were both thrown by John's challenge to Max's authority and were desperate to get the meeting back on its usual, predictable course. Elspeth, a German friend of Anita's who'd only been in the House for a month and still didn't have a great grasp of English, merely said she expected to miss Michael and left it at that. Her Irish boyfriend Sam said pretty much the same but added that he thought numerically speaking, ten was more stable than eleven. Another two minutes of silence followed his short speech.

Chris however, elected to follow John in rebellion. Chris was from Chicago, gay, and living in San Francisco under an assumed name in order to hide from the authorities in Illinois where he was wanted for questioning about a few minor drug offences, some outstanding debts and a certain matter of draft-dodging. Anita had met him at an underground house and begged Max to take him in a year earlier. Chris had always been well aware that any time he overstepped the mark he ran the risk of Max turning him in, which meant he was usually content to go along with the group. He had found that, contrary to his expectations, he quite liked living in community and could almost overcome his innate distrust of Max, but this time he felt buoyed up enough by John's attitude to bring some of his own feelings into the equation. He was also heartbroken.

"John's got it. There's some stuff going on here that isn't right. Just look around – Paul's really happy for Michael to have gone. Of course he is, he's got what he's wanted all along – now he's sitting there at the right hand of God. Father and Son, yeah Max? Isn't that how you see yourself? Only of course, now Michael's gone we'll have to think of him as the Holy Ghost, am I right?"

"No conversation, Chris."

"Fuck your rules Max. We've lost a friend, a brother . . . "

Paul looked across the table to Chris.

"Don't you mean lover?"

There was a pause while Chris looked at Paul, sizing him up and everyone else stared at Chris.

"Yeah, OK Paul. Lover. Michael was my lover. Do you have a problem with that?"

Max stood up at the head of the table, his voice trembling with the effort of affecting a calm exterior.

"This is a conversation. This is against House rules. You cannot do this."

"One minute, Chris."

Chris turned and snarled at Anita.

"Put your fucking watch away Anita, I know what's been going on."

Max and Anita both looked at each other and John noticed Anita's hands begin to shake. Max put his left hand over hers and pulled her slightly closer to him as he sat down again.

"Fine Chris. If you're so determined to bring it all up, perhaps you should say this in front of the whole group. If, that is, you really feel it's what Michael wants everyone to know?"

"Fuck you, Max."

"No. Not me. Go ahead. Here, let's get rid of this."

He took the stopwatch from Anita's hands and flung it against the wall.

"Now you have all the time in the world. But I warn you. You started this. If you can't handle what comes of it, you had better be prepared to leave the House yourself."

"I'm ready."

"Go ahead then. The floor is yours."

Max sat back in the chair, waiting for Chris. Only John

noticed that his grasp on Anita's hand was so tight that the tips of her fingers were starting to turn blue.

Chris looked at Max, then around at the whole table and began to speak.

"OK. Michael and I have been lovers for about three months. We were planning to leave together and Michael believed Max wouldn't let him go. That's why he started to do all these Processes. He thought that if Max saw how committed he was to the Group and to the Process, then when he actually said he was leaving, Max would allow him."

"I've never stopped anyone leaving before now, have I?"

John looked across at Max.

"No one's ever wanted to leave, so we have no means of comparison. But, then again, you were never in love with anyone who left before now either."

Rose sat up from John's shoulder and Doug and Jake shifted uncomfortably in their seats. Anita wrenched her hand away from Max's grasp and Max burst out laughing.

"Is this what all the fuss is about? You think I was in love with Michael? Christ! That's incredible!"

"You were. He told me you were."

"No Chris. I expect he told you he was in love with me. Didn't he?"

"I . . ."

"He never said I was in love with him, did he? He said he was in love with me. There's a big difference there. That is what he said. Isn't it?"

Chris just stared at Max, uncertain of what to say and certain that he had probably got himself in far too deep. Anita turned and took Chris's hand.

"Well, as it's all truth here today, I've got something to say too."

She raised her hand as both John and Max started to remonstrate with her.

"Don't worry, I'm talking to Chris, not you. You see Chris, I know Max."

"You don't know what ... "

"Oh yes I do. It's not that he has a problem with it, the homosexual thing, though maybe he does, but actually, I really don't see that he would have had the time."

"What do you mean?"

"I mean that as Max was screwing Rose for the first couple of months she was with us and Elspeth ever since Rose got too big for him to be comfortable with it, and me whenever he could, he hardly had time to fit Michael in as well."

Seeing Max was about to speak, she continued.

"Don't bother to deny it Max. I know you. Very well. How these silly little girls thought I didn't know, I'll never guess. But you see Chris, that's how I know Max certainly wasn't screwing Michael. He may have learnt the lessons of free love admirably, indeed, I think I taught him too well, but he hasn't quite managed to outgrow his traditional fear of queers. Have you Max?"

Max smiled at Anita.

"Thank you Anita. You're right, I still haven't quite crossed the border to explore my 'man loving' side. Stop snivelling Rose, it doesn't matter that much. It's only sex, at least Elspeth and Sam acknowledge that. Well, there we are – those are my secrets, but it still doesn't address Chris's hostility towards me. Shall I tell you what it is you're feeling Chris? Simple jealousy. Sure, you two were lovers, big deal. But Michael loved me and I rejected him. That is why he left us, that is why he's gone and that is why you won't ever see him again. I didn't want him and so he didn't want any of us. Michael is gone Chris, without you. Gone because it was me he loved, not you."

Chris sat slumped in his chair, tears trickling down his face. Max was about to start in again when John interrupted him.

"OK Max. You made your point. As it happens Chris, I think what Max says is true. I also knew Michael was in love with Max, but I didn't know he'd told him. I knew something was wrong but I wasn't sure what it was. I'm sorry, I don't think I'd have spoken up if I'd known it would end like this."

Anita looked up at John. "It's probably for the best. I shouldn't have let the girls keep thinking I didn't know what was going on. And it's good that Chris knows how Michael felt. It's good we all do. I mean the truth ... well, you know how it is ... the truth will set us free. At least that's what it's supposed to do." She looked up at Max who was sitting beside her. "Isn't it?"

Max smiled at Anita and then around the table at the whole group.

"Let's hope so. Now, shall we go on?"

The meeting continued for over three more hours. Secrets told and dissected, torn apart and digested. Until finally it was two in the morning and there was a room of ten tired people. Ten people of whom three were very relieved because there were still two secrets left and they'd managed to manipulate the meeting so successfully that neither of them was touched upon.

wavewalker

There is more to it than you know. It isn't clear from
outside.
You see it once you're in there. Too late.
It is hidden, in code, in the hieroglyphics of his magic.
But I have seen it, touched it.
I know the truth.

The code is close to breaking now, the sea lapping at its
edge.
Soon there will be a washing away, sweeping all the lies
before it.
I want it now, but even I cannot command the tides,
they come when they are ready.

I have laid a channel.
It is coming sooner than he thinks.

CHAPTER 13

Anita had been relieved to unload the burden of her Christmases past following her Process but she certainly hadn't told Max any of the details of the Christmases present she'd been spending with John.

John and Anita had met within the first week she was in the States. Both of them being new to New York and new to big cities, they'd met at a club and played babes in toyland together for a while, before settling down to some serious drug-taking and countrywide roaming. They were able to take in most of the midwest, half of Canada and even some of Alaska before Anita's money ran out. After a year of travelling – physically and psychically – John had gone back to his wife to give it "one more chance" and Anita went on to feed her wanderlust alone. She attended lectures, seminars, arts events, camps and concerts, all funded by her clever knack of turning pleasing young men into even more tender currency. By the end of '69 she knew all about the underground movement and the antiwar movement, but as with so many other "free" young women of her generation, the woman's movement remained another world.

Then she met Max. She gave him a window on to a whole new way of life and he gave her cash. Cash, cheques and two charge cards. Anita thought it was a simple transaction, Max thought it was love. Eventually, she decided to persuade herself it was love too, after all, it would be easier to take his money that way. And for a while it had been love, persuasion becoming reality, but then the House, Anita's dream creation, had taken over. With the House came Max's new strength, leaving Anita much less able to be free and run her own life as she had been used to. Running her own life had, until Max, usually meant running away whenever things got a bit too involved. But with the House as a base and Max's growing confidence, it all got bigger and bigger until one day she woke to find herself living with the exhausting trappings of marriage – children in the shape of the House members requiring constant attention, personally subject to the authoritarian demands of her partner, often denied access to the "patriarch" by his lackeys – all without a hint of the security of a real marriage. Which was when she answered John's letter from Virginia, telling him that as his wife had decided she didn't want to try any more, he was welcome to come join them in the House and resume their relationship where it had been left off – in secrecy of course, but that would no doubt give it the extra frisson her relationship with Max was sadly lacking.

John duly arrived, was welcomed into the community, joined in the running of the House and joined Anita whenever he could. Which, given Max's paternalistic pre-occupations, was more often than not. And when Anita became pregnant with Jasmine, she just let Max assume the baby was his. John lived in the House and, as the whole community was present at the birth anyway, he missed out on none of the upbringing of the child who may well have been his daughter.

Anita didn't know whose child Jasmine was. John, with three children of his own back in Virginia, didn't care and Max didn't even know there was any question of paternity. It didn't occur to Anita that it might one day matter to the child. Once she had John to play with it was all working out rather well for Anita, Max's burgeoning power complex notwithstanding. Or it had been until Michael used her winter quilt to mop up what remained of his life.

Max's secret was a different matter. He told Anita that the night Michael crawled into their room and curled up on the chair at the foot of their bed he had heard something. In the foggy aftermath of sex and on the edge of falling into deep sleep, he had seen a figure at the bottom of his bed and had heard Michael's gentle sobbing gradually die away. He told her he had been too close to sleep to react. Too close to that part of sleep where the brain is still just conscious but the limbs and exterior senses are not capable of functioning. But Max did know that he had chosen to ignore Michael, chosen to let him cry, he knew that he had chosen to sleep with the iron scent of blood heavy in his nostrils.

Max knew and then made another choice – to actively block the memories. Not to remember how during the Process he had told Michael he would be better dead than in so much pain. Had told Michael that he was creating his own suffering and could also provide his own succour. Had told Michael he didn't love him. Told Michael he would never love him.

Max knew it all and then, like any good Processee, chose not to know. To look at his own reality and then put it away. He never expected to have to look at his memories of Michael again.

CHAPTER 14

For Saz, making contact, or at least being in the same room with Maxwell North had been the easy part. Trying to talk to his wife was proving almost impossible. Saz had chosen to pose as a journalist and unfortunately, Caron North was not only unwilling to talk to the press, she had positively rejected the idea even as a possibility. As her agent explained, not especially patiently, to Saz when she called.

"For a start Miss . . . what did you say your name was?"

"Hannon, Ms Hannon."

"Well, Ms Hannon, I assume you mean Caron McKenna?"

"Oh, she uses her own name for work?"

"Most artists do, Ms Hannon," he continued, stressing the Ms as if it might choke him, "I'm sure you will understand that Miss McKenna is a very busy woman. She has two new commissions and an exhibition opening within a couple of weeks."

"That's why I'd like to talk to her."

"And that's why she wouldn't like to talk to you."

"I'm sorry?"

"I'll be plain Ms Hannon. Caron McKenna has, to be frank, absolutely no need of publicity. Her work sells for phenomenal sums, a fact which, quite naturally, delights me. She is clearly one of the most gifted artists of her generation."

"I know how good she is, that's why I want to talk to her."

"Yes. Of course you do. And so do the ten or eleven other journalists who have called me this morning. Now, I appreciate your interest, but I can assure you that even if Miss McKenna needed the publicity, she would not have the time to take up your kind offer of an interview. She gives one interview a year only and I'm afraid the *Arts Review* took up that opportunity last month, having arranged the meeting six months in advance. Try someone else Ms Hannon, I'm sure there are thousands of eager young artists just dying to achieve the kind of exposure you're offering. Caron McKenna is not one of those artists. I'm afraid you're wasting your time. Good morning."

And he hung up on her. Which didn't put Saz in an especially good mood as she was still deeply in the throes of packing and had to wade across the room through two half-filled suitcases and eight boxes of papers in order to find her diary and obtain the next number she had earmarked as a possible introduction to Caron McKenna-North.

"Bloody elusive artists, bloody aggressive old misogynist agents, bloody damn bloody fucking horrible packing!"

"Did I hear you expressing a less than generous attitude to our Caron's agent, and do you really want to keep this?"

Molly came out of Saz's kitchen with a very old, very time-worn frying pan.

"Of course I do. That is my mother's cast iron frying pan and was her mother's before her."

"But you never use it. You don't fry anything."

"It's a sentimental attachment. Like the one I have for you. And it makes great pikelets. Put it in the big plastic bag over there, I do want it. But even more than that, I want to talk to Maxwell North's bloody elusive wife. It's

ludicrous, I mean I know she's good but she's hardly
Greta bloody Garbo."

"You tried her agent?"

"Doesn't need the publicity, doesn't give interviews."

"The gallery?"

"They told me to call the agent."

"Any charity work?"

"None. Well, she goes to the events with him, drug
rehabs and stuff like that, but doesn't have any all of her
own. For a society wife she doesn't seem to have much
to do with society."

"Maybe she isn't really a society wife?"

Saz looked up from the fourth box where she was trying
to decide just how much she would need to have sixteen
small boxes of childhood photos with her at Molly's flat.

"Huh?"

"Well, she does seem to have a life of her own. All that
press stuff you've got on her is almost all about her work.
No specific charities, only a few balls with her husband.
Except for the odd event with him she seems to devote
herself to her work. So maybe you should stop thinking
along the society lines and try career woman instead.
She sounds a lot more like you or me than like one of
those ladies who lunch and get their hair done all the
time."

"Good point. So what do you suggest?"

"I don't know, you're the detective, do you always get
your lovers to help you?"

Saz finally dumped all the photos in the box and earmarked it to remain in the cupboard full of things she
was planning to store at her sister's house.

"Only the ones who look so stunning in a T-shirt, old
socks with holes in the toes and nothing else."

"Don't forget the frying pan!"

"How could I? It's what makes you so damn sexy."

"Your mother's cast iron frying pan makes me look sexy? Very Freudian!"

Saz launched herself over the boxes to Molly and pulled her down on to a pile of old clothes destined for Oxfam.

"Shut up, lie back and think of Dunoon."

"Hold on, we can't do this here, these are going to the charity shop this afternoon, I've just folded them all nicely, they're for recycling, not shagging – oi! Leave my socks on, I don't want to get my nicely pedicured feet all messed up wading through your rubbish!"

Saz had removed Molly's T-shirt and the frying pan and was attempting to take her socks off but left them at her complaint, and proceeded to warm Molly's body with her mouth instead. Warm breath replacing the goose bumps of sudden naked chill with those of desire, cold skin turning to warmth with gentle sweat breaking out, as Saz's hot and fully clothed body alternately writhed and rested on Molly's naked skin. With the rough scratch of a still unfolded winter coat beneath her and Saz's fingers playing her, Molly came quickly. Saz looked up from where she lay, her mouth at Molly's breast.

"Was that it?"

Molly sighed sleepily, "I'm afraid so darling. You're just too good. I never met anyone who could make me come as easily as you do."

"But I'd only just begun!"

"You, me and Karen Carpenter – speaking of which, shouldn't you get back to Caron North?"

"McKenna."

"Whatever. Her. The artist."

"I guess so, I'd rather lie here with you though. Shall we do it again?"

"No. Look dollybird, you're only half-packed, you've got Caroline moving in here tomorrow and you still haven't even exchanged pleasantries with Caron North-

McKenna-Thingie. Slaying me yet again with your undisputed sexual prowess is going to have to wait. Unfortunately. Besides, I'm due at the hospital in an hour."

"You're so damn responsible!"

Molly smiled and stood up, rubbing her shoulder which held an inverted imprint of Saz's winter coat.

"I'm a doctor Saz, surely you've seen all the movies? My work is my life!"

"So's mine. Doesn't stop me knowing a good shag when I see one."

"Thank you. Actually, the truth is, I can't afford to be late yet again this week. Get a move on, I'm unhappy enough about your ex-lover moving in here as it is, I don't want her moving in and finding we've made a love nest of all your old clothes."

"Beggars can't be choosers. If, like Carrie, you are wont to suddenly decide that New York isn't where you want to live after all, quit your course, pack your bags, book a flight back to London the same day and still expect to have somewhere to live when you get here because you could never live with your own mother for more than two days, then you have to take things as you find them."

"Maybe so, but I don't especially relish the idea of her taking me where she finds me."

"Neither do I, you're all mine."

"Right. So get on with it!"

"Yes ma'am!"

Four hours later most of Saz's life was piled in twenty boxes and three suitcases in the hallway of her flat, she was hurriedly dressing and, with her mother's frying pan in her hand, racing over to Caron North's house.

Caroline had rung to arrange picking up the keys and when Saz told her about the problems she was having getting in touch with Caron North she burst out laughing.

"All this fuss just to get to talk to her?"

"It's not funny, it's proving bloody impossible!"

"Do you not read the papers at all Saz?"

"What?"

"Yesterday's *Guardian*, media section. An article about Caron McKenna, artist and cook."

"I was told she wasn't giving any interviews."

"This wasn't an interview, it was an article. Apparently she's an artist who loves to cook."

"So?"

"So she's incorporating cooking utensils and food things into her new exhibition."

"I knew that, all the papers have said that. That's hardly news Carrie."

"Did they all also say that she was planning to use 'found' objects?"

Saz picked up two unmatching socks from the carpet and threw them into a black plastic bag full of items even Oxfam couldn't possibly want.

"What's a 'found object' when it's at home?"

"Well, my little philistine, usually it's just that. Something you find, at home, in the street, wherever. But in this case, McKenna is accepting items from anyone who wants to give them to her. At least until she's got enough."

"Are you serious?"

"Of course. It's one of those 'involve the general public in the arts' things. Makes the Arts Council feel better about the massive grants they keep giving her. Not that it ever works of course, because the general public don't read the *Guardian* media section all that much. Now, in New York . . . "

"Hold it! Where is she going to collect these items?"

"Don't know. It didn't say. I suppose you could just take your egg timer to her house and hand it over."

"Carrie, I love you. I love your eclectic head that remembers all kinds of rubbish, I love your inability to stay in any one city longer than eighteen months, but most of all I love how you always seem to know just exactly what I want you to know."

"Yeah yeah, I know."

CHAPTER 15

Two hours later Saz was still waiting to see Caron North. Having left her place in such a hurry she'd panicked halfway there when she realized that Max might be around and may even recognize her from the workshop. Two tube stops later she'd calmed down with the thought that even if he did happen to be home and not at his office in the middle of the day, she'd just lie and say she'd seen Caron's article in the paper and felt the need to bring along her pan. It was at least as likely as any other lie she could come up with in the next eight tube stops to South Kensington.

She'd been shown in to the big white house by the Australian cleaner and directed to the drawing room next to the entrance. And left there. She'd had plenty of time to examine the coffee table, loaded down with neatly piled glossy magazines. She'd looked out the back window to the garden – standard landscaping and pond, though with one or two interesting sculptures breaking the South Kensington mould – and she'd looked out the front window to the almost identical tall white house opposite. She'd accepted a pot of coffee from the cleaner who came back to explain.

"I'm Kirsty, I'm the cleaner. Caron's busy working, but she likes your frying pan and needs to know the story behind it, so if you don't mind waiting, she'd really like to talk to you."

Saz didn't mind at all, in fact she was perfectly happy to spend the next hour or so drinking coffee and sneaking through the attractively "distressed" cupboards – artfully, if somewhat pretentiously, hiding the TV, stereo, fax and answerphone. And when the telephone rang unanswered for the fourth time and she heard the answerphone click on, she checked the hallway for any signs of the cleaner and very sensibly turned the answerphone monitor up. Which is how she got to hear Maxwell North talking lovingly to his dear wife.

"Caron, it's me. If you're there, pick up the damn telephone. I know you're busy but there is something I need to discuss with you . . . are you there? . . . Well, when you get in please call me at the office immediately."

And ten minutes later for the second time.

"Caron, I've just spoken to your father who assures me you are at home, he spoke to you this morning and you told him you'd be in all day. Now answer the damn phone! . . . I don't care if you are working, I need you now . . . Caron? . . . Kirsty are you there? Caron? . . . "

He waited a short while and then hung up. And finally for the third time,

"Caron, call me. I want to speak to you. It's urgent."

Maxwell North sounded worried. Certainly not the Mr In-Control who'd run the Process a couple of weeks earlier. Still, Saz figured, even existential gurus couldn't always have the perfect homelife. Overhead she heard footsteps on the stairs and very quickly turned the monitor off and picked up an old *Vogue*, settling herself on the sofa. Kirsty came back in.

"Look, I'm really sorry this is taking so long – do you want anything? More coffee?"

Saz looked up at the woman. Classic Australian good looks – tall with long legs, long blonde hair, great tan and bright blue eyes.

"No, thanks. I think I'm about to overdose on coffee.

Um ... the phone's been really busy – sounds like the answerphone's probably overloaded too."

Kirsty went to the answerphone and played back the messages quietly so that Saz could barely hear them, she rewound the tape with a barely audible "Shit" and bounded out of the room and up the stairs.

"Caron! ... Max has been calling, get on the bloody phone!"

Saz heard nothing more for about ten minutes until Caron North herself walked into the room.

"I'm so sorry to have kept you waiting all this time. I didn't get your name?"

"Molly – Molly Steele," Saz lied, standing up quickly and bruising her knee on the too-close coffee table.

"No, please, sit down, make yourself comfortable. And call me Caron. I never know whether I should say McKenna or North anyway, so Caron's always much easier. Now tell me about this wonderful pan of yours."

Caron McKenna got out a little notebook and Saz told her about her mother's frying pan, all the while studying the artist who was taking notes in front of her. Her delicate, thin hands still covered in plaster, elegant features, small frame, the long fair hair. Everything about the woman was pale and fine, practically translucent yet also strong at the same time. Her clearly muscled forearms were covered in a fine dusting of plaster powder. According to the press cutting she had to be thirty-eight, not an awful lot older than Saz, though all those years of good breeding and family wealth gave her an assurance Saz never had without a fair amount of effort and bravado coming into play. And there was something else, something she couldn't quite put her finger on. It was to do with a distance, an air of "otherness" that Saz felt she recognized but couldn't quite place. At least not until Kirsty came back in with a tray of sandwiches.

"I thought you girls might be a bit hungry. I'm out of here now Caron, sorry I can't stay longer. See you next week, bye!"

Then Saz caught the look from Caron to Kirsty's long legs and fine mane of hair as she flounced out the door and she knew just what it was.

"She's a dyke Moll. Caron North is gay and she fancies her very tasty Australian cleaner."

"You're mad Saz. Caron North is an upper-middle-class Englishwoman. She's one of 'those' women. She's married to one of the most successful men in the country . . . "

"Too flash to be gay?"

"No. But she really doesn't need to lie."

"Don't you believe it. A family like that? They're not going to ruin their reputation just because their little girl's queer. And the woman's an artist for God's sake. I know she sells well now, but what about all those years when Daddy was supporting her, and then when North was supporting her? It's an arrangement Molly my darling, a good old-fashioned traditional arranged marriage."

"Hardly what my Mum would call traditional."

"Nor mine. But I bet that's what it is."

"Possible."

"You know when you spot one."

"Yeah right. And I could spot a poof at sixty paces, and all blacks look the same. You sound like a fascist."

"That's not fair! All I said was I think she's a dyke."

"OK. Anyway, the dubious nature of Caron McKenna's sexuality aside, what else did you learn?"

Saz screwed up her nose and started on another cup of coffee.

"Not a lot. Classic rich person's house, most of the decor straight out of the Conran Shop. Nothing spectacular. I was hoping to get to see the studio, but no chance, they kept me well caged in the drawing room."

"So what now?"

"Not sure, I'll sleep on it. I get my ideas better that way." Saz gulped down the rest of her coffee and took Molly's hand leading her to the bedroom.

"Only I don't intend to have any ideas for at least a couple of hours yet."

CHAPTER 16

Saz rose early the next morning and went out for her run before the rest of London even knew Sunday had started. Leaving Camberwell had been hard in many ways, giving up her freedom being just one of them; though she and Molly had seemed to spend all of their free time with each other, it wasn't until they moved in together that she realized it wasn't quite the same as never being able to get away and "go home". And she missed the "cosmopolitan" nature of Camberwell – blacks and whites, Asians and Greeks, living side by side, if not in complete harmony, at least with a fair degree of non-violent co-operation. After only one week she missed the Greek bread and the little gift shop and she especially missed the chip shop with Jamaican patties for which no amount of Hampstead Haagen-Dazs was fair compensation. But at six in the morning on an early summer's day, she would gladly have traded it all yet again for the pleasure of having her early morning run on Hampstead Heath. For four years she'd been running, in all seasons, in Camberwell, Vauxhall, Stockwell and Brixton, now she ran through trees and over fields. She'd quickly discovered she could run for an hour and not meet anyone – as long as she left home early enough. This morning she left their flat and ran straight across the heath to the women's pond where three old ladies were already swimming, up another hill to take a five-minute breather at her favourite resting point – just two trees and a stunning view of London. Today in the warmth, the view was hazy and she thought she could just make out St Paul's, but in late winter when she'd first met Molly, it had been cold and crisp, the whole of London clearly imprinted on the southern sky, making the pain of leaving her new lover in bed and running in freezing weather almost worth it. From the hill she turned again and ran through the wooded area, then past the car park to the tearooms where the staff were arriving at work. They knew her well enough by now and she was able to buy fresh coffee hours before opening time. This morning she took her polystyrene cup, borrowed a copy of *The Sunday Times* and went back outside to sit on the grass.

She was halfway through the review bit, having discarded the other sections, with an apology to the many trees dying for newsprint she wasn't even vaguely interested in, when the wind whipped up the pages, scattering them all across the little hill. She ran around frantically, gathered them together and was carefully replacing them to return the paper as neatly as possible to its owner, when she saw Caron North's name, in one of the longwinded articles she never normally could be bothered with. The article said little of interest, mostly it was about the difficulty of finding good staff and how hard it was for a busy woman to run home and family. It did however mention Caron North as one of the few women who seemed to have it all – husband, home and career, all in glowing health. Though even she was quoted as saying "What I wouldn't give for the perfect assistant" and ended with the writer chiming in with the old cliché about every successful woman needing a wife to come home to. Saz laughed to herself, "Yeah, but I bet you don't have any idea of just how much Caron would welcome that wife!"

She ripped the article out of the paper, gave it back

over the counter, threw away the rest of her coffee and ran home.

Five hours later Saz bowled up to Maxwell North's Kensington home, her head stuffed with the names of every sculptor and British artist of the past fifty years that Molly could recall.

"How do you know all this?" Saz asked groaning, her head sagging on her hands, her hair brushing the chunks of fresh parmesan she'd loaded on top of her pasta.

"It's not that I know so much," Molly replied. "It's that you know so little. And get your hair out of your lunch. Didn't you ever watch *The Late Show*?"

"Not by choice."

"Well it's too late now. Anyway this still seems a little stupid to me, what if North finds you in his house? What if he answers the door?"

"Doesn't matter. I gave them your name when I did the course in the first place."

"Great."

"And it's Sunday. He's probably taking a course."

Molly stood up and started to clear away the empty plates.

"What if he's not? Don't you think he'd be surprised to find you there?"

"I might be very interested in art for all he knows. Just because I've done the Process, doesn't mean I can't talk to his wife. Anyway, Maxwell North has run two courses a week for the past three years, all over the world. I don't think that even I could have made that much of an impact on him. Now if you'll kindly stop depressing me and give me your car keys, I'll be on my way."

Molly handed over the keys with a kiss and the last piece of olive ciabatta.

Caron North answered the door. She was obviously very surprised to see Saz.

"Oh . . . Molly, isn't it? Do you want the pan back?"

Saz smiled and held out the newspaper article.

"No. Look, I know this is weird, and I'm sorry to disturb you like this, but I saw how busy you were yesterday and then I read this today and I know it's a bit of a silly idea but . . . "

She took a deep breath and launched into the lie she and Molly had rehearsed while making lunch.

"I thought maybe you could do with an assistant. And I could do with a job. Just for however long it takes until the exhibition – it is soon, isn't it?"

"Ten days."

"Right. You see I'm going back to college in the summer. Adult student. I'm going to study art – not fine art, but gallery management, history, all that stuff, only I don't really know much yet and I know how busy you are, well it was obvious really, and then I read this, and I wondered . . . if maybe you'd take me on."

Caron opened her mouth to speak but Saz interrupted her.

"You do need some help don't you?"

Caron just looked at Saz and then burst out laughing.

"I really don't know what to say. You have to admit this is a little odd."

"I know, I'm sorry, I did think I ought to call first but I just got all enthused and then . . . "

"Don't apologize, I appreciate your enthusiasm. Not that I'd actually thought about taking anyone on . . . Kirsty comes in twice a week to help with the house. What can you do?"

"Type a little, answer phones a lot. I make great coffee – espresso, cappuccino, latte. Depends what you need really."

Saz waved the article under Caron's nose.

"It says here you need a wife."

"Journalistic licence. I really need someone who doesn't mind doing all the crap legwork until the show opens."

"I'll give it a go. Eight quid an hour."

Caron asked Saz in and gave her coffee and individually wrapped Turkish delights, read through the non specific references – dug up that afternoon by Molly, one from an old landlady and one from her grammar school headmistress. They then talked briefly about sculpting, though, luckily for Saz the discussion was rather more about Caron's own work than anyone else's. She then sent her away with orders to show up the next morning at nine. And an amended wage down to six pounds an hour.

After five days Caron North was declaring she couldn't survive without her "new helper" and Saz, with only five more days until the exhibition, was becoming more and more frustrated. As she explained to Molly,

"It's not that she doesn't talk to me, it's just that when she does it's never about anything that matters."

"You've only known her a week, you can't expect her to divulge her life's secrets just like that."

"You did."

"That's what you think, like your Mrs North, I'm still an untapped mystery waiting to be discovered."

"Yeah, but I don't have time to wait. For her I mean. My job's done in five days' time. I'm stuck on this one and going nowhere fast."

"You seem to be going all over London."

"The circuit from their house to Caron's agent, encompassing Harrods' Food Halls and Harvey Nichols, is hardly my idea of seeing life."

"God, she really is one of those women isn't she?"

Saz munched thoughtfully on her thumbnail.

"Kind of. I mean she has all the trappings – boring clothes, black velvet headband, BMW – all that. But she just doesn't quite fit in with them. You know, I've met two of her friends so far and they really are those 'ladies who lunch' – hairdresser at ten, nails at eleven, little walk to Sloane Square at twelve and then a glass of champagne and three lettuce leaves at any one of those identical trendy bloody Kensington restaurants for lunch. But she's different. It's like there's something going on. More than just the artist thing. I mean at least she actually has a job, she's doing things with her life, she's not just defined by her husband and his work. But there's definitely something else."

"So what are you going to do?"

"Stick it out for these last few days. Try and snoop around a bit more. I haven't had a chance to look into her bedroom yet. I haven't even had any reason to go upstairs. I think she's starting to trust me. I know she's not going to talk to me like a normal woman friend or even a new boss might, but maybe I can get her to tell me a bit about Max. Or whatever else might help. I'm just certain something's not quite right. And I really do think she's a dyke."

"Then get her drunk. Even posh ladies talk when they're drunk."

Saz laughed, "Yeah, but so do I."

"In which case, my darling, you'll have to stay sober, won't you? It's easy, work late one night, ask her if she fancies going to the pub for a quick half, she'll be shocked and horrified at the thought and offer you a glass of the lovely champagne that's chilling in the fridge, you get her to drink most of it and then ask her how a refined, fancy girl like her comes to be married to Dr North, guru to the establishment."

"So that's what they teach you in medical school."

"That's right. Bedside manner always was my forte." Molly rolled over until she was on top of Saz, she held her face in both hands and began to kiss her; nose, eyes, mouth, chin, shoulders, each body part rapidly surrendering to her touch. Molly muttered as she kissed, "Bedside, fireside, heath side, beside you, down your side, underside, overside, outside . . . "

"Inside?" Saz whispered and pulled Molly even closer.

CHAPTER 17

Saz's first chance to get inside Caron North's head came the next day. Kirsty had just left, having finished dragging the vacuum cleaner up and down the four flights of stairs, and Caron had received an urgent call from her agent begging her to come down to the gallery and "chat pleasantly" to the owner. Caron was expecting an upholsterer to come and look at the sofa she wanted to cut in half for another installation and her agent left her with no choice but to go out. She assured Saz she'd be back in a few hours and left her with a long list of questions for the upholsterer about the best ways to mangle sofabeds. Saz put Caron into a cab and then jumped back up the steps, closing the front door behind her and grinning in anticipation. She ran up to Caron and Max's bedroom on the second floor.

The room was ageing eighties chic – swagged curtains, ragrolled walls, dominated by a huge old bed, draped with a slightly threadbare, obviously handcrafted patchwork quilt. On what was clearly Max's side of the bed was a small bedside table, with a neat stack of medical books and a halogen lamp as the only marks of his presence. On the other side of the bed there was a slightly larger, matching table. This one held three or four fashion magazines, a pair of reading glasses, a selection of homeopathic remedies, an open bottle of mineral water, two alarm clocks and a photo. A signed photo of a young woman, smiling directly at the camera, using one hand to hold back a swathe of long dark hair from her eyes. Across the bottom of the photo was an inky scrawl.

To my darling Caron, all my love, Deb

It was signed with three large kisses. The head and shoulders shot was taken at a beach, Saz could just make out a shoreline in the background and she guessed it must have been at least a few years old, the colours in the picture were starting to fade slightly. She slipped the photo out of its heavy silver frame and turned it over. It was an ordinary enlargement of the kind of photo taken on any summer holiday and then made into Christmas presents by the subject, elated to finally have a picture of themselves good enough to give away. Written on the back in Caron's tiny, neat handwriting were the words – "Deb. Summer '86. Sifnos." Saz carefully replaced the photo and then began going through the drawers.

One by one she gently sifted through Max and Caron's clothes, underwear, hankies, socks. She went into their bathroom and rifled through the bathroom cabinet, no condoms, diaphragm or pills anywhere, no obvious signs of any heterosexual activity. She went into each of their walk-in wardrobes and slipped the jackets and shirts and neatly drycleaned dresses backwards and forwards on the sliding rails. She scanned the small bookshelf by Caron's side of the bed but it scarcely revealed a hidden passion for dyke novels, being largely full of weighty tomes on expressionism and the postmodern in the present day. Finally, she went through the big desk against the end wall of the room. It was obviously divided in half – three drawers for Max and three for Caron. Max's drawers were singularly unspectacular. One was completely empty, one was full of old cheque book stubs and an international assortment of coins and the last one held a range of writing paper and stationery with both names and their home address elegantly printed across the top. Max obviously kept all his work-related things quite separate from his home life. Caron's drawers were much more full but initially, equally unhelpful. A mix of old letters in the top drawer, from various interior designers, builders and plumbers confirmed that Caron took control of all their joint household requirements. The second drawer down contained another neatly piled bunch of used cheque books and assorted foreign monies. In the bottom drawer Saz came across a pile of old cards, from Christmases and birthdays long gone. She was about to dismiss them when, shuffling them into a neat pile to put them back, she noticed that a couple were not in the same cheery colours as all the rest. She pulled them out of the middle of the pile and opened them. They were sympathy cards. One signed with Max's thick, calligraphic pen which the manufacturers had thoughtfully left blank inside to allow Max to pen his own message. It read

I'm so sorry my darling, we'll never find another Deb, I will comfort you all I can.

And the second, a much more formal card from a neighbour just saying,

We were all terribly sorry to read about Deb. If we can help at all, please let us know.

Saz was just starting to replace the cards when she heard the front door slam downstairs. She shoved the cards back into the drawer and hurried out of the room, quietly closing the door behind her. She stood frozen on the landing for a couple of seconds wondering which way to go – upstairs to Caron's studio or downstairs to greet whoever had let themselves in. Maxwell North's voice came up the stairs.

"Caron? Are you home?"

Saz clenched her fists and answered, forcing herself to walk calmly as she called out, "No, she's had to go to the gallery. Can I help?"

Max stood at the bottom of the stairs, going through his mail piled on the hall table, he was engrossed in a letter and didn't even look at Saz until she was within three feet of him.

"No. I was just hoping to have a chat with her, you must be the new assistant, I'm Dr North. Sorry we haven't met before – I'm terribly busy, haven't been home for most of this week. I'm on my way to a meeting right now, just passing . . . "

Max finally looked up from his mail and Saz was more than a little surprised to see the recognition in his eyes. He smiled.

"Oh Molly, it's you. How's the swimming training coming on?"

Saz groaned inside and planted a smile on her face.

"Ah – great. Yeah, it's fine, thanks Dr North."

Max nodded and picked up his briefcase to put his letters into it.

"Did you tell my wife that we'd met, Molly?"

"No. No I didn't. Should I have?"

Max closed his briefcase and continued to smile pleasantly.

"I don't know. I guess it depends why you're here. Why are you here?"

"Ah – to help?"

"Help who?"

"Well, Caron of course."

"But she told me her new assistant wanted to know

more about art – about which she also says you seem to know absolutely nothing. So maybe you're really here to help yourself, yes?"

"Kind of, I mean if you look at it like that. Yes I am. To help myself know more."

Saz could feel herself turning bright red under North's unflinching smiling gaze, her neck was straining from having to look up at him and she hoped he couldn't tell quite how nervous he was making her. With a mental note to herself to stop being so soft she remembered her mother's story about how school bullies were always cowards at heart and decided that North was likely to have her bleating out the truth in seconds if she didn't take control of the situation, so she smiled back at him and turned to walk downstairs to the kitchen.

"I must say I'm impressed at your feat of memory Dr North, I can't imagine how you do that. I wouldn't have thought that even I was that memorable. I was just about to make a cup of coffee, would you like one?"

North's smile dropped and he stared back at her.

"No, thank you. I'd rather you answered my questions. Which came first – me or my wife?"

Saz turned and leant against the banisters.

"I can't say for certain, I mean I knew I was doing the art course already, but when I did the weekend Process, everything just seemed to fall into place."

She grinned at him, "I'd acknowledged I was scared about starting in September, so I decided to do something about it. Look for an artist to help, get involved. A friend told me about the found objects – for the installation. So I brought Caron my frying pan. Then I saw the article about her and I'd already seen how busy she was, so it occurred to me that maybe she'd take me on. Just to help with the exhibition. And she did. It was simple. Everything seemed to follow so easily after I did the Process. What was it you said? Take the step and the path will appear? Well, it did."

Max looked at her, obviously still a little suspicious, but not quite able to argue with what seemed to be one of his own success stories standing right in front of him.

"And you didn't find the need to tell Caron that you'd met me?"

Saz shook her head,

"To be honest Dr North, as I said, I'm stunned you even remember me. And I didn't want to seem as if I was sucking up to Caron – through you I mean. I actually really like her work and I thought it might be a bit off to come in to see her and then start praising you."

Max smiled again, apparently put at ease with a big dose of flattery, he picked up his briefcase and walked to the front door. With his hand on the doorknob he turned back to Saz, no smile at all now.

"You know Molly, I'm really glad that the weekend Process was so beneficial to you. But hey, if you're lying, you can be sure I'll find you out. And if you are – I will find you. Is that clear?"

Saz looked back at Max, she too had stopped smiling.

"Sure Dr North. Whatever you say."

Ten minutes later, when her hands had just about stopped shaking, Saz opened the door to the most tedious upholsterer she'd ever encountered – the only upholsterer she'd ever encountered – who talked to her for what seemed like the whole afternoon about the best ways to dismantle a sofa and who was still there when Caron came home an hour later, leaving Saz no time at all to look through the rest of the house. She went home that night with an even greater curiosity about Caron, a growing grudge against Max and more knowledge about the secret life of the sofa than she thought was truly decent.

CHAPTER 18

By the time Saz finished her last day's work for Caron she knew more about Deb Mitcham than she could ever have hoped for. She had roped in her tame policewomen friends for added backup. Judith and Helen had been together for almost seven years and Saz, like most of their friends, found their constant vacillation between being either passionately in love or on the brink of breaking up fairly infuriating – if only because she could never be sure if both or just one of them would turn up to dinner when invited. They were however, able to access information Saz could never find by herself – and they also brought very nice champagne whenever they did make it over for dinner. Following a great deal of subtle digging they were able to let Saz know that not only had Deb lived in the house with the Norths, she'd died there too. On a hot night in August, twenty-seven-year-old Debra Mitcham had killed herself by cutting her wrists. Lengthwise, the right way. She'd wrapped herself in a winter quilt, which had quite effectively soaked up most of her blood. Maxwell North had found her at about four in the morning and had immediately alerted the authorities but, as a doctor, he could confirm that she'd already been dead at least an hour. She'd cut her wrists with North's specialist razor – "a fine shave for refined gentlemen". She'd lived in London for five years and with the Norths since 1984, where she'd been gainfully employed as an assistant to them both and had, by all accounts, seemed happily settled. According to the policewoman who'd interviewed her, Caron North had been devastated, but as Carrie remarked to Saz, "Well, even if they weren't shagging, she's not going to be too happy to have all that blood over her carpet, is she?"

That night, Saz asked Caron if she could take her for a drink, "To thank you for this past week."

To her surprise Caron did exactly as Molly had predicted. Turned down the suggestion of the pub and told Saz to open the bottle of champagne in the fridge. Three hours and two bottles of champagne later, and again, fulfilling Molly's prediction, Caron North was fairly drunk and Saz was, with not a little feeling of regret, almost completely sober. She finished a mouthful of her smoked salmon sandwich.

"I have a friend who used to live round here. She said there was an Australian girl staying with you, I thought she meant Kirsty, but she said this was years ago."

Caron nodded.

"Yes, there was."

"Did she use to work for you?"

Caron nodded again and poured the last of the wine into Saz's glass.

"I'd rather not talk about her Molly, if you don't mind."

"Sorry – I just heard something, and I wondered . . . "

Caron ran her finger around the top of her glass until it began to sing.

"You know, this is really interesting. Max said you were snooping. But I told him you couldn't be."

She looked up at Saz.

"He was right wasn't he?"

Saz put down her glass and looked directly at Caron, as honestly as she could manage.

"Kind of. But not snooping on him, or you. For Deb . . . Deb's friends. For one of Deb's friends. I met this Australian girl at a club and she said . . . we got talking . . . and she said she couldn't believe Deb had killed herself . . . "

"I saw her. I saw her dead. I know she killed herself. It was a long time ago. I can't believe you're bringing this all up . . . "

"I know, I'm sorry. But I told her, this girl, that I'd done the course, Max's course I mean . . . "

"He told me."

"And I said, if you took me on, I'd try to find out for her. Find out about Deb."

Caron stood up and took their empty glasses to the dishwasher, her grip on the glasses was white knuckletight.

"I see. And what should I do now, Molly? Now that you've been in my house and touched my things and my work and all under false pretences?"

She turned around and flopped down until she was sitting on the ground, leaning against the dishwasher and looking up at Saz. She was crying.

"What should I do now? You've come in here. You've lied to me, taken advantage of me and brought up past things that I'd hoped were safely put away. What shall I do?"

Saz got off her chair and knelt on the floor beside Caron. She tried to reach out to comfort her but the older woman shoved her away.

"Look Caron, I'm really sorry. I have liked working with you. It hasn't all been lies. Um . . . was she, Deb . . . was she your lover?"

Caron glared at her, "You really are pushing it now, aren't you? Just get out before I have you thrown out, go on, go. Get the fuck out of here."

When Caron finally stopped screaming and crying Saz

held her close, stroking her hair, the two of them sitting among the shards of shattered glass.

"Fuck, I really am sorry Caron. I had no idea, I mean . . . Christ, I don't know what I mean. I never intended to upset you like this. I'm really sorry. Please, listen to me, it would be really good if you didn't do anything. Don't speak to Dr North about this. Not yet."

Caron didn't answer so Saz pressed on.

"You have no reason to, but if you could just trust me, if you'll just hang on for a little while, I'll . . . oh shit, I don't know, I'll do something."

Caron sniffed and wiped the back of her hand across her eyes.

"Very eloquent. You sounded a lot more convincing when you were lying."

"Yeah well. As I said, I'm sorry."

Caron pulled herself up and leant against the table.

"Molly – is that your real name?"

"No. Sorry again."

"Right. I . . . ah . . . I'm quite interested in what happened to Deb myself. I would like to know too. I . . . "

Her voiced petered out and she started to cry again, then with a shudder she seemed to pull herself together. As Saz later remarked to Molly, it was like seeing the stiff upper lip in action.

"I really don't even want to think about this right now. My exhibition is very important, it is all I care about. I have to be in control. I'll give you ten days. Sort of a reciprocal arrangement, after all, I've just had ten days of your time. If you cannot adequately explain yourself by then, I will tell Max everything and we will have you arrested and charged with . . . I don't know, but there must be some charge that covers lying and cheating and getting into someone's house and life under false pretences. Now get out. If I don't hear from you, rest assured, I will find you."

"And I left with my tail between my legs."

"Sorry babe, so my plan wasn't foolproof."

"Not proof for this fool anyway."

"Do you think she'll say anything to Max?"

"I'm not sure. But they hand out remarkably similar threats. Before I fucked it all up by asking about Deb she did talk a bit about them. About her relationship with him. It sounds like they really do lead completely separate lives, different friends, different interests. Or at least that's what she said, but then again, she could have been lying. She certainly sussed that I was."

"Ten days huh? It's not long."

"No, I know. And I don't even know where to start."

"I do. This arrived while you were out. It's addressed to you but I opened it anyway."

Molly got up from the table and shoved a large unstamped envelope in front of Saz. Inside was a return ticket to San Francisco, a map of the city, a card with a gift shop name and address on it and one thousand dollars in cash. Molly sat down beside her.

"I didn't think your mystery woman had this address."

"Neither did I."

"Can you find out about the shop from here?"

"Helen or Jude could try, but it might take a couple of days for them to do it discreetly."

"Well I'm afraid you can't wait that long."

"Why not?"

"Look at the tickets. The flight leaves first thing in the morning. Your bag's packed and I've put petrol in the car so I can take you to Gatwick."

"I love you Molly, you know that?"

"Prove it. I want a lot of presents on your return and I want a lot of you – right now."

Saz did as she was told.

CHAPTER 19

By the mid-1980s Maxwell North's career had done far better than even he had dared to hope for. The boy who had "run away from home" at twenty-seven was hugely successful and widely respected, with practices spanning the Atlantic. He had a beautiful wife and beautiful homes. That his marriage was a sham and that his work meant he was almost never in any of his lovely homes, mattered not at all. Maxwell North was successful, but far more important than his own life, the Process was successful. The Process worked.

When Anita had left him to live with John and taken Jasmine with them, he had been happy to agree to her stated belief that the little girl was probably John's child. After a year or so he convinced himself that she was John's child anyway, that his relationship to her had been that of a father figure. Not a father but a carer. Just as he cared for all the other people in the House. After all, sorrow and trauma were for others, the Process could heal them of their pain, but Max was the creator of the Process and had no time for any grief of his own. In Max's mind the Process always came first and anything attempting to stop that would be dealt with – as severely as necessary.

The first time had been easy. Michael was practically alone, even within the House, even with Chris as his lover. In the early days he had caused a slight hiccup and then been removed – like a successful surgical operation.

Michael's parents had never even tried to trace him, happy to accept that their son, the good all-American boy they'd determined to raise, was lost to them and readily believing Max's story of Michael's departure. They let Michael out of their lives with relief. And Max accepted their dismissal of their own child with even greater relief.

To Max, Michael's death made perfect sense because Max believed in the Process. Believed the Process was the way – the healing future – and he was starting to produce results that showed the same. Someone threatening to tell the world that the House in San Francisco had not always been so successful, had not always run along the perfect lines that Max proclaimed and the many psychology and sociology thesis writers who had studied the House attested to – that someone was against the Process. That someone was stopping the work. Those someones were stopped. Just as Deb had to be stopped.

Max's marriage to the British furniture heiress had made all the papers in the late seventies, it was a match made in heaven – at least for the writers of the tabloid papers. Beautiful young British artist marries dashing not quite so young American doctor. Actually it was a marriage made in Max's ideal scheme of things. He and Caron had met through mutual friends, liked each other fairly well and were intelligent enough to know that they could work for each other. After a first dinner Max had sussed that Caron was gay and, well aware that her contacts in the British establishment would do him good, he immediately proposed marriage. When Caron had stopped laughing Max explained exactly what he meant by marriage, adding that he expected the two of them would find enough in common to allow them to get along, that he expected nothing of her sexually and, as her parents would no doubt pressure her into marriage eventually, it might as well be him. The next week Caron completed the Process and four months later they were married in the crypt of St Paul's Cathedral. Over the ensuing years their mutually assisted careers flourished and they developed a good partnership, just involved in each other's lives enough to make the story work, just separate enough to live the lives they'd planned. They slept in the same bed when they were at home together, they ate together and they knew exactly how far to go with each other. Both of them had occasionally had lovers and when, after seven years of marriage, Caron had asked Max how he felt about her young Australian girlfriend moving in with them, there had been no hint of dissent. Max moved into the spare room – which was, of course, Deb's room whenever there was company – and Deb became a part of their lives. Max and Deb got on well, Deb working for them both as their housekeeper, for Caron as her PA and occasionally helping Max. It was a system that worked for all three of them, and if Max sometimes resented Deb's intrusion or Caron was very occasionally threatened by a slight fear of Max's need for power, neither of them was prepared to rock the boat. Neither of them had any desire to swim alone in uncharted waters. Deb however, was a great surfer and had no fear of sharks.

On a late summer night in 1986 Caron McKenna-North got up from the supper table and went upstairs to the canopied bed she shared with Deb on the third floor of their huge Victorian terrace. She left Max and Deb to finish the washing up, kissed them both and climbed the stairs smiling. She was sleepy and safe in the knowledge that her husband and her lover were colluding in a new line of attack on a difficult ex-patient, sorting out Max's problems and leaving Caron free to her work. Deb was doing what she did best, making life easy for all three of them. At least, that's how Deb's conversation with Max started. But an hour later things had changed markedly, and four hours after that Max woke Caron to tell her about Deb. Sticky wet and cold blood dead on the second landing of their staircase. The blade beside her was from Max's old-fashioned razor and must have been taken from his bathroom while he worked downstairs in his study. Caron held Deb, the still damp blood sinking into her own pyjamas and Max went back upstairs to start tidying Deb away.

The following week Anna Johnson repeated the actions of her mother nearly forty years earlier and jumped off the Dover to Calais ferry. She'd never learnt to swim. Her case, like all of Max's cases, remained strictly confidential and Dr Maxwell North was praised in most newspapers for refusing to give in to the temptations of the tabloid tenner.

wavewalker

He can't help himself, can't stop himself.
Neither can I.

I am almost too close now, the tide is going out, there is
not much longer I can remain unseen.
Nor do I want to.

The confrontation is imminent and I begin to enjoy the
thought of it.
I will have to let him know I am near, am here.
I want to see him look for me as I have searched for him.
See him look around corners and under beds.

I know he is afraid, he is so scared of losing it.
He should be.
I am getting ready to make him pay.
The wages of his sins will bankrupt him.

CHAPTER 20

Holding Caron in his arms to tell her about Deb, Max thought she was going to throw up. Her whole body strained against the knowledge he was forcing into her. But the police were already on their way and it was vital that any hints of Caron's life with Deb were removed before they came in with their intrusions and prying and contacts in the press. Max tidied away the photos and telltale books and Caron went slowly downstairs, to the corner where Deb stained away her life. She looked at the form, Deb but not Deb, lying at her feet, her body wrapped up warm on a muggy summer night, sticky in an old winter quilt. Wrapped up warm but body cold.

Ten minutes later Max came downstairs and led Caron away.

"Now, all you have to do is tell the truth. You were asleep. I woke you. You came down here to see her, then I took you back to bed."

"That's not the truth."

"It's enough."

"No Max, you're supposed to tell the truth, the whole truth."

"There is no point in telling them the whole truth. And it's not fair. Think about Deb's family."

"Don't you mean my family?"

"If you like. Caron, we certainly don't have time to go into all this now. Deb's dead, for some reason, despite all we've done for her, she has decided to kill herself. Now I'm sure this is hard for you, it isn't exactly easy for me, but just for the next couple of hours, let's see some of that famous English reserve and stiff upper lip and get on with it. OK?"

The doorbell rang and Caron had no choice.

When the police finally left it was already day, Max went into his study to work on the new paper he was to deliver to the BMA and Caron went up to her studio at the top of the house and looked around. There was Deb, or the beginnings of Deb, in the block of ebony she'd been working on. Deb as hidden woman, coming out of the shadows of the dark material. Deb emerging. There too was Deb in the pile of things collected for the new installation. Deb's influence, Deb's attitude, Deb's strength, hung like a dark curtain over the whole room. Hot morning sunshine was flooding in from the windows all around the top of the studio, bouncing off the white walls giving the clear light she loved for her work, but Caron could hardly see for the fog in her head and the tears in her eyes, so she sat on the floor of her studio, little bits of dried plaster, shavings of wood and brick sticking to her gown. Too tired for tears, she sat and rocked herself and finally acknowledged Deb's death, and worse, the manner of her death. An hour later she stood up, threw off her gown and started to work in the pale pink silk pyjamas she always wore to bed. Pyjamas stained with Deb's dried blood. She worked on the ebony head of Deb, refining and defining it, all the while sorting out in her head what she already knew to be reality.

She had gone to bed at midnight, Deb was downstairs with Max, they were doing the dishes from the late supper the three had shared. Cold beef and new potatoes, the beef a little pink, the potatoes drenched in melted salty butter. Max had been lavish with his favourite Italian wine and both Caron and Deb were a little drunk.

Caron had kissed them both and gone to bed, leaving the two of them as she so often did, Deb and Max sorting out yet another of Max's traumas. some patient with a grudge against Dr Maxwell North, determined to make a fuss about yet another life unfulfilled.

Max regularly had these traumas and never seemed to know how to deal with them. Or rather, he did know how to deal with them, knew exactly what needed to be done, but it was almost as if he didn't trust himself to go alone. Caron had often wondered what would happen if he did go alone. She supposed Max was scared that they'd irritate him so much he might just blurt out the truth, that these rich women needed to get a life, not more therapy. That their mutual arrangement was so much more beneficial to him than it was to them. That their exorbitant fees supported the work he really believed in, the group work, the work with addicts, with manic depressives, with schizophrenics. The work Max was proud of. The work he loved. She knew how much he despised the "paying guests" as he called them and was happy to help save him from his own anger when she could. After all, she too had lived off her father and husband in the early years until the success of her own work. She didn't want Max to hurt these women who could so easily have been herself or any of her friends and, even more, she didn't want him to hurt himself. She was not Max's lover, but she was his wife, and cared for him. Their arrangement worked for her and it had worked for Deb as well. He'd call Caron at home, worried that Lady So-and-so was about to tell the world all the secrets of his methods, his precious Process. Of course they never did. All they wanted was more of his time, usually for free. More time in the presence of the great Dr North. Caron would soothe his fears and then Deb would go to speak to them. To remind them of the contract they signed when they entered into therapy with Max, the "no revelation" clause, the demand for secrecy, both for their sake and his. And, faced with the implied threat of disclosure of all their own sad little secrets, they would reveal to the sweet young Australian that all they really wanted was more time with him. The healer. Like Max, Deb was an outsider, beyond the class distinctions they defined themselves by, they could tell her the truth. The trust fund couldn't afford it, or their husband, grown jealous of hearing Max's name constantly invoked in a haze of glory, had refused to pay and now they wanted just that little bit more . . . Deb would offer three free sessions, just to "tidy things up" and the sad woman with too much money and not enough life would relax and give herself over, again, to Dr Maxwell North.

So, Caron had left them doing just this. Planning Deb's methods for the next day. Going over the complainant's case history as they scrubbed out the roasting dish, disposing of her fears as efficiently as the grease-cutting liquid they were using dispersed the congealed fat and blood of the dead animal. It was all perfectly normal. Yet four hours later Deb was dead. It wasn't just Caron's love for Deb that made it impossible for her to accept the suicide. She and Deb had talked about it. They'd been lovers, living in the same house and working with a man who dealt in that world. The world of unhappiness and suicides, it wasn't strange for the three of them to talk about it for hours. Well, Caron and Deb would anyway, Max would just contribute a few statistics and theories when it came to that topic of conversation. He'd pass Deb and Caron off as ghoulish and try to alter the path of the discussion. Caron knew it was a sensitive subject among the people he worked with. There were few mental health professionals who had not lost a patient to their own despair and she knew that among their friends in the field it was a cause for concern, either dealt with in angry defence or silent guilt. Or, as Max preferred, dismissal. It had happened, it was sad, it was over. But Caron wasn't able to dismiss this suicide so easily.

She looked down at the work under her hands. It was Deb. Deb's head, Deb's long, soft hair. The head was life-size and Caron pressed her own lips to those carved in the rich ebony. She kissed the head of her dead lover as if she could breathe life into it, as if with her love it could live and speak the truth. It didn't speak out loud, but Caron heard the voice inside her own head. Heard what she'd been too scared to acknowledge inside her own silent head. Caron placed the carving carefully on a shelf at the back of the room. She went downstairs to wash and rest, to think about what she was starting to know. She was beginning to think she understood Max better than he wanted her to and, looking clearly at herself, beginning to realize just how little she was prepared to do, even with that knowledge. It would take a stronger woman than her to deal with Max. Until then, Caron would wait and harbour her truth. She had carved Deb's head just as Deb's bloody body had been carved, Max would be less yielding than the ebony.

CHAPTER 21

If Saz had any summer of love illusions about San Francisco, they were soundly dashed about ten minutes before the plane touched down. She'd been hoping for one of those glorious late evening landings into any unknown city – losing altitude while the captain drones on about local times and weather variations, to come gliding through the clouds and make out famous landmarks, in this case, specifically the Golden Gate Bridge. No such luck, even in summer, Saz's *LA Law*-fed visions of California were brutally dashed as they landed in rain, a light breeze and an unrelentingly wet, if gentle, mist.

Having had no time to prepare herself for the journey meant that Saz avoided the usual problems of queuing at baggage claim. Molly had very sensibly packed the smallest travel bag they possessed, and Saz merely had to lift her "cabin allowance" from the overhead locker, replace the shoes she'd removed almost nine hours earlier at Gatwick and walk from the plane, through customs and visa check and straight out to a waiting cab.

The mystery employer had given her strict instructions – flight to San Francisco, cab into the city and a week-long room reservation at the Amsterdam Hotel which, according to the list of instructions that came with the tickets, was "near" Nob Hill. She'd done little surveillance work, but enough to know that "near" could mean anything from round the corner to about two miles away and she assumed that the vast majority of San Franciscans didn't realize the English, on hearing the address, would only think of a silent "K" but, as everything was fully paid for in advance, she felt little need to complain. And she'd also been given plenty of cash for incidental costs. More cash in fact, than Saz could possibly expect to spend in one week, though obviously, all the presents she would have to buy Molly for leaving her at such short notice would cost a fair bit.

She checked into the hotel which appeared perfectly normal if a little quainter than what she was used to in the States, rather more like a B&B in Canterbury than a hotel in California. She went out into the street and round the corner to the little café where she was confronted with an alarming array of types of coffee.

"Coffee please."

"Espresso, double espresso, cappuccino, cafe latte, cafe mocha, iced?"

Suppressing a desire to tell the over-friendly young man that in her advanced state of jetlag even Gold Blend would do, she ordered a cappuccino and apple muffin "to go" and retired to her room to waste the afternoon and evening hopping between the twenty or so cable channels until she could fend off sleep no longer. Nine hours later, she woke up simultaneously alert and exhausted at 5.30 a.m.

"Come on Saz, sleep for God's sake. This is no way to start a week of wandering."

But even an entire run through the in-bed relaxation routine Molly had been teaching her, the non-sensual version, did no good and after another half hour of trying to sleep with no result, she got out of bed, pulled on her running clothes and went out of the hotel and into the city for a quick circuit to get her bearings. The run down-hill to Market Street and then along the waterfront round to Fisherman's Wharf got her acquainted with the central downtown area, and the walk uphill back to the hotel got her acquainted with her hamstrings and the necessity of abandoning running and taking up mountain climbing as her preferred form of exercise. After a shower and a somewhat more circumspect flick through the huge array of TV channels than she'd subjected herself to the night before, she was ready to go out. And, eschewing the hotel's proffered complimentary "continental" breakfast of Danish pastries and coffee, she went out for her favourite meal – the real American breakfast.

Saz tucked into her "Farmers' omelette" – sausage, eggs, bacon, potatoes, peppers and tomato, all cooked up in one big cholesterol enhanced mess – with rye toast and jam, with all the abandon of a woman used to fierce regular exercise and fervently in lust with her lover. That is, she didn't once think "I'll get fat".

She finished her meal, paid the startlingly cheery waitress and headed out. She had her San Francisco map sent to her by the unknown employer, which she'd discovered on the plane also had two crosses on it – one by the waterfront corresponding to the address on the business card and one on a street in North Beach. The guy on reception had also very kindly provided her with a quick précis of the transport situation – BART, MUNI and buses – though as she had so much cash, taxis seemed by far the simpler option. She had an extra jumper just in case the sunshine suddenly disappeared behind what Carrie called a "San Fran bastard of sudden fog" and she was ready to go to work. She stepped out into the street and as she did so the dazzling sunshine was swallowed up by a bank of mist that seemed to roll up the road to meet her. Saz pulled on her jumper and looked around for a cab.

"Bloody brilliant, I was planning on Baywatch and I get Brigadoon. Let's hope I don't cross the magic bridge

without noticing or my ruby slippers'll never get me back
to Kansas."

Saz told the driver her destination and sat back in the
taxi marvelling at how many hours she must have wasted
to have such a thoroughly sad knowledge of Hollywood
musicals. It took less than ten minutes for the driver to
cut through a dozen back streets and take her to the
shop back down by the water, but the cutting was so
fast Saz couldn't quite keep track on her map and was
thoroughly disorientated by the time the cab pulled up.

She wandered past two street performers, one a young
– and very bad – juggler, the other an old – and much
more entertaining – banjo player, and a dozen or so
"emporiums" until she reached the one listed in the information pack delivered along with the tickets. She stared
in through the gift shop window. It was fairly ordinary in
a retro-hippy, stars and moons kind of way. Good-looking
teapots and hand-etched Mexican wine glasses lined the
shelves, various astrological and astronomical items
hung from the ceiling and the back wall was lined in
star-spotted blue velvet. Saz was a little disappointed to
have come all the way to San Francisco to see half of
Camden Market and most of Molly's bathroom recreated
in the gift shop she'd been directed to by her employer,
but she entered Midas's Daughter, reminding herself that
this was work, not tourism, and there was no reason at
all that San Francisco shouldn't be overcome by the same
fashion blimp that had so thoroughly engulfed London.
She went in, loosing the breeze on a field of wind-chimes
above her head as she did so. A head popped out from
behind the velvet curtain.

"Hi, looking for Jake, or just looking?"

The young, and very gorgeous, black woman came out
into the body of the shop. She had long curly dark hair,
copper black skin and huge eyes. Tall and slim, God had

obviously meant her to be a dancer when forming her long legs with perfect turnout. Her bare right shoulder sported a white tattoo of a dolphin.

"Only Jake's not in just yet. I'm Milly."

"Oh . . . well. I'll just look around if you don't mind. A . . . ah . . . friend of mine – in London – told me to come in while I was here . . . "

"Right. Must have been Jasmine?"

Saz thought it was as likely as not, so she readily accepted the proffered name, glad of even a tenuous hook on which to carry the source of her travels.

"Yeah. Jasmine. She said I should come and . . . so . . . "

"Well Jake'll be really disappointed not to hear how she is. I know they were really close before she went. I don't really know her that well myself, I mean I wouldn't. You know we only knew each other as little babies, so I don't really remember, and then recently I only met her a couple of times with Jake and she wanted him all to herself, you know – talking, talking, talking. I'm not real interested in all that past stuff myself."

"Oh. I don't know, that is, she and I aren't really close either. She just wanted me to . . . give her regards . . . to Jake. Do you know what time he'll be here?"

"Usually comes in around three."

"Fine."

Saz looked at her watch and wondered what to do with her next five hours. She needn't have bothered, Milly was already coming at her with rampant enthusiasm.

"You know, I can't leave the shop, but here – I'll make a list for you."

"A list?"

"Sure. All the places to see. Round here. In a few hours. Unless you already know San Francisco?"

"No, not at all, I only got in last night. First time."

"Good. There's a bunch of things you could do. Shop –

that could easily take a couple hours. Or you could go and get one of the boats. Around the bay, or maybe over to Alcatraz? Take a look and then come back for Jake."

Milly was scribbling on a sheet of paper which she gave to Saz.

"You got a map?"

Saz handed it over and watched Milly number the seven places she insisted were "just the best places to see, if you don't mind being with tourists", marking her map with corresponding numbers.

"I see you've got Jake's place marked out already."

"Sorry?"

"Jake's place. In North Beach. Did you go there to find him?"

"No. Um . . . Jasmine did that for me. She gave me the map. In case he wasn't here."

"She sure is thorough. Not like me. I think Jake thinks I'm a kinda . . . goofy . . . you know? I mean I'm not really, it's just most of the time I'd rather think about college than all this stuff."

"What are you studying?"

"Law. I mean I will be. I start in the fall. I've spent a few years playing around, but I figure I'm ready to get serious now."

Milly looked earnestly at Saz, hair falling over her face, standing there in a pink and orange thigh-length halter-neck dress and what looked like an original pair of platform shoes. Saz suppressed a smile.

"Well Milly, this looks pretty organized to me, maybe he was just more used to Jasmine?"

"Could be, but he's known me all my life and he only met her again a couple of years ago!"

"Yeah. Jasmine said," Saz lied, wondering how much information she could fish without becoming too obvious.

"Well hey, sorry but I've gotta get on – there's boxes of these really cool Indian rugs to unpack, you wanna look?"

Saz retrieved her map and Milly's list.

"Maybe later. I've got a lot of sightseeing to do. I'm only here for a week."

"OK, I'll tell Jake to expect you. Oh hey . . . what's your name?"

"Sarah . . . ah, Sarah Hannon."

"OK Sarah, I'll be sure and tell him. Cool! See you later!"

Saz smiled at the cuteness disappearing behind the velvet curtain and walked out of the shop. The mist had cleared and the sun was shining down on the bay, hot and fierce.

"So Jasmine, you have a name! Good. That makes two of us."

CHAPTER 22

Saz took a leisurely uphill walk from Jake's shop to the house marked out for her in North Beach. The streets seemed to go from Italian to Chinese and back again within half a block. Halfway there she started to wonder why Jake hadn't just turned his own house into a shop, there seemed to be several just like Midas's Daughter in the area. When she got to the house she realized why. It was far too beautiful to waste as a place of mere commerce. The house was wide and big and looked to be in very good condition. Sited halfway up a hill, she imagined the top windows ought to have a fantastic view of the bay or at least much of the city. It was right on the street, three storeys high, painted white with detail picked out in a pale golden cream, large bare bay windows (no hanging crystals in these), and six new marble steps going up to the stained glass panelled front door. Beside which was a sign:

> PROCESS HOUSE
> Dr Carla & Jake Epstein
> "Where there's a will, there's a way –
> through, over and beyond."
> WELCOME

Saz was just deliberating whether or not to ring the bell when the decision was made for her. An extremely pretty young man opened the front door.

"Are you ready?"

"What?"

"Are you ready?"

"For what?"

"For IT of course!"

"I'm sorry – can we start again?"

"Can't do that, can't go back, can only go forward. So are you ready?"

"But I came to look for ... "

"Oh! Looking! Bad, very bad. Don't look, just do it!"

He grabbed her with a tanned brown arm and pulled her inside. Saz was just about to start fighting him off, pulling her arm back to deliver a swift blow to his solar plexus, when a woman intervened, grabbing Saz and holding her with a cool hand.

"And who are you tormenting today, Grant?"

"She's looking Mom, she must be ready."

"She's English. She may not even know who we are. Isn't that right?"

Saz looked from mother to son, the similarity between the huge brown eyes and fierce cheekbones being too striking for any lesser relationship.

"I'm a bit – shaken – do you mind if I sit down?" she asked, stalling for time while she thought of an answer that wouldn't pre-empt her meeting with Jake later in the day.

The woman led her through to what looked like a sitting room to the left of the entrance.

"Of course, I'm so sorry. Grant go and get some iced water – or would you prefer tea?"

"No, water will be fine, thanks."

Once the boy had gone, the woman continued.

"You must forgive Grant. He has a ninety-year-old's wisdom rather unfortunately coupled with an eighteen-year-old's enthusiasm. He's lived in the House all his life you see. He's used to living his every moment in open interaction."

Saz, recognizing the phrases and buzz words from her day with Max North, nodded.

"Yeah, I'm just starting."

"So you did mean to find us?"

"Kind of. Um – I'm Sarah Hannon. I did one of the Process weekends in London. And I was interested . . . "

The woman nodded, pushing her short greying hair out of her eyes as she continued Saz's sentence.

"To see where it all started? Well, that's not unusual. But it is the Past. And we do our work from the Now. Capital letters. Surely you learnt that from Max?"

"Yeah. I did. I'm here – just for a week, a working break, really. I just wanted to look. Look around."

"Of course. That's fair. Well, Jake's not here at the moment, but I'd be happy to give you a tour of the House. I'm Carla Epstein, Jake's wife. I run the women's groups and the one-to-one self-assessment course."

"And I run the youth stuff. And some of the sex stuff too."

Grant was back with a tray, grinning ferociously over three glasses and a jug of iced, mineral water.

"That'll do fine for now Grant."

"But you're real busy today Mom, you've got a family session at noon and a talk at two. I'll show her round, I'm not working until this evening. You can even stay to lunch if you like?"

Saz looked at Grant and saw a tall, dark-eyed young man staring back at her, completely open, totally at ease with himself and with an extremely winning smile, in spite, or perhaps because of, a chipped front tooth. In all her visits to the States, she'd rarely seen less than perfect teeth on anyone under about seventy-five and this made him seem especially attractive.

"OK. You've got me."

Grant sat down seriously beside her.

"No, you've got you. I've engaged you. See, words are just the format of conversation, just the beginning, but you've got to be precise or you can't attain the whole entity of anything. Words make the Now more possible, but only the correct words ... "

"Grant, she's done the Process in London. She just wants to look around. Give her a break!"

Suddenly Grant's enthusiasm surfaced again and he jumped up off the sofa.

"London? Cool! Did you see Max? What was he like? Was it good? Are you changed?"

"Well, maybe changing ... "

"Grant! The tour? You can ask her questions later – and sweetheart, it might help to remember that Max is just another guy. Just an ordinary guy who happens to know some stuff? Stuff we all know if we ask the right questions?"

"Yeah Mom. Sure. Come on, we'll start at the very beginning, in the Process Room!!"

Grant grabbed Saz's hand and pulled her to her feet, Carla just managed to grab the glass out of her hand before it went down the front of Saz's shirt and, hanging on to her bag and map, Saz allowed Grant to drag her out of the room, leaving Carla laughing behind them.

"I'll see you later Sarah, have a good time!"

They went through the House, Grant pointing out the first ever Process room and the six others, smaller and slightly more modern, which were part of a loft extension at the top of the House. Saz asked him about Max's involvement in the early years.

"And this is where Max set everything up?"

Grant frowned a little and turned away to look out at the bay view.

"Kind of. Look, Max isn't really cool about us discussing all the past stuff. He says it blocks the Now. I'm sure you're interested, but you don't need to know about then. The early years were all trial and error. This is the real thing."

He pulled her into the meeting room where House meetings were carried out once a week.

"It used to be once a month, but with six people living in-House and about another fifty involved in the regular work, let alone the occasional seminars, once a month wasn't nearly enough for everyone to get clear."

They went on to the family room on the third floor – a luxurious open space paid for by "a very kind donation from a grateful ex-resident". And finally he collected some bread, cheese and apples from the kitchen and took Saz out into the courtyard at the back. They sat under a lemon tree with ripening fruit and, after he'd had time to devour half a loaf of sourdough and most of a ripe Camembert, Grant looked up at Saz. He wasn't smiling now.

"OK, so if Sarah isn't your real name but you have done the Process, I can tell that ... then why are you lying?"

Saz just about choked on her apple.

"Fuck! How?"

"You had to think about your name too long when you were talking to Mom at the door ... "

"You weren't even there! Were you eavesdropping?"

"Of course, Carla is always far too trusting of new people, Jake and I are always having to remind her. We have to be careful here and what's more, you didn't answer me twice already when I called you Sarah. Simple really. So, do I call the cops now and have them take you away for lunching under false pretences or are you going to tell me what's going on?"

"I was asked to come here."

"Who asked you?"

"I don't know."

"Are you spying for Max? Doesn't he trust us to do the work?"

"It's not Dr North. Look, someone bought me a ticket and gave me the money to come ... they thought I might find it interesting."

Saz wondered if Grant was as hot on half-truths as he obviously was on whole lies.

"I honestly don't know who it was that sent me ... they wanted me to meet Jake and so I came. They told me where the House was and they told me where his shop was ... I went there this morning."

"You met Milly?"

"Yeah, she was really helpful."

"Yeah, I'm sure she was. My sister can be brilliant when she wants to."

"Sister?"

"House sister. She's Rose's daughter. She was born here. So was I, a few years later when Carla came to live in and got it on with Jake. There's a whole bunch of us kids who grew up in the House. Most of us are still heavily into the work, but Milly is really ... I don't know, into the world. She wants to live out there."

"Well you can't all stay here forever, can you?"

"Why not? And anyway, we don't. Some of us have already left to found a Youth House in Toronto. And there's others who are travelling. I think they'll come back though."

"And Jasmine?"

"Do you know her?"

"I think she's the person who sent me. Milly told me about her."

"Really? Look Sarah, Milly . . . oh God, what's your real name?"

"I'm called Saz."

"Cute. Short for?"

Saz grimaced, "Sarah."

"Listen Sarah, Jasmine isn't OK. She kind of . . . she went a bit strange. She's not like the rest of us. She was born here and then her Mom left the House and took her away when she was small and then her parents died. She was brought up by someone else, her aunt. She came back a few years ago, but she only stayed for about six months. She didn't fit in, couldn't do it. The House thing. Community. It was best that she left. We all agreed. I think Jake saw her a few times after that, but . . . you mean she gave you the money to come here and you've never even met her?"

Saz figured she could lie to Grant about the grand efficacy of the Process and he'd probably swallow it.

"All I know is, that I did the weekend Process. I really liked it. I told lots of people I liked it. I mean lots."

Grant nodded, "I understand, I have that joy in it too."

"And then the money and ticket came. In the post. Along with a map with the House marked on it and the card for Jake's shop. I put two and two together after talking to Milly and came up with Jasmine."

"Crazy."

"Maybe."

Saz was starting to get nervous about giving away too many secrets without knowing which were the ones she was supposed to be keeping. She stood up.

"I have to go, I told Milly I'd go back to the shop to meet Jake."

"OK. Listen, will you call me? I'd like to know what you find out."

"Sure. It would probably help to talk it over anyway," Saz lied, getting more nervous by the minute. "Are you free tonight?"

"No. I'm running a meeting. It's about adult children and their parents. Wanna come? We could do something afterwards. I'll show you around, we could go to China-town. Come on, it's not exactly far away."

Saz groaned.

"I don't think so. It's not really my kind of thing."

Grant smiled up at her from the grass.

"Your immediate reluctance indicates that this meeting could be good for you. In fact, I demand you come. What else have you got to do, all alone in San Francisco?"

"That's hardly changing my life of my own free will, is it?"

"It's close enough."

He got up from the ground.

"Go through the back gate, out on to the street, take the second left and you're bound to see a cab. I'll see you tonight, 7.30 p.m. Sharp. I have a punctuality thing – and you won't like it if I have to spend half an hour uncovering your reason for lateness in front of sixteen other people."

"How old did you say you were?"

"I didn't. Carla did. But I'm eighteen, and pushy with it. You'd better get going, Jake has a timekeeping thing too."

"But he's not even expecting me."

Grant took a bite of the small, hard lemon in his hand, he screwed up his face and spat out the bitter flesh.

"Jake's waiting for you, we all were, Milly called as soon as you left the shop. She's not very goofy at all actually, but that orange and pink girl thing really works for her."

"Wha . . . ? Then why did you . . . "

"Get you to tell me all about it? Confession is good for the soul. And you'll feel an awful lot better after tonight when you've told me the whole truth instead of these half-stories. Bye!"

He leaned over and held her head, kissing her on the forehead, Saz could smell the bitter lemon juice on his hands. Then he casually sauntered back into the House, leaving Saz wishing that she'd been asked to investigate dodgy landlords, timeshare dealers, even a good traditional case of adultery.

"Anything rather than these bloody see-through-my-lies-new-age self fucking actualizers!"

CHAPTER 23

Within the first five minutes of meeting Jake, Saz was
starting to worry about her lying ability. Jake was obviously well endowed with his son's charm, though without
the pushiness, and a huge dose of what could only be
Max's perception. She sat talking to him convinced,
though with no clear reason she could name, that he
knew just exactly what she wasn't telling him, along with
a whole lot more. He had that ability to keep silent, while
smiling and looking interested that always made Saz
want to scream, silence that made her say much more
than she really wanted to. He looked like Saz's archetype
of a grown-up hippy – sun-tanned with curly dark brown
hair, just beginning to go grey and a well-trimmed,
slightly more grey, beard. His eyes were big and pale
blue above the fine, prominent cheekbones he shared
with his wife and had handed down to his son. This
man looked exactly like the Woodstock generation was
supposed to – and exactly not what most of them had
turned into. He greeted her with a hug, severely disarm-
ing her protective South London cool. He was friendly
and warm, but with a touch of distance that Saz found
extremely difficult to reconcile with his hippy
appearance.

Jake pulled the blinds on the shop window shutting
out the direct afternoon sunlight and leaving them in a
soft yellow glow. He made them both mint tea, sat Saz
down in an old velvet-covered armchair, fed her carrot
cake and then settled himself on a massive pile of

embroidered cushions opposite. From her chair, Saz asked questions, answered more questions than she asked, drank tea and listened intently to what answers she did get; the only sound other than their voices was the murmur of tourists passing by outside and the Tibetan windchime above the cash register at the desk. Jake had questioned her about her family, her sexuality and her home – all of which Saz answered completely honestly, glad not to have to lie to someone she wasn't sure she could even trust with the truth. He then explained to Saz that he'd moved into the House at almost twenty and had "grown to a man within the disciplines and freedom of community". He seemed to have "it" with a vengeance – the fervour, the belief, even more strongly than the people she'd met on the course in London, though perhaps with a slightly clearer sense of the ridiculous than the serious-minded Processors she'd met there. He was a charming, seemingly responsible and very engaging grown-up. Which made sense, given that Maxwell North had left him in charge of the whole operation in San Francisco, but also made her less able to trust his bluff, cheery persona. Saz felt like she was being shown just one half of Jake and that the one she really wanted to talk to was the silent Jake who watched her like a hawk whenever she spoke. Jake had shut up shop and sent Milly home in order to have a "clear space to dialogue" with Saz.

"Well Sarah, Milly told us that Jasmine sent you. Which is really great because I've been very concerned about her. Jasmine should have been at ease with us, in the House, you know? I mean, you've met Grant and Carla and the others are cool too. But it was very hard for her, for Jasmine. So I thought you and I should spend some time together and maybe you could help me understand what happened, what went wrong."

Saz plunged in, having decided her best course of

action was to tell at least some of the truth and hope Jake would fill in the gaps.

"Actually Jake, I honestly don't know Jasmine that well. I've only just done the weekend Process myself. About a month ago. We met there."

"She was doing the Group Process?"

Jake's cool dropped just a little but it was too late for Saz to back out now.

"Ah – yeah."

"That must have been difficult for Max?"

"He . . . well, he didn't seem to have a problem with it. I mean – she was in my group and he was taking one of the others. So they didn't really do all that much together."

"Right – but she's OK?"

It went on for about ten minutes, Jake asking questions about Jasmine and Saz trying to fob him off with answers ranging from the possible to the almost probable, terrified to commit herself in case she got it completely wrong and was found out. Then Jake dropped a bombshell and Saz couldn't escape the nagging feeling that he had intended to drop it to see which way she would run.

"Whatever. Listen, it's cool, Sarah. I can see you're not comfortable answering my questions. I guess if she'd wanted me to know the details of her life she'd have contacted me directly. Perhaps now she's made her peace with Max she doesn't need me as an alternative father figure."

"Father figure?"

"Oh. You don't know?"

"What?"

"About Max."

"No," Saz answered, profoundly relieved to be able to tell the truth for once.

Jake smiled back at her.

"Me and my big mouth. Carla's always reminding me to shut up – at least occasionally. Jasmine probably doesn't want any of the London people to know. Max always was hot on treating all the Processees exactly the same. No concessions for blood or bread we used to say."

"Jasmine is Max's daughter?"

"Maybe."

"But you just said she was."

Jake frowned at her, his smile quickly gone.

"No. Clarity of words, Sarah. Something we're pretty hot on round here. I was talking about father figures, that's not the same as fathers."

"I don't get it Jake. What do you mean? Is Max her father or not?"

"Who knows? Look, it isn't a big secret or anything. Jasmine was born in the House – our first House baby. I'd only just arrived then. We were real proud of her. Anita, her mother, and Max were living together, had been for some time, ever since they founded the House and for a while before that too, I believe."

Saz interrupted him, "So Max was here from the beginning?"

"It's a matter of public record."

"Well, it's just that I've read articles where he doesn't mention it at all."

Jake smiled.

"Past present problems again."

"What?"

"Max is hot on keeping the past in the past. We believe in living the Now, now."

"Yeah, so I gathered, but . . . "

"So if journalists want to know about the past, Max sometimes feeds them misleading information. If they're the kind who refuse to talk about the Now."

"But why?"

"No reason really, just to keep it clear. This is the present. We live now. And anyway, I thought you wanted to know about Jasmine?"

Saz forced a smile, hoping she didn't look quite as pissed off as she felt.

"Yes, please."

"Now, I'm only telling you this because the past has a relevance to our present, you do understand the distinction?"

Saz lied and smiled. "Oh sure."

"OK, Anita was Jasmine's mother so naturally Max was Jasmine's dad. Then, a couple years later, Anita revealed she'd been having an occasional affair with this other guy who'd moved into the House – John – since long before she met Max, so you see . . . "

"Jasmine could have been his baby too?"

"Yeah."

"Ouch!"

"Well, it certainly upset things for a while. But Max was really sane. Talked to us all about reality being what it was perceived to be and not what it was treated as."

"There's a difference?"

"It's subtle. You'll come to it."

"Like Christmas. Then what happened?"

"There'd been some problems in the House. One guy, Michael, had only recently moved away. Then all this stuff with Anita and John. We weren't used to dealing with . . . interpersonal problems. We didn't yet have a system to get on top of them."

"And now?"

"Sure we do. But at that time, even a year or so into the project, it was all so new – exciting, but really hard work too. So, when Anita said that she and John were moving to Idaho and taking Jasmine with them, whoever's daughter she was, I think we were all just happy to put it behind us. They left, the House got bigger and better, things changed, people moved on. Chris moved south and then Rose went to Mendocino and took Milly with her. Then when Max went to England, he left Paul in charge and when Paul eventually went to Toronto, I took over – with Carla of course, she'd moved in by then."

"Max didn't see any more of Jasmine?"

"I don't think so. She was brought up by her aunt when Anita and John were killed."

"Killed?"

"Arson attack on their farm. Poor kid can't have been more than about seven at the time. I think when she came to stay with us she was hoping to find some sort of family, but I guess we just weren't quite what she needed. She certainly needs some form of stability."

"Why?"

"Nothing really. Nothing real I mean. And everyone needs stability, don't they? I think maybe she needs it more than most. Jasmine was our first baby, she's a special kid."

Saz chatted to Jake for a while more but her heart wasn't in it. She was terrified that she'd shown too much of her ignorance, worried that Jake knew more about her than she wanted him to and a little suspicious that he'd only told her all about Jasmine for his own ends. Whatever they were. As soon as she could get away without seeming too rude, she left and caught a cab back to the hotel. She lay on her perfectly made bed and felt sick. Sick at having lied to Jake who seemed like he spotted every lie anyway. Sick when she thought that she had to go out and spend the night with Grant who she trusted even less. Sick at being so far away from Molly in a strange city where they should have been together, wandering around Castro, diving head first into a rainbow forest of gay culture, but instead she was alone and spending her time ferreting around in a house of people with uncertain pasts who had been well and truly convinced that looking at the past was a waste of time. But worst of all she felt sick about Jasmine. She was ninety-nine per cent certain now that Jasmine was her employer, and if that was the case, then Jasmine already knew all about Max. So why had she sent Saz here? What else did she expect her to turn up? And most worrying of all, who else was lying?

She called home and left a "miss you" message for Molly and then rang her lawyer friend in London, asking Claire to get her anything she could on arson attacks in Idaho from about 1976 to 1979. Claire Holland was a freshly tattooed, soon-to-be senior partner in a highly reputable and extremely expensive central city law firm. Her company's offices in Covent Garden always meant good lunches for Saz as long as Claire was buying and Saz's good ear for juicy tales of Claire's serial non-monogamy meant that Claire was usually pleased to hear from her, as it gave her a chance to offer blow by blow descriptions of her latest conquests. It was a healthy relationship founded on mutual respect, a history of good clubbing (at least until Saz had discovered the joys of home life with Molly) and a shared liking for vegeburger and champagne lunches, with not a little use of Claire's contacts thrown in to sweeten up Saz's side of the friendship.

"Are you even vaguely serious? Just anywhere in the whole state of Idaho?"

"Yeah. Sorry."

"America's not England you know. It's huge."

"I know. I'm here."

"This'll take forever to find."

"Maybe not. There must have been a court case, he said they got the guy. And arson must be a fairly big crime even here where they have guns everywhere, it's treated very seriously at home."

"I'm the lawyer Saz."

"And it was part of a 'spate of attacks' I believe you'd call them?"

"Only if I still worked for the CPS. In defence mode, that's a series of completely unrelated incidents you're talking about, doll. Anything else?"

"Just that there were two dead – one woman called Anita and a man called John. Probably both in their mid-twenties to early thirties."

"Very specific. It didn't occur to you to get surnames?"

"These people were living 'in community' Claire. I don't know if they even had them. They probably gave them away as part of a protest about Vietnam or something like that."

"Great. Sounds like half the dykes we know."

"Well, I suppose you could see Greenham as a continuation of the United States oppression and world domination . . . "

"Shut up Saz, some of us have real jobs to get on with. You're sure it was Idaho?"

"Positive. I owe you."

"Yeah. I'd say a case of champagne if this works out."

"Make it a half bottle and you're less likely to be disappointed. Can you fax it to me here? Soon as?"

"Probably by tomorrow morning, your time. I'll have to call on some favours of some other friends of mine in the States, and I don't imagine they'll like being disturbed in the middle of the night any more than I do."

"Surely you weren't sleeping already? It must only be about two in the morning there!"

"Sometimes Saz, I behave like a normal everyday girl.

Besides that, I was saving myself for tomorrow, I've got a hot date. You know, you should be bloody glad I don't charge you in six-minute increments like all my other clients."

"I am babe, I am. Thanks."

Saz gave her the fax number and then went to have a shower, hoping the harsh water would wash away the threat of unease that was starting to prickle her scalp. There were a whole bunch of things that she didn't like about all this – not least the fact that her lying skills didn't seem to be up to much any more. There had to be some good reason that Jasmine had bothered to send her over here to find out about Max – a man she must already know all about – but whatever it was, it wasn't likely to present itself to her on a plate. She had just five more days to work out what Jasmine wanted her to know and then she had to decide what it might be that Jasmine wanted her to do with that information. And she only had two days after that before Caron North was going to go to Max and the police and tell them all about meeting her and therefore do away with any anonymity Saz might still have. And when she did get back, much too busy and laden with all this information, she'd have a very neglected girlfriend to deal with. Somehow in the next five days she was going to have to do some serious "forgive me" shopping.

By the time she dragged herself from the shower it was just after seven. She dressed in crumpled clothes straight from her suitcase, ran directly out of the hotel into a cab and arrived back at the House with two minutes to spare, a welcoming smile from Grant and the greetings hugs of ten complete strangers.

CHAPTER 24

Max kept in constant, weekly contact with the various Houses throughout the world. Jake had proved to be an excellent deputy, becoming his assistant when Paul went to Canada, and eventually taking over sole charge of the House in North Beach. Jake loved the work, he'd spent the past twenty years working in it and for it. Once a week Max received a three-page report detailing future activities and every month they sent him a ten-paged faxed report on the work from both the San Francisco and the Toronto Houses, the reports detailing the various Process functions – and their successes, no one of course, had any failures. Or any worth reporting. Max's wrath at an incomplete Process or failed attempt meant that both Houses had devised ways to keep his favour – sins of omission rather than commission. Once a year Max tried to go to each House in person, but with his current research investment, both of time and money, that had been impossible for the past eighteen months. The Houses had managed very well without him, telephone and fax communication being regular and immediate, if not quite as immediate as the presence of the flesh.

Telephones and faxes meant that occasionally things were missed out. People's names and ages for one thing. Which was how Max never got to hear that Jasmine had briefly been living in San Francisco, back in the House in North Beach where she was born. Jasmine was only there for a few months and most of that time had proved difficult for all concerned. Her hasty departure had her classed as a "no reference needed" and Jake decided it was best not to tell Max. It would not do Max any good and, more to the point, it would not do Jake any good either. As he told Carla, "There's no point. It will only hurt him."

"Isn't Max beyond that?"

"I don't know if anyone is beyond pain. Even Max. In this case, especially Max. He really believed Jasmine was his daughter."

"And then Anita made him believe otherwise?"

"The way she told it, didn't seem like there was much doubt. She was certain Jasmine was John's daughter."

"And you believed her?"

"Yeah. Why not? She was the kid's mother."

"Nothing really. Just it's something that comes up in my mothers' group all the time. It's not exactly politically correct to say, but for a woman denied power, which from what you've told me about the early days was exactly what happened to Anita, annexing the child is a great form of revenge. Sometimes the only revenge possible. Feminism or not, it does happen."

"Who knows? It was a long time ago and John and Anita are extremely dead. It was just one of those things that happened back then. We thought we were a family – I guess we thought it was OK to just swap dads."

"Really?"

"Hey, we were cutting-edge radicals, there were plenty of other things to deal with. It was just the beginning of the Process. Max suffered for a while when they first left and then put it behind him. So did the rest of us."

"I'm glad I came along after all that. I don't think I would have been able to cope with such . . . "

"Indifference?"

"Callousness."

"We were young. And very excited. We were only just

discovering it all. The House, the Process. Nothing else really mattered much."

"And then you met me."

"Let's be clear here. You came to the House to be part of the work like everyone else, you loved it and you dedicated yourself to it . . . "

"Like everyone else."

"Exactly, and . . . well, eventually I realized just how lonely a single-minded dedication to changing the world can be."

"I love you Jake."

"I know Dr Epstein, but we don't have time to go into our sex life right now. The point is that Max's private life really doesn't have much to do with us these days and maybe I should have told him when Jasmine first came here anyway. I chose not to and I don't want to have him – or you – questioning that. OK?"

"Sure. You're the boss. Now, can we get back to work?"

"If you're cool with this, then I guess so. I don't exactly think we can leave our son to run the whole House by himself."

"He'd love it."

"Yeah, he's so much like Max."

Carla Epstein wasn't sure why the comparison made her uneasy, but she didn't bother to mention it to Jake. She was well-aware that Grant was dedicated both to the work and to Max and she was very much hoping that first real love would bring him round to a slightly less intense reality as it had at least done with her, if not with his father.

So neither Carla nor Jake had bothered to mention Jasmine to Max while she was living at the House, then time passed and it became even less relevant. Which is why he was horrified to receive a note at the bottom of his ten-page fax from San Francisco.

By the way, we met someone today who knows Jasmine in London. I guess she must have caught up with you after all these years. She wasn't with us long and it wasn't exactly successful, so I thought it better not to bother you with it. Hope I did right? Anyway, I'm sure working with you will be great for her. Give her our love and tell her I met her friend this afternoon. Sarah seems like a nice girl, though a little too interested in the Past by your standards, I guess the Process didn't quite clear her, huh? Maybe we can speed her Forwards from here!

With best regards as ever and holding our breath for the inevitable great results and the next research project, Jake & Carla.

Max turned white and threw up into the rubbish basket beside his desk. His head was reeling with untenable thoughts. Jasmine was in London. Anita was dead but her daughter was here. Their daughter, the child Max had carefully excised from his thoughts, choosing to believe she was John's daughter. Preferring to believe, on the rare occasions he looked at his past, that he had created an orphan rather than killing the mother of his own child. It sat far easier on his conscience to see Anita and John as a separate family than as a genetic link to himself. Only now she was here, not in his thoughts by his choice and for him to deal with privately, but of her own volition and with her own agenda, and just maybe she was his daughter after all. Why hadn't she contacted him? And who the hell was this Sarah that Jake met today? Except that it wasn't today any more. Whoever it was had met Jake yesterday. Had spoken to Jake yesterday. Max felt out of control. He couldn't bear being out of control, it terrified him. He undid his tie and the top buttons of his shirt, panic perspiration making his fingers clumsy, his gleaming white and chrome office spinning around him. The girl who might be his daughter had come back into his life and chosen not to make herself known to him. Which in Max's confused thoughts could only mean one thing. That she knew. She knew about him and she knew about his past and now she knew him. He didn't even know her name, because no one in his London group was called Jasmine, he was certain he would have remembered that. Max threw up again and from the pit of his stomach where the memories were kept he disgorged both his breakfast and a picture of Anita. Anita lying in his arms, kissing her on holiday in Mexico, kissing her in the garden of the House, kissing her as her last breath came from her. Kissing Anita and holding Anita and killing Anita. Very much in the same way he had first held Michael and kissed Michael as he handed him the razor blade to kill himself with, leaving him at the door with a quiet "Goodnight". Very much in the same way that almost ten years ago he had held Deb and kissed Deb as he cut her wrists for her. Very much in the same way that he had eventually convinced Anna Johnson that drowning would be a soft and pleasant death.

Max was nearly fifty-three and had spent almost half his life developing and refining the Process. With his family and establishment contacts and the several favours which had been owing to him since Anna Johnson's death when he had let it be known to one or two key figures that he was hanging on to her secrets, he had built up a position so that now he was ready to take the Process to the public arena and over a third of the hospitals nationwide. It was to be the culmination of his desires. Sure, the money and prestige would be nice, but the value of the Process was way beyond that. It would be available to all. This was no longer any silly youthful delusion of grandeur, this was exactly what he'd set out to achieve all those years ago – something that mattered. Then it had been a vague dream, now it was reality. And now this girl was here, this loose cannon. Two loose cannons. Jasmine here, and this Sarah, whoever she was, in America.

To take the Process this far Max had pretty much given up on personal relationships, on the possibility of a family. Had pretty much given up everything. And he'd been fine about that, happy to make the sacrifice. The only thing he would not give up was the Process. This girl was a danger and a worry, but she was not an insurmountable problem. Max went to his cool office bathroom and wiped his face with fresh water and a lemon scented towel. It would be all right. He'd deal with this girl, just like all the others. Once he found her.

wavewalker

The woman takes my hand and leads me between them.
Between the two men and I do not know which is mine.
Though I have chosen.
The small waves hit against my small bare feet and I
wait for the seventh wave. I count the first six.

At the great wave I will unleash myself.

He does not know me still, but he will.
She is guiding me, walking very near me. She is taking
me close.
I am the puppet master and I will take control.

The woman is pleased with me.
I am pleased with the woman I have chosen.
She too is coming close.
Can he smell the women returning?
Is he scared?
I hope he is. I am hungry for the taste of his fear.

The woman is very pleased with me.

CHAPTER 25

It wasn't so much that Saz didn't enjoy the "adult children and parents" meeting. It wasn't even that she didn't grasp a few valuable insights of her own. It was more that all the while she was discussing the difficulty of becoming friends with your family, and all the while she was "opening her heart and mind to the possibility of a New Loving Paradigm", she would have preferred to be opening the records and files of the House to the somewhat more juicy possibility of uncovering the truth about Maxwell North.

The group were the usual eclectic bunch these things turned out and Saz was glad she had at least attended the one-day Process or most of the concepts and jargon bandied about the whitewashed room would have been incomprehensible to her. Saz had long ago accustomed herself to the fact that her parents were fallible and as likely to make mistakes as anyone else and she was echoed in her thoughts by Grant, who tried his best to get the group to pass on from their anger and into something slightly more constructive – like looking at the future, even if it was only tomorrow. He was fairly successful with all but one man who, in his early forties, was still blaming his mother for his inability to relate successfully to women. Saz thought that might have a little more to do with his rampant sexism, but forbore to say so, as he'd already bridled perceptibly when she came out at the beginning of the evening.

Over a cup of jasmine tea for Grant and pure caffeine-ridden coffee for Saz at the end of the session, the two of them agreed that the most obvious thing they'd seen in the meeting was that those who were prepared to forgive and then just get on with it, did so fairly readily, once the concept of "letting go" had been clearly explained to them. But those who were scared of actually having a life were the ones most likely to want to stay exactly where they were. As Grant explained,

"God Saz, if that guy Bob actually had the guts to do it, he'd probably be a great actor – I've seen his work. He's good. But he's just too damn scared. So he gets to say 'Mommy didn't love me' and at forty-two he's going nowhere fast, because he would rather blame others for his failure than have a life of his own and risk the possibility of failing on his own terms."

When Saz nodded her agreement, Grant asked, "So perhaps you'd like to take a risk and be honest with me now?"

Saz just managed to put down her cup before she spilt it all down her front and stuttered, "Ah, sure . . . um, OK."

Grant smiled and patted her hand.

"Good. I'll just farewell the others and then you can tell me all about it. I love stories."

Saz, cursing herself for consenting to come to the meeting when what she really needed was a good night's sleep, swallowed her coffee and muttered, "Yeah, well I hope you're going to love this one."

Grant said goodnight to the last of the participants and then took Saz two blocks down the road to a small, dimly lit Chinese restaurant with a huge sign proclaiming "NO MSG" on the door. It was quite warm and they sat by the open front window while Saz told Grant all. Or made it look like she was telling him all. Grant was charming

and terribly good-looking and very friendly and perceptive, possibly even more perceptive than his father, but
while Saz could have used his co-operation, she was not
prepared to risk her own safety at the hands of this
boy. This boy who was bending over backwards to make
himself look like a good guy. This boy who obviously
worshipped Max. Admonishing herself for her lack of
trust in the world, Saz nonetheless told him a heavily
censored version of the whole story. She told him about
the first letter, about going to the weekend Process and
coming home to find the flowers. She told him about some
of the discrepancies in Max's past dates – how in most
press records his early years at the House just didn't
feature at all. And when Grant, like Jake, tried to tell
her that this secrecy was to protect the House from the
pointlessness of delving into the past, she nodded and
told him she was sure he was right. For good measure
she told him a little about her relationship with Molly
and the strain it was under due to her preoccupation
with the case. She told him about her time with Caron
McKenna but she didn't tell him about the apparent
suicide of Caron's PA. She told him she thought there
was something odd going on, and that she didn't know
what it was. Knowing that Grant wasn't especially
enamoured of Jasmine, Saz told him she thought it was
all connected to her. That she now believed Jasmine to
be her mystery employer, but she still wasn't clear why
she'd been employed in the first place. When she finished,
she waited, studying Grant's impassive face. He asked
her,

"So what do you think all this has to do with Max?"

"I don't know. Apparently he wasn't even in the country
when everything went wrong for Jasmine, when her
mother died. But I think maybe she blames him
somehow."

"Think or know?"

"I don't know. I don't know anything for sure. It's not as if I even know Jasmine either. And from what both you and Jake have said, she may not be the most trustworthy witness."

"I wouldn't have thought so. What do you want from me?"

"You could look up the records. Tell me who else was living in the House in the early days. Jake mentioned Michael, the guy who left? I'd love to find out where he went, talk to him. Anyone who was there really. People from the early days."

Grant was quiet for a moment, stabbing his chopsticks into the glazed vegetables in front of him. Then he looked up and smiled at Saz, running his hands through his long hair, it was the first clear smile he'd given her since the session began earlier that night and she was surprised to find she was glad to have him smiling at her, pleased that he seemed to like her. Which disturbed her even more.

"Leave it with me, yeah? It's been a long night. I'll go through some things in the morning, Carla will be teaching and Jake's got to be at the store first thing, I'll have plenty of time. You go back to your hotel and get some sleep."

"OK, thanks. I'm really grateful for this Grant. I needed an ally."

"Sure."

At the door to the House Saz hugged Grant goodnight and wasn't surprised that she didn't get much response from him, she reasoned that she must have confused him, and he was only eighteen after all.

"Night Grant. I'll meet you around lunchtime, yeah?"

"Uh-huh. See you later, Saz."

Grant slammed and locked the door behind her and Saz walked out into the night, and commencing the brief but painful trek up the hill she turned to smile back at the view, feeling pleased with herself as she correctly turned the corner to the hotel and tucked another chunk of San Francisco cartography under her belt.

As Saz walked slowly back to her hotel, enjoying the glittering map of San Francisco all around her, Grant ran upstairs to his bedroom and put in an urgent telephone call to Maxwell North.

CHAPTER 26

Jasmine met Caron on the third night of her exhibition, a "gallery evening" designed to keep the flow of press coming after the first day and keep Caron's name in the papers. It usually worked very well. The exhibition had been warmly received, as was to be expected from a Caron McKenna show, the stark white gallery was bright with the tinkling glasses and affected smiles of all the right people. Only Max was absent from the opening but Caron had passed that off as a pressing work commitment on his part, which was not far wrong. His obsessive behaviour and constant phone calls to San Francisco could only be work-related, though he wasn't likely to discuss it in any detail with her. Her artistic entourage were long-used to seeing Caron as a woman in her own right and didn't really care whether Max was available to chatter to the press or not – only the press seemed to mind about that. For her part, Caron was glad not to have to talk to Max since she'd been forced into remembering so much about Deb. Caron's "Kitchen Works" installation was particularly attracting a great deal of favourable interest, used pots, pans and other kitchen implements hung at different heights and revolving incredibly slowly on a wire washing line around the perfectly placed pieces of a shattered ebony head. Deb's head. Jasmine introduced herself as an old wrought iron pan scraped past the shards.

"Ms McKenna? I'm Jasmine, Anita's daughter. Maybe Max has mentioned me?"

Caron nearly dropped her glass of barely touched wine when the young woman stepped in front of her and introduced herself, quickly reaching out her hand to steady the glass.

"Careful, wouldn't want any blood spilt, would we?"

Caron took in the younger woman's small, terribly thin body dressed, highly inappropriately for the gallery, in old jeans and a dark red shirt, her hair was long, fine and white blonde, her high cheekbones cutting a fine line under startlingly pale blue eyes. Max's eyes.

Seeing another reviewer coming towards her, Caron regained her composure and taking the younger woman's hand from her glass, pulled her into the gallery office, excusing herself from the *Evening Standard* feature writer who was almost upon her now and was desperately trying to extract a witty quote to contrast with what he knew would be a scathing attack from the paper's arts critic. Caron shut the door behind them and turned to look at Jasmine. She sat herself down on the office desk, legs folded under her, chin resting on her right fist. She smiled and Caron couldn't escape the fleeting image of a malevolent elf.

"What are you doing here?"

"I came to see you."

"Couldn't you have chosen a slightly less public place?"

"Why? You don't think these people would be interested in your long lost step-daughter?"

"Oh, I know they'd be fascinated, but I'm afraid I'm not interested in providing them with salacious gossip for their tacky rags."

"Oh well, I guess you'll do for now. I'm not exactly desperate for publicity myself."

Jasmine's mouth smiled at Caron, her eyes scrutinizing the artist's face.

"Did he kill her?"

"What?"

"Max. My father. Daddy. Did he kill her? You know, your assistant? Deb, wasn't it?"

"Suddenly the whole world wants to know. Shame none of you asked this ten years ago. Deb committed suicide."

"Oh, yeah. Silly me. Now, just tell me this, did you see her do it or did he tell you?"

"I saw her body. She was very dead."

"Who saw her last?"

Caron stepped back towards the door looking through the little side window at her guests.

"Look, I really don't know why you're here or what you want, but this just isn't the right time. We can meet for lunch if you want."

Jasmine swung her legs off the desk and walked the few steps across the little office to Caron.

"No I don't want, I don't want any of your nice English lunch shit. Just answer the question, who saw her last?"

Caron looked at the floor, bewildered.

"It was a very long time ago. I don't think about it much. I don't like being made to think about it. I don't want to talk about her . . . "

Jasmine reached out to Caron's face and turned the older, trembling woman around, her small cold fingers pinched Caron's jawbone.

"Listen to me, I don't mean to scare you, I know I'm acting weird . . . acting? God, I probably am weird and maybe this has nothing to do with you, I don't know . . . it's him, Max . . . look, will you just tell me, who saw her last?"

Caron looked down at the glass in her hand and almost whispered.

"He did."

"Yeah, right, and he told you she'd killed herself?"

Caron pushed Jasmine away and leant back against the wall.

"Well, forgive me, but it certainly looked like it from the pool of blood she lay in."

Caron was crying now, tears dripping down her cheeks and into the glass, her agent pushed the door open and looked in.

"Oh ... Caron ... I'm so sorry, I'm intruding. I apologize."

Caron took a deep breath and turned to face him, smiling.

"No Paul, it's fine, I'll be with you in a moment. I'm sorry."

Paul closed the door behind him and Jasmine laughed.

"Christ, you're all so God damned sorry."

"No, we're just English. Now look, Miss North ... "

"De Vries, I use my mother's name, not his."

"Fine. De Vries? Well, quite frankly, I can't deal with this just now. I'd love to, but I can't. I'm not interested in any of your questions, any of you. This exhibition is very important to me, my work is all I have left and I have no intention of making a mess of this too."

Caron relaxed as the holds of social constricts and etiquette took over and she found herself in control again, if not of Jasmine, then at least of her own emotions.

"I do however, very much want to hear what you have to say. Why don't you meet me for lunch tomorrow, say one o'clock? I'll pick you up, give me your address."

Jasmine scribbled down an address in Camden and as Caron relaunched herself on the scrimmage of her own party, Jasmine helped herself to a bottle of wine and several smoked salmon canapés, leaving via the back door.

By two thirty the next afternoon Caron had finished

pursuing her lightly grilled fishcakes around the thin pink plates in the very private restaurant and Jasmine had managed to eat all of her own meal and most of Caron's. By the end of their second bottle of wine, again mostly imbibed by Jasmine, Caron knew everything her step-daughter could tell her about the deaths of Anita and John and all she'd managed to infer from what Chris could tell her about Michael's abrupt departure from the House, which he believed to be, and Jasmine was happy to interpret as, another covered-up suicide. Caron had already decided in her own mind that Max had somehow been involved in Deb's death, this diatribe, the scene in her kitchen a week earlier, only served to convince her further. Jasmine had not one jot of evidence against the man who was probably her father, but she laid a very convincing case of damning circumstantial possibilities. Max had been in the States when Anita and John were killed. Caron knew he'd gone to visit them, not that he'd ever told her they'd died then, and Jasmine herself had only found out by accident that he'd been around at the time.

"It was years later that I knew he'd been over. The guy they got for the arson has always protested he was innocent – at least of burning down their place – but it wasn't until I moved into the House two years ago that I had a chance to look through the records. Max was in the States the week they died."

"How do you know?"

"He called Jake. Jake's got this thing about accuracy. He records everything, you know? I mean everything. I asked him to tell me about my dad, I mean Max, there is a chance he isn't my dad. I mean, I'd be much happier if he wasn't, but anyway, Jake brought out this huge file – sort of like a diary, with every single time he ever talked to Max. He even recorded this phone call when

Max was only calling to say hi. Max didn't want people to know he was in the States, Jake said it was because everyone would want Max to come to the House."

"Wouldn't they? People do think he's something special. They do want to see him all the time."

"Yeah, I know Caron. I am the child of a guru. Believe me, I know it real well. But I think it's just a little odd that he happened to be there when my mom was killed."

Caron thought so too, even more so when Jasmine told her a little about Michael's death. She found herself shocked that she could so quickly believe the man she had lived with for such a long time was capable of any of this. But she could, and almost easily, because she knew just how devoted he was to the Process. As Max was so fond of saying, most people loved their work if they were lucky, loved their families if they were lucky. Most people liked things a bit, disliked other things a bit and then just trusted to fate or God or the Universe or whatever was going to get them through, but he wasn't like that. Max really believed he could make a difference. It was part of what made him so attractive. Their marriage had certainly been one of convenience, but Caron had also really wanted to mix her life up with Max's, to have some of her safe, planned, upper-middle-class life touched by his fierce ambition. And sitting opposite this girl, Caron found herself convinced that Jasmine was Max's daughter. Physically, she was nothing like him except the eyes, but what was so attractive in Max was recreated in her. And if what was attractive about Max was also frightening, it was doubly so in Jasmine. In Max the desire to make a difference and his fierce ambition had a channel in the Process, in Jasmine it was all directed towards Max himself. She looked across at the fierce young woman and found herself wondering if she wouldn't be making as big a mistake choosing to trust Jasmine as she had in choosing to trust Max. She decided to leave it up to the girl.

"Jasmine, this is really scary for me. Other than with my work, I'm not actually that good at taking control. I've always let Max do that for me. And Deb for a while. I honestly don't know what to do. I'm confused and yet I think I believe you, but I don't know what to do about it at all."

Jasmine poured the last of the wine into her glass and raised it to Caron, smiling at her.

"That's OK Caron, I know exactly what to do. Cheers – as the English say."

Saz had every intention of doing just as she'd told Grant and was longing for her bed, but when she got back to the hotel the little red light on her telephone was flashing and she called the desk to be told there was an urgent message to call Carrie, which she did immediately.

"You'll never believe this Saz, but yesterday afternoon Caron McKenna called me."

"How did she get your number? My number?"

"You gave it to her when you took the frying pan."

"Oh shit, I'm so fucking stupid sometimes, I forgot all about that."

"Obviously. She called last night. She thinks he did it."

"Who did what? What are you talking about?"

"Caron McKenna thinks Maxwell North killed her assistant, their combined PA and her lover of four years, Deb. Last name not specified. Nationality Oz."

"Fuck!"

"That's what I said."

"Why did she tell you?"

"I told her you were in San Francisco and she said you should be careful and I said why and . . . well, that's why. She said she's suspected for ages that Deb's death had something to do with Max."

"You can't make someone commit suicide, Carrie."

"Maybe not, but Caron says that a patient of Max's killed herself just a couple of weeks afterwards."

"And?"

"Well it's not many people who have two suicides in their lives within two weeks."

"Perhaps we should be feeling sorry for him in that case."

"I think not. According to McKenna he's obsessed. Would do anything to protect the Process. She thinks this patient who killed herself was going to reveal some problem with it."

"What problem?"

"I don't know. She doesn't know. That's why she's worried."

"Couldn't she have been worried ten years ago?"

"I didn't ask."

"Well it sounds like you asked her everything else."

"We get on very well."

"I doubt she's going to be another of your conquests, Carrie."

"I wouldn't be so sure about that if I were you. Anyway, I'm not paid to be your secretary you know, I've got to get something out of it."

"OK. So what else? I can't just go on her feeling of 'worry'. Not even Helen and Jude would help me out on as little as that."

"Shut up and listen. And be grateful that I'm bloody good at chatting up complete strangers on the phone."

"Obviously."

"Do you want to know or not?"

"Sorry. Go on."

"The night Deb died, Caron McKenna left Deb and Maxwell North sorting out the problem of the problem patient. So she goes to bed leaving them talking quite amicably and the next morning Deb's sharpened her wrists into oblivion, snuggled up in a bloody quilt and then just the following week the aforementioned problem patient dives off the cross channel ferry, only without her water wings."

"You have such a choice turn of phrase, Carrie."

"Anyway, Caron McKenna's moved out to a secret address and as soon as you get back she wants to talk to you."

"She's moved? Why?"

"Didn't say and when I tried – very subtly of course – to find out, she went all reserved and middle class on me."

"And you've always been so good at subtlety haven't you Carrie? Well, I'll look forward to seeing her."

Saz then told Carrie about her meetings with Jake and Grant.

"I hope you're right to trust this kid, Saz."

"I don't trust him. I just hope I can use him before he starts using me. But he is cute, more like incredibly bloody attractive really . . . "

"Oh yes?"

"No Carrie, I'm not you, I'm not likely to fuck him just to see if I still remember how to do it. I wouldn't have the time anyway, tomorrow morning I'm going up to Mendocino to look for Milly's mother, she was living at the House during those early years. Maybe she knows something."

"Or maybe they're all mad and dangerous."

"Whatever. I'm fairly well into this now. I can't just leave it and come home because it's getting a bit messy."

"I don't imagine Molly would agree with you."

"Yeah, but she's not going to know about all this because neither of us is going to tell her, right? I'll just keep calling her everyday and feeding her some soothing little stories . . . "

"Lies? To your new love, your only true love? Surely not!"

"Don't push it Carrie, or I'll ask about the next rent cheque."

"Why the next? You didn't even get the last."

"It's so good to be able to rely on one's friends ... so, I'll tell Molly what I think she wants to hear and then she'll have no reason to worry, will she?"

"Whatever you say, landlady."

Saz hung up after asking Carrie to call Caron McKenna and assure her that things were under control. It was stretching the truth more than just a little, but it made Saz feel better to at least act as if she knew what was going on. She touched her face with some warm water and brushed her teeth, then climbed into bed massaging her calves, still a little sore from the unaccustomed uphill treks and was just starting to drift off between crisp white sheets when the phone rang yet again. It was the long-suffering front desk where an urgent fax had just arrived for her. She ran downstairs and rifled through the pages quickly as she returned to her room, blessing Claire as she realized that not only had she sent the details of the fire and the inquest report on the deaths, but she'd also managed to get the name and address of Anita's sister who'd been appointed Jasmine's guardian and, best of all, a high school photo of Jasmine printed ten years ago in the local paper. Smiling back at her from the fax was a slightly blurry but unmistakable younger version of the Janet she'd met a month ago at the London Process. She sat down on the bed in shock as she realized that her lie about meeting Jasmine on the Process had actually proved to be true – as had her lie that Max knew his daughter. What she didn't know was whether or not he knew he knew his daughter. And if he didn't then what was this Jasmine/Janet planning to do?

Saz opened her suitcase and, congratulating herself for

not bothering to unpack, pulled out her tattered California road map from underneath her clothes and perused it closely for a few minutes. Then she set her alarm, climbed into bed, turned off the light and fell asleep almost as easily. Two and a half hours later she dragged herself from the bed, showered yet again, changed into clean jeans and a T-shirt and checked out of the hotel. Following the directions of the desk clerk, she hired a car from the place in the next block, praising the efficacy of the American all-night system and, having crossed the bridge, hit Highway 1 up to Mendocino. It wasn't the fastest route but promised to be the most interesting and she'd get there too early to call on Rose as it was. Things were starting to fall into place and she reckoned it would take her most of the next five days to make the round trip driving from San Francisco to Rose Connell in Mendocino and then travelling across to Idaho where Anita's sister still lived and Jasmine had grown up. All in time to make it back to catch her plane back to London on Sunday.

The hours of driving ahead would give her time to work out minor details like what lie she would use to meet Rose, how exactly she would make the interstate journey and, possibly most difficult, how best to delicately get information about the long-dead Anita. Meanwhile she drove as fast as US speed restrictions would allow – which was admittedly, much slower than she preferred – with the Pacific on her left side and Thelma and Louise on her mind.

CHAPTER 28

Saz took the hairpin bends and sheer cliff drops on the road north at a leisurely pace and made it in just under four hours, including a break for petrol, toilet and the purchase of twelve Reese's peanut butter cups. The sickly sweet and sour of peanut butter and chocolate and booming Billie Holiday on the rented car stereo kept her going despite the lack of sleep. Chocolate at regular intervals to keep her blood sugar up and constant singing along to "my man done me wrong" torch songs pumping oxygen into her lungs and through to her brain.

She arrived just after eight in the morning and spent an hour eating pancakes until she thought it might be late enough to start making her phone calls. She sipped her coffee and watched the sun reclaim the sky. She called home, wasting coin after coin on a sleepy and disgruntled Molly who resented being woken in the middle of the afternoon having been on call all night and resented Saz being away and just wanted things "back to normal, now, yesterday". Saz finally pacified her with the promise of a Greek island late summer holiday and about another ten dollars' worth of sweet nothings to put Molly back to sleep.

She then turned her attention to the matter in hand. On the drive up, she'd decided to make a clean breast of things with Rose. Wondering in passing, just how clean her own breasts were, as she felt more than a little hot and sticky having spent half the night driving and nibbling the ultimate in chocolate. She figured she could probably be fairly honest with her, after all this was a woman who'd managed to leave the House and bring up a daughter alone, and whose child was considered by current members of the House to be slightly strange for wanting to actually live in the real world – compared to the rest of them, Rose sounded really quite sane.

Finishing her third cup of coffee, she went back out to the call box and looked up Rose's address in the telephone book. The waitress explained where she should go and Saz followed the convoluted directions up to a cliff overlooking the ocean. There, Rose's house with its unpainted wood walls and redwood shingles, seemed to gently emerge half-hewn from the surrounding rocks and forest that leant out over the Pacific. The view from the front door was amazing, which is why, when Rose opened her door, she saw Saz's back first.

"Sarah?"

Saz spun around and came face to shoulder with a woman who had to be six foot if she was an inch. Six foot, redheaded, blue-eyed and with such white skin that for once the expression "alabaster" wasn't an extravagant hyperbole. Saz immediately found herself wondering how easy – or not – it could have been for a white woman to bring up a black child around here. When Rose opened her mouth and revealed a still strong midwest accent, Saz realized that it had to have been easier here, than wherever Rose had left behind.

"You must be Sarah. I'm Rose. I spoke to Milly last night. I wondered if you might drive up here. Come on in."

Saz followed Rose into an enormous living space with one entire wall made up of floor to ceiling windows facing the sea. What walls were visible were lined with untouched wood and completely covering the opposite wall was an assortment of feathers. All sorts of feathers.

Huge gleaming peacock trophies and the tiny downy ones that Saz collected in the morning after Molly had pulled them from her pillows in her sleep.

"Air and water. I'm Scorpio with Aquarius rising. Moon in Gemini."

"Sorry?"

"One wall's water. That's the sea, courtesy of the universe. The other is feathers – flight, air, courtesy of Milly. What are you?"

Saz answered her without thinking, surprised at herself that she even remembered how to reply to such a question,

"Ah . . . Aries, March 28th, Leo rising, moon in Gemini."

"Interesting. No earth – initially, I mean. You must have some somewhere."

"You're an astrologer?"

"I also write, tell stories. And so do you – tell stories – from what I hear."

"Milly or Grant?"

"Oh, definitely Milly. I don't have a lot of contact with the House these days. But maybe the story-telling is part of your job?"

"Um – yes. At least until I know who to trust."

Rose motioned for Saz to sit down on the quilt-covered couch.

"Can you trust me?"

"Hell – Scorpio with Aquarius rising and moon in Gemini? I would have thought I could."

"You know astrology?"

Saz laughed.

"Not at all. I had my chart done once at a lover's insistence. We broke up soon after. But I do have a good memory for whole sentences."

"Useful. So, can you trust me?"

"Well, I decided to very early this morning, around

about the third time I had to remind myself to drive on the right side of the road."

"Good. Then come through to the kitchen and tell me all about it while I make breakfast. You must be exhausted."

Rose sat Saz on a high stool beside the window and then bustled about in the long narrow kitchen that ran the length of one wall – sea view windows at one end and a cool pantry built right into the rock of the hill at the other. She assembled a breakfast of yoghurt and honey, small warm bread rolls and fresh coffee, handing Saz a tray, the coffee topped with whipped frothy milk and sprinkled chocolate.

"You look like a cappuccino girl to me."

And Saz laughed as she explained she was also a six-mile-a-morning runner but had barely even looked at her running shoes since she first arrived. They carried their trays into the living room and sat, either side of a low wooden table. When Saz had finished her yoghurt and started on the bread, Rose looked up.

"So, what is this all about? I suppose you've come from Max?"

Saz shook her head and wiped the crumbs from the corner of her mouth with the back of her hand.

"Look, I really don't know what to say. How much to say. You seem really nice Rose, but ... I just don't know how much I should give away."

"As much as you want. It really won't make any difference to me. I have no contact with Max and no desire to be touched by him. Whatever you say will go no further than this room. These rooms. That hill. The ocean. Unless it affects my baby, of course?"

"I don't think it does. At least not directly."

"Good. And whether you believe it or not, we're

protected here. The sea to wash us clean and the air to fly us clear and the rock," Rose said, patting the floor, "to ground us and make us air and fire girls see some sense."

Saz smiled at this long, thin giant of a woman describing herself as a girl. With her hair tumbling down her back and smiling unmade-up eyes, she made no concessions to the passing of time. Admittedly she was not even that much older than Saz, though certainly with enough years to be the mother of a grown womanchild. Then, taking a deep breath and hoping she wasn't wasting her time on someone who might not know anything after all, she started at the very beginning.

CHAPTER 29

When she'd finished, Rose looked up, her face even whiter than usual.

"He hasn't stopped then."

"Stopped what?"

"Killing people."

"Fucking hell! I mean, um, sorry . . . what?"

"There's no need to apologize. Oh God. You know, Max, he . . . well, you know . . . "

"No Rose. Actually I don't think I do. Just what do you mean by 'killing people'?"

"Well, I mean helping people kill themselves. See, when I first was at the House, there was this guy, Michael? And I was in love with him. I was only just seventeen, I was pregnant. I'd been in San Francisco for a month or so. Anita found me and took me home."

"To the House?"

"Yeah. Well, it was better than my own home where they'd kicked me out. Sixteen-year-old girls just don't get pregnant to black men in Bellefontaine, Ohio."

"I wouldn't have thought they were supposed to get pregnant to any men."

"Not in 1971 anyway. Actually, I don't suppose they do now, either. But black man, white woman? That's the kind of prejudice America's built on."

"And the rest of the world."

"Yeah, I guess. So I left – or was kicked out – a little of both. I decided to go to San Francisco because it was where the flower people were."

"Just like in the songs?"

"Sure. Only I was just a greyhound bus away. Actually it was three buses and far too many truck stops. Easy. Or it should have been, unfortunately I'd missed that particular bus by a couple years. Charlie Manson had come and gone by then and the whole hippy ideal was being questioned – even by the hippies. People weren't exactly dancing in the streets, San Francisco isn't that warm all year round and I'd landed there with hardly a cent and a rapidly swelling belly. I met Anita at the zoo, she took me in, made me a part of the House and within twenty-four hours, I'd fallen in love with Michael."

"Was it reciprocated?"

"Michael was gay."

"Then he'd come to the right city?"

"I don't know, honey. Seems all the misfits found Max. Michael was gay but not cool about being gay."

"I thought being gay was always cool in San Francisco?"

"Sure, it's a nicer place to be out – or so I understand – but the environment can't make it better if you're not OK with it yourself. You'd know that?"

Saz smiled.

"I didn't know I was that obvious – I thought I grew out of my dyke uniform in 1984."

"You'd certainly pass, but you have a very proprietary use of the word 'gay'. You don't say it so it means 'them'."

"I wouldn't want to either, I've been out so long I wouldn't know how to go back in. This Michael, he didn't come out happily?"

"He didn't come out at all. It was all hidden and pre-tending straight."

"Pretending with you?"

"Yeah. Not that I didn't know, but for me at that time,

any man to latch on to was better than none. And unfortunately I chose two."

"Two?"

"I'm not proud of it, but for the first couple months I was in the House I was also having sex with Max."

"Really?"

"He was a good lover. A great lover actually. I thought he was wonderful, thought he knew everything. But of course I didn't expect Max to actually talk to me as well. I was getting sex from Max and affection from Michael. I hadn't yet worked out that I was entitled to expect both from one man. And Michael was very sweet. He and I kissed and cuddled and he thought no one knew he was gay, so . . . "

"He was blindingly obvious?"

"Exactly. He was having an affair with Chris, another guy in the House and they were planning to leave together – of course, I didn't know this at the time – and then, one night, Michael just disappeared. There was a big fuss and Max told us all that Michael had declared his undying love for him."

"For Max?"

"That's what he said. And it wasn't really beyond belief. Max was beautiful. Very charismatic. Max said that Michael was in love with him and when he realized it wasn't reciprocated, he must have run away."

"You don't think so?"

"I think Max made Michael kill himself."

"You do?"

"See, Max told us all that Michael had left but, years later when we'd got away from the House, Anita told me that Michael was dead. She said he'd killed himself on the night that Max told us he'd run away. She said Max had 'taken care of everything' because he didn't want anyone from outside coming in and disturbing the House. The House, the Process – they mattered more."

"And what did the others think?"

"We all took Michael's disappearance hard. It meant we didn't ask a hell of a lot of questions. Later though, once I knew Max had helped Michael to kill himself, then I knew it wasn't my fault."

"Does it have to have been because of Max? It seems a bit extreme, don't you think he could have really wanted to die?"

"No I don't. See, Michael hadn't been happy as a teenager and yeah, he wasn't really OK with the gay thing either, but since he'd been with Chris, I thought he'd been a little better, and . . . well, he told me he loved me. He was really looking forward to the baby. I don't mean love like that . . . we both knew it wouldn't be that, but he said he wanted to be the dad. I don't think he was lying. He was sad and he was confused and, for all I know, he may well have been in love with Max, it wouldn't surprise me. As I said, Max is very attractive."

"And very straight?"

"I'm not the expert but I certainly don't think Max is gay. At the same time though, I'm just as sure that Michael didn't mean to kill himself. Not even for Max. I think that Max somehow made him do it and then tidied it all away. And if that is so, then maybe Max did the same with these other people?"

"Look, hang on, I really don't understand. I mean, why would someone as well-respected as Max, with so much to lose . . . why would he run those risks?"

Rose picked up the empty trays and took them through to the kitchen.

"I guess you have to weigh it all up. If Michael was going to spoil the balance of the House and if maybe this girl in England was likely to do the same – well, Max doesn't care about anything as much as he cares about the Process. You have to admire him, the dedication – it's all paid off. And he had to overcome so much resistance to get it off the ground – from his family to the State Medical Board – it wasn't easy. I just can't see Max letting someone get in the way of that."

"So why didn't you call the police?"

Rose turned to Saz and laughed.

"And tell them that I, astrologer, hippy and single parent, thought that Dr Maxwell North – of the Boston Norths – made a young gay man commit suicide? I don't know about you Sarah, but I do know that many straight men think being gay is a good reason for killing yourself. And who's going to believe me? But if you could get some real evidence, that's another story . . . "

Rose trailed off and looked out at the ocean, steadying herself against the wide wooden window frame. Saz tried to stop herself but a yawn shuddered out anyway as she asked, "OK, so you didn't tell, but what about Anita and Jasmine?"

Rose smiled at her.

"Look, I'll run the tub for you and then you can wash and rest up a little."

"But I need to get on – I'm going to Idaho to talk to Anita's sister."

"I understand that, just listen. You're too tired to do anything right now. Take a bath, have a short sleep. While you do that I'll pack some food, call the bus people and see what's available. Then I'll take the rental car back for you and take you to whatever is going to get you to Idaho fastest – with a sleep on the way."

"But I . . . "

"It's cool, I'll call Julia and let her know you're on your way, we've had a little contact over the years and she'll be glad to know someone's finally doing something about all this. So, you've got as far as the journey to Sacramento to hear what I know about Anita and Jasmine. There isn't a whole lot actually, but I'm sure you'd rather get it part-awake than half-asleep?"

Saz grinned at Rose and shrugged her shoulders.

"Lead me to the bathroom."

CHAPTER 30

While making Michael kill himself had been somewhat disturbing for Max, it wasn't really that difficult to achieve. They were living in the same house, Michael was completely dependent on Max and Max knew that he could ask Michael to do anything he wanted. And he did.

Anita and John had been more difficult. Their hasty departure a few months after Michael's death had caused a huge amount of disruption. The ensuing problems took weeks to die down, Max had to work for long hours on the new House dynamic, on the remaining members and especially on himself so that he again appeared to be completely in charge. Eventually though, largely thanks to Max and the blossoming talents of Paul and Jake, the House got back to normal – better than normal, since Max and Anita were no longer regularly arguing and a year later, Max's future seemed secure enough to allow him to move to London and begin planting the seeds for the British version of the House.

Max left the States, began his new life in earnest and felt that his past – at least the past he didn't want to acknowledge – was well and truly behind him. A difficult time that had nonetheless set him up perfectly to conquer Britain, hardening his resolve and fostering his belief that his Process was the only way. All the more disturbing then when, three years after his arrival in London, having set in motion the beginnings of the Toronto

House, after successfully handing the San Francisco House over to Jake and having more or less excised those difficult early years with Anita from both his real and remembered CV's, and just as he was beginning to build up a fairly impressive client list of minor royals and major celebrities, the first dangerous call came in. Out of the blue Anita contacted him at his London practice and told him she needed money. Max knew Anita well enough to know that this wouldn't just constitute a one-off payment and that he would have to deal with her face to face to sort things out.

Two months after their flamboyant society wedding, Max told his brand new wife that Anita needed help. Confronted with the story of his ex-girlfriend who was the mother of the baby he had delivered – while believing it to be his, Caron couldn't possibly object to the return trip, knowing Max's story of how heartbroken he had been when Anita told him the truth back in San Francisco. Caron told her husband to fly to the States and sort it all out. She paid for his tickets. She took him to Heathrow and wished him bon voyage.

Max traded in the tickets at the airport. Instead of San Francisco, he flew direct to New York and booked into a hotel there to cover his tracks. He then flew to Idaho where he stayed just two nights with Anita and John. They were living in a squatted farmhouse with no electricity and no heating, their hippy ideals transported into a dubious plan to give them a home and security. The owner, who lived in a much more prosperous farmhouse seven miles down the unlit road, had no objections to them living in the almost ruin, as they had assured him that within a year or so their work on the land and some other "investments" would mean they would have enough capital to buy the house from him along with the five acres of fallow land it stood in. They certainly did need money, reality not having been as kind to Anita's theories of universal providence as it had to Max's counter-culture implementation of the Protestant work ethic. John and Anita however, did not want a loan, or even a gift. They had a carefully worked-out blackmail scheme that would entail Max sending them £2,000 a month. Forever. As Anita put it to Max in his first discussion with them, "You know, we did the work in the House for you, we helped you discover your theories, now you're doing so well, we should benefit from them too. After all, you'd still be in Boston if it weren't for me."

Max argued with them both, even offered to give them the deposit for the house and land, and further help by guaranteeing a bank loan to set their development plans in motion. After a morning of fighting with Anita, Max and John went for a long walk. John explained that, now he had married Anita, he wanted to "do right by her". To make their lives secure, to make a safe home for Jasmine. He told Max that he would have been prepared to accept the loan but that Anita really saw the Process as being as much to do with her as with Max. She honestly believed she was entitled to benefit from the regular income it generated and she wouldn't be fobbed off with just a single payment. The two men talked for hours, then over dinner that night, Max tried to talk to Anita again, he agreed that to a large degree his present success was very much due to her influence, but he disagreed that he should have to pay her for it. They argued through the meal, Anita getting more vehement the more wine Max poured for her. John refused the alcohol but tired himself out anyway with several joints. Max stayed sober. The three of them went to bed with the situation unresolved and Max's return flight to New York booked for the next afternoon.

That night, Max lay on his bed for three hours until

he heard the sounds of Anita and John's lovemaking die away and their rhythmic, sleeping breathing through the thin wall beside his head. He then got up, quietly walked into their room and killed them both with a lethal overdose of heroin, John while he slept stoned and heavy, and Anita as she looked into the eyes of a man she had once loved.

He left Anita and John in their bedroom and went to the spare room where he'd been sleeping. He washed the syringe, took off his thin surgical gloves and then washed his hands thoroughly. That done, he put on clean gloves and went back upstairs to John and Anita's room, slowly and methodically going through all their cupboards and drawers – the few that there were. John was already dead and Anita was comatose, he had no need to worry that they might wake up. He did the same downstairs in the kitchen. When he had collected every letter and note about himself that he could find – there wasn't much, just a note about his arrival time, a few photos of a holiday long ago and a couple of old letters he'd sent Anita when she first left the House – he put them in his briefcase with the syringe and locked it. He put his bags in the car. He let the cats and dog out into the yard and collected three cans of petrol from his car. He walked through the house spilling petrol everywhere, but especially in the hallway outside John and Anita's bedroom. At the back door he stripped off his clothes and threw them behind him into the petrol-soaked kitchen, washing his hands again with the garden hose and walked naked to his car.

He slowly dressed in the clothes he'd left sitting on the back seat, took out his father's pipe, filled it with tobacco and lit it. He was tempted to actually smoke the pipe, but he knew too much about the dangers of tobacco to do that and threw it through the open kitchen window.

He stayed long enough to see the smouldering tobacco catch light and then the fire destroyed his clothes and spread quickly through the rest of the house. He drove off as John and Anita's bedroom went up in flames. The pair of charred bodies lying in a burnt-out bed would look just like any other couple of dead fire victims. If the small town police made an effort they would find that John had died before the fire and, Max hadn't bothered to check before he left her, maybe Anita had died after – asphyxiated in her sleep and without even the chance to wake up and acknowledge that she was dying. Or maybe they both just died of an overdose while the place went up in flames – a gruesome suicide pact. What Max knew for certain was that none of the local officials would waste too much time raking over the ashes of a couple of dead drug addicts.

By the time Max arrived back in New York, the police were sifting through what was left of the still smouldering house and the local busybodies were discussing the unsurprising fate of the "godless hippies". The identification was confirmed by their dental records and the sad news conveyed to their families. What Max hadn't reckoned on was that the local police were much more interested in catching the arsonist, which they did about six months later after another two arson attacks on local barns. This wasn't the first fire in the area and the police logically assumed they were all down to the same trouble-maker, doubling their efforts to find him. When they did, catching Morgan Davis in the act of setting fire to the small local drugstore, he admitted to the barn burnings but said he'd never been near the hippies' house. He got life anyway.

Michael's suicide and Anita and John's murders were happily buried in the past as far as Max was concerned.

Difficult but necessary adjustments had to be made occasionally, for the far greater purpose of the Process of course, and these had been just those sort of adjustments. Max had expected Michael would try to kill himself, had encouraged him to do so. Michael's infatuation with Max was becoming apparent to the House and beginning to make waves. Max was prepared to give his whole being to furthering the cause of the Process and, having finally started on his mission, he certainly wasn't prepared to let a mixed-up kid like Michael get in the way. When Anita and John had tried their little blackmailing trick, they too had found that Max's belief in his work, its future and power, meant that their banking scheme was as nothing compared to his single-minded dedication to his purpose.

He covered his tracks from Idaho well, flying back to New York and then to London, taking Californian wine with him as a present for Caron. He didn't bother to tell her when Jake informed him that Anita and John had been found burnt to death in their farmhouse and he very thoughtfully remembered to send Julia a huge bunch of white roses for the funeral. Unfortunately he didn't remember to send a sympathy card to his own daughter on the death of her mother. But then Max had never had a lot of sympathy for Jasmine anyway. Nor was he likely to get a lot from her.

CHAPTER 31

Saz pulled over and got out of the car, relieved to stretch her legs. This wasn't her first visit to the States but, as always, the sheer vast scale of the place had caught her off guard. When Rose had woken her after her long bath and a horribly short two-hour sleep with a travel schedule that took a little more than the next twenty-four hours, she'd felt tempted just to dig into the hillside and stay there. That however, was not part of her job.

Rose managed to persuade her that even though public transport would take a little longer and go a less than direct route, it was more likely to get her safely to Anita's sister than the more dangerous option of attempting to drive herself through the night again and Saz, still feeling jetlagged from the combination of flight and fancy, eventually acquiesced to the timetable that was pressed on her. They drove down to Sacramento where she just made it to a bus that took four hours to get to Reno, both the fabled city and the landscape conjuring up a million late-night movies in her head. In Reno she caught her breath for forty-five minutes before boarding another bus which, after sixteen and a half hours with two tedious "layovers", and a night of painfully disturbed sleep, got her into Twin Falls, Idaho just at lunch on Wednesday. She then drank another cup of strong, sweet coffee and hired a car to drive herself the last leg of the journey to Julia's farm near the tiny village of Bliss about forty miles north of Twin Falls.

During the drive into Sacramento, Rose had told her

all she knew about Anita and Jasmine. It didn't amount to much but it gave Saz a better background on Jasmine. Anita had brought Rose in when the House was just getting started and, as Rose put it, she'd seemed the very epitome of a groovy European drop-out.

"There I was, just a kid, pregnant and lost. She was only four or five years older than me in age but several lifetimes ahead in experience. She took care of me."

According to Rose, although the House had originally been Anita's idea, it soon became clear that Max was really in charge.

"You have to remember Sarah, feminism wasn't really in existence then. It was still all talk."

"Yeah Rose, right. Not like now of course."

"No. Really, not like now. For all the talk of finding a new way of life, we were still pretty much stuck in our old patterns. The patterns of our parents. Pre-war attitudes. And, by the time Jasmine came along, Anita was more or less relegated to House mother. Not that she wasn't damn good at it though."

When Anita and John decided they'd had enough of the House life, the two of them left together with Jasmine.

"Max didn't know if Jasmine was his baby or not, but in a way, we all were the parents – you know, like everyone shared the caring for Milly too – so he didn't really seem to care. No, care's the wrong word, he didn't seem to mind. We were all trying to be very aware, very evolved – that thing of, you know, you weren't supposed to be possessive in relationships. And more than that, Max didn't really need a child of his own to father. He had all of us. Maybe it was a relief for him when they went. It gave him more time to devote to the Process anyway."

That afternoon, Saz arrived at Julia's farm knowing nothing about the woman except that she was a prolific mother, had married a "straight down the line good ol' boy", and was, according to Rose, as far removed from the idea of her dead sister as could be imagined. So when the tall, slim, forty-something woman opened the door, dressed in what looked suspiciously like a Donna Karan suit and flicked back her sharp cut grey-blonde hair from a perfectly made-up face, Saz was a little surprised to say the least.

"Ah . . . Julia?"

The woman laughed and asked her into the house. Saz could only just make out a faint accent as she explained,

"No doubt you were expecting the Beverley Hillbillies? Well, that's geography for you, I believe they came from a little further south than here. Don't worry, it's a fairly common reaction when people come to visit. I do have an office in New York now, but very occasionally I still have to deal with the surprised ones. My middle daughter Tracy – she's moved to LA – she has a good line about Twin Falls, says all the men round here have belt buckles bigger than their brains."

"Sorry?"

Julia smiled at her ruefully,

"Means she couldn't stand most of the boys she went to school with and she got out of here the day after she turned eighteen. She likes LA, she's an artist there. I like the city too, but . . . my Kevin is a farmer and so we've made it work for us."

"I'm sorry, I didn't mean to be rude."

"You weren't. I live on a farm, my husband is a farmer. I'm not. I was once, when we were just getting started, we badly needed the money and we both had to work very hard, but I never enjoyed it – I've always preferred silk to denim – and, once the children were older, I found I was much more use to Kevin if I was earning my own money."

Saz looked around at the startling interior of the farm-house, most of the inside walls had been removed and the space was white and huge and full of light.

"I design homes."

"You're an architect?"

"No, unfortunately I have very little formal education – not a mistake I wanted my own children to make – I left school far too early so I could follow Anita here. I thought my big sister had all the answers. Well, that's for later . . . I work with an excellent architect who creates wonderful shells for the designs I then lay on top. I make things the way I like and other people seem to like it too. And quite a few people are willing to pay me a lot of money for making things how I like them. I'm in New York one week a month and the rest of the time I work from a studio here. Which is all very pleasant."

Saz looked around at the huge room, vast windows in clean bare lines from floor to ceiling.

"Yeah, it must be."

"Follow me to the conservatory and we'll talk there. From what Rose said, I understand you don't have much time and I want to make sure I tell you everything you need to know. It seems to me, things are starting to get a little messy and, as you can see," she said, leading Saz down a skylit, white painted hallway through into another open, white room which was completely empty except for a dark green sofa and a carefully ordered bookshelf, "I don't like a lot of mess."

CHAPTER 32

Only once she was safely on the plane did Saz allow herself a moment to look back on what Julia had told her. Their conversation couldn't have lasted more than two hours, but it was enough to send her straight back to Twin Falls to catch an internal flight to Boise, then on to another to San Francisco with only minutes to spare, where she checked into the airport hotel so she could be on the first available flight in the morning. She felt worried enough about events in London that she was prepared to spend rather more of Jasmine's money than she would normally have chosen to. She called Molly from the departure lounge at San Francisco airport.

"Moll? It's me."

"Me? Which me might that be? Oh yes, me. The woman who moved into my home and then moved out just moments later. That me. Missing me?"

"Yeah, too much. I'm coming back tonight."

"Really? Well, that's thrown a completely different light on my aggravated tone. Angel of my heart, this is brilliant news, when do you get in? When will you be here? What airline are you flying and do you want me to pick you up?"

"Are you pissed?"

"Ever so slightly. Your nice mystery employer had a rather nice bottle of champagne delivered this afternoon. And so I . . . tasted it for you." Molly giggled.

"Molly, listen to me,"

"I'm listening, I'm listening, I love your voice, your

delicately flattened South London vowels. Speak again
sex kitten, which airport is it? I'll get you from Heathrow,
or from Victoria if it's Gatwick, I don't think I can bear
driving round on the M25, not even for your sexy strong
runner's thighs – actually, on second thoughts . . . "

"Molly! Shut up and listen!"

Immediately Molly's voice descended several notes to
her serious doctor's register.

"Oh. Right. What's wrong?"

"I think you should go and stay with Judith and Helen."
Molly laughed uneasily.

"Aha. I see. You're kicking me out of my own flat? Are
you bringing someone nice back with you?"

"Molly, listen. Please? I think, just to be on the safe
side, that you should go and stay somewhere else. I'll
follow you there. I don't think your place is very safe."

"What do you mean, safe? It's got double locks, window
locks . . . "

"The woman that's employed me, I've found out some
things about her. I think she's the one who left the flowers
and I think she's been following me in London."

"Right, so she's after you and she's going to bump me
off, is that it? Maybe this is poisoned champagne."

"Who knows?"

"Come off it Saz, you're starting to scare me, this isn't
very funny."

"Sweetheart, I'm not trying to be funny. I have proof
that she's been following me, she's got the address to my
flat and she's got the address to your flat."

"Our flat. Anyway, we knew that already."

"I know, but I'm not . . . I don't feel very good about it
now. That's why I'm coming home."

"Not just for my body then?"

"No."

"My cooking?"

"Christ Molly, will you take this seriously?"

There was a silence and then Molly said wearily, "I'm sorry Saz but I honestly don't have the faintest idea what you're talking about."

"She's not after me, she's after Maxwell North, but I think that she might be ... well ... maybe ... "

Saz's voice petered out on the other end of the phone, Molly waited a while and then picked up the conversation, her voice now much calmer and colder.

"Are you trying to say she's dangerous?"

"I know it sounds melodramatic, but yes."

"So I have to move out of my own home?"

"Just until I talk to her."

"You don't even know who she is."

"Oh yes I do, only too well."

Molly groaned.

"Saz, I can't stand this, I never see you and you keep waking me up in the middle of the night and it's not for great sex!"

"It's not the middle of the night now."

"It is when you're on night shift and you've got to be back on the ward in five hours."

"Then you'd better get sober pretty fast, hadn't you?"

"God Saz, give me a break. Look, I know relationships can't maintain the fever pitch of the first few weeks, but this is ridiculous. Why couldn't I just have fallen in love with a nice normal lezzie, someone who stays at home, signs on for a living and likes cats?"

"Sorry babe, I don't have time to go into my pet phobias right now. I'll make my own way home and you just promise me you'll go and stay with someone? For a couple of nights?"

"Saz, I want to stay with you. I want your body, your skin, your smell. I miss you ... "

"I'll take some time off after this. I promise. Look, I've got to go. Will you move out?"

"If you say so. I'll call Helen and see if they'll have me. You'll have to tell them all about it you know."

"Maybe not. Just tell them you got lonely. They'll understand, they hate being apart. I love you Molly, I'll call you when I get in. It'll be fine."

"I suppose I don't get my 49ers cap then?"

"I'll see what duty free has to offer. I'll call you tomorrow. OK?"

"As if I have a choice. Love you."

"You too. And babe, they're Kent vowels, not South London. Bye!"

Later on the plane, Saz regretfully turned down the uniformed barbie doll's offer of a tiny bottle of wine with her plastic meal. She was still terribly tired and, much as she would have loved to devote the flight to eating, drinking and watching movies, she knew that what she really needed was as much sleep as possible to render her fit to deal with whatever was ahead. She swallowed a few mouthfuls of the dry chicken with soggy rice and then folded up the dinner carton to give herself a little more room. The man beside her was already on to his wife's dessert and she could see him eyeing her untouched bread roll.

"Help yourself, please. I'm really not hungry."

The elderly, fat man reached for her tray and placed it on top of his own.

"Dieting huh? Very wise. Shame I didn't try harder."

His wife on the other side of him looked up from her giant crossword smiling first at Saz and then at her husband.

"You said it Jim, you sure said it!"

The two of them then caused the entire row of seats

to rock with their laughter. Saz, cowering against the rapidly icing-over window and desperate to avoid one of those "fly here often?" conversations, quickly pulled her file on to her knees and smiled sweetly at them both.

"Well, I'm not so much not hungry actually as just very busy. It's a working trip, you see, I've got a lot to get on with."

The old lady smiled at her and reached over her husband's stomach to pat Saz's hand.

"Then don't you worry darlin'. Jim and me, we won't say a word. Not a single word. Now give me that after-dinner chocolate Jim, and shut up."

Saz, relieved, looked down at her notes and then spent the next two hours going through all she knew about Jasmine North/de Vries. It didn't make very comforting reading.

Jasmine, who from the photos Julia had shown her was definitely the same woman as the Janet from the Process workshop, was convinced that she was Max's daughter. Julia told Saz she agreed with her. She'd never actually discussed it with Anita, but although there was only a remote possibility that Jasmine was John's daughter, it seemed that both John and Anita had been happy to maintain the uncertainty. But, as Jasmine had grown older and more sure of herself, it was the driven Max not the laid back John that seemed most obvious in her character. So, she thought of Max as her father, which was not a problem as far as Julia was concerned. As she told Saz.

"After Anita and John died, we became her family. Having lost both of them, it made sense that she wanted to make Max her real dad."

However this belief in Max as her father didn't stop

there. When she was nearly nineteen Jasmine had suddenly dropped out of college.

"It was a real disappointment. Our own children are fairly bright, but nothing like Jasmine. She's actually close to genius. We were so proud when she got into Harvard."

Jasmine had been accepted at Harvard Medical School. Julia expected her desire to go there had been as much to do with following in her father's footsteps as anything else, but she'd made the mistake of contacting Max's family. Julia was fuzzy on the details, but she knew Jasmine had a horrible altercation with Max's father.

"Apparently he was an ogre even when Max was young, but Jasmine just turned up unannounced at the home of this old man in his eighties. I understand he's very proud of Max these days, but for a long time the relationship with his family was terrible. They never accepted Anita, they never even met her and when Max told them about Jasmine, they refused to acknowledge her as his child. As far as Max's father was concerned, Anita broke up their family and took Max away from them. He may be world-famous now, but I'd chance a guess that they'd still have preferred him to stay in Boston. So they never met Jasmine and they never wanted to. Apparently he wouldn't even let her in the door. Just kept her standing on the step as he shouted at her. That's when things started to go wrong."

Jasmine dropped out of college and came back to Idaho with just her bag and the clothes she'd been wearing the day she went to visit Max's father. She stayed with Julia and Kevin long enough to take a shower and sleep for sixteen hours solid and then drove off in the morning. The next thing they heard she'd turned up at the House and told them she was moving in.

"Jake called us so we wouldn't worry. He said that of

course they'd take her, in a way it was her family home. Kevin went to get her things from college and then, other than a monthly phone call and visits at Christmas and Thanksgiving, we hardly saw her for almost a year and a half until she turned up here at the end of last year."

Julia sighed and looked out at the late afternoon sun lighting up the land. She frowned out at her property as she spoke.

"You know, Jasmine really did love Max. As a teenager she used to get the English magazines sent over to her and she'd cut out all the articles and little mentions about him. She must have filled about three or four scrapbooks. She thought he was a god. I guess that's what comes of never having really known him. Anyway, to cut a long story short, she found out some stuff about him. I don't know how, she wouldn't tell me exactly what happened. She went through some old House records of Jake's when she was staying there. It apears Max was in the States the week that Anita and John died."

"So?"

"Well, she wouldn't tell me anything really. Just that she contacted some of the people who'd been living in the House when she was a baby. She went to visit this guy Chris in San Diego and he told her about Michael. Rose must have mentioned Michael?"

"Yeah, the guy who killed himself? Rose says she thinks Max did it."

"So does Chris apparently. And once she knew that, she kind of just went mad."

"Mad?"

"Crazy. She burnt all her stuff about Max. And not just Max, she burnt everything. I came home from a trip to New York and she was out in the back yard throwing everything on to a fire. Photos of Anita, cuttings about Max, a little corn doll John had made her and she'd kept

for all those years. All in the fire. I screamed at her and
tried to put it out – they were photos of my own sister
she was burning. But she was real cold, just said he'd
killed them all. The next morning she'd gone, booked a
ticket to London and gone. We thought she must have
contacted Max, but now that you're here . . . and you say
he didn't seem to know Jasmine was in London, well . . . "

"But the money. How could she afford all that time
with no work? And the flights? More to the point, how
can she afford me?"

"Insurance. Not Anita of course, that would have been
far too sensible for Anita, but John. He had quite a bit
of money put away – which made it even more awful
that they'd died in that rundown old place. There was
some legal loophole and John's first wife and children
weren't eligible. I never really understood why, but it all
went to Jasmine. Lump sum, cleverly invested by my
very clever husband and Jasmine got an eighteenth
birthday present of fifty thousand dollars. There was
talk of her contacting John's children and giving them
something, we hoped she would, but I don't think she
ever did anything about it. I think the Max obsession
kind of stopped her thinking about anything else."

"So why do you think she's employed me?"

Julia turned back from the window and smiled.

"Do you have children Saz?"

"No. I'm gay."

"That's not exactly a reason not to have children."

"No, but it kind of stops you getting pregnant by
accident."

Julia smiled. "I guess it would. Anyway, before I was
a mother, I thought I'd love them all the same, care for
them all the same. I thought it would be equal."

"It's not?"

Julia shook her head.

"Not with me. I have five children of my own. The result of a fantastic sex life with a man I've loved since the day I met him. They're all of them very different and very special, but the truth is, that while I do love them all, the only one I've ever felt completely . . . at one with, was my sixth child, my extra baby we used to call her. I've always felt I really knew Jasmine. And um . . . oh damn . . . "

Julia was crying as she looked up.

"I don't feel good about this Saz. I think she might be using you to get back at him."

"I don't know how. She already knows much more than I do."

"Proof then. You're collecting proof. I expect she means to confront Max with it."

"And then?"

"Then I expect she'll kill him."

Julia smiled at Saz through her tears,

"And you know? If it's true, if Max did kill my sister, then nothing would make me happier."

wavewalker

I am impatient now. Hot for it.

This is like waiting for a lover, a slow lover.
The anticipation is physical pain, the culmination will
be hot blood release.

I want to hurry, to do it, to have it done.
But I will work according to my plan.
They are so close now. We are all so close.

I bite my lip to stop myself calling out, to lock in the
words that promise betrayal.
I bite deep enough of my own flesh to bleed and taste
the iron.
I like it.

I am my father's daughter.

CHAPTER 33

At first it only rated a small mention in the *Telegraph* –

Esteemed doctor, Maxwell North has been reported
missing having failed to attend his central London
clinic for the past two days. Investigations continue.

After another two days, when it became clear that
the routine police investigations were leading to nothing,
pressure began coming in from higher quarters. Certain
"pillars of the community", having relied on Dr North for
discretion, were not in the least pleased to discover that
he really did seem to be missing. The ambitious detective
who had reluctantly taken on the case was forced to take
it a lot more seriously than he had at first expected and
approached Caron about taking the search on to a wider
level. Originally, he'd seen little glory in finding yet
another missing doctor – in his experience they regularly
turned out to be stress-related suicides, carbon monoxid-
ing themselves to death in the garages of their country
cottages – but now it looked as if things could get juicy
and he impressed on his wife the chances of glorious
promotion and on Caron the seriousness of his mission.
Caron McKenna, almost installed in her new home
assured the charming young policeman that he should
do whatever he saw fit.

"Of course Detective, Max and I have very recently
chosen to lead separate lives, but naturally I'm concerned
about him and it certainly isn't like him not to let the

office know. I'll co-operate fully. You should just do whatever is necessary."

He did and the next day most of the tabloids carried pictures of the handsome Dr North, his wealthy and beautiful artist wife and jumped to the, obvious to their readers, conclusion that as Caron had moved out of their marital home, Max must have run off with another woman. And after another day of fruitless if salacious speculation the papers gave up, no one called the police, the journos went back to their stories of randy vicars and Max remained resolutely missing.

Max and Grant had talked long into the San Franciscan night about Jasmine and just what she could be planning.

"I'm sorry to say this Max, but she isn't really all that together, you know. I know she's Anita's daughter, maybe even your daughter ... and all, but ... "

"You really don't have to wrap this up neatly for me Grant, whether Jasmine is my child or not is hardly relevant. There have been vital advances in our work in the past few months and I will not allow anything to damage our standing. It may be that she has come here to discredit me, certainly from what this Sarah has been telling you, that's what it sounds like. It's the kind of thing the English press would adore. With the results just in from the Toronto House and your efforts in San Francisco, things are going extremely well – she must not be allowed to harm the Process."

"You know Max, I don't know if she really cares at all about the Process. I think it's much more likely she'd want to actually talk to you."

"Well, if all Jasmine wants is a father figure, then we really don't have a problem. But from what you've told me, I'm concerned that we shouldn't underestimate her."

Max questioned and Grant answered for over an hour, but the result was the same in the end. Unless Jasmine or Sarah showed up again, there was nothing either of them could do. Max called the next day to ask Grant about the English woman.

"I don't know, I don't feel like she's entirely trustworthy, that's why I called you in the first place, but then again, she didn't seem to know that much either. I'm not even sure that she does know Jasmine."

"But she knows about her?"

"She does now, Milly says she's been up to visit Rose and you know how she talks."

The conversation went on and on, Max becoming more frustrated as his questions, only half-formed due to his own need for secrecy, remained unanswered. He finished the conversation with an urgent plea that Grant call him if anything – or anyone – turned up.

"You know, a photo of Jasmine might be nice, I haven't seen any pictures of her since she was about eleven, I wouldn't know her if I fell over her."

And indeed, Max didn't know her when she woke him at four the next morning. Although it didn't take him long to find out who the woman was standing at the foot of his bed.

"Hi Daddy, it's me."

"What?"

Max reached for the bedside light and Jasmine shone a torch in his face.

"Don't do that Daddy. Don't turn the light on. It's only me. Surely you remember me – you know, Anita's daughter? You remember Anita? You were the last person to see her weren't you? Alive, I mean?"

"What do you want?"

Jasmine laughed.

"Now that's not very friendly is it? And after all these years too! How about a nice father daughter chat? Come on, get up, it's time to go."

And the thin young woman with long blonde hair like her mother and her own father's shockingly pale blue eyes, laid down the torch and reached along the length of the bed until she was almost level with Max's chest, close enough for him to smell her skin, touch the softness of her hair as it fell on his chest, feel the cold grip of fear as she placed one wiry hand against his throat and with the other held the point of a sharpened steel knife to his rapidly beating heart. In the darkness she cut into him just a little, just enough to make him bleed a drop or two. Max tensed against the shock of the knife and Jasmine laughed.

"Gee Dad, aren't you pleased to see me?"

CHAPTER 34

Saz flew in to Gatwick, stood up long before the seat belt sign had flashed off, pulled her bag out of the overhead locker and hugely irritated several first class passengers as she clambered her way to the front of the plane and the exit, thereby pointedly not earning herself a friendly "Thanks for flying with us" from the irritated crew. She ran out of customs through the blue channel and directly to the taxi rank where she caught a cab to Helen and Judith's flat in Clapham, paid from her rapidly thinning wad of cash and let herself into her friends' home. They'd given her a key three years ago when she first started investigative work – "just in case". She knew they'd both be at work but was hoping she'd find Molly in, sleeping after another long night shift. She wasn't disappointed. Saz pushed open the door to the spare room and saw Molly stretched out on the futon on the floor.

She lay sleeping, flat on her back, pillows either side of her head with a thick strand of long black hair twisted in her left hand. Saz smiled and put her bags down very carefully. She undressed as quietly as she could, shivering a little as her bare feet touched the cold floor tiles. Molly stirred a little, twisting the strand of hair she was holding and moving the sheet down from her shoulders. Saz could see Molly was wearing her red tartan nightshirt and grinned, it still had the gaping holes around the neck where Molly had ripped it off her the first time they'd gone away together. An early relationship weekend with Molly's parents in Dunoon and Saz had been too cold and too shy to be naked in Molly's mother's house. But Molly hadn't.

Saz was naked now and shivered again, this time with the mounting pressure of desire. The past few weeks of Maxwell North obsession had limited their sex life to the occasional kiss and hug or brief, purely orgasm-destined, functional fucks. Saz looked down at Molly and remembered just how much she loved playing in Molly's arms. Twisting and turning and taking hours to do it or not to do it, the coming a by-product, not the only goal of their coupling. Molly knew exactly how to do it to her – and fast, but Saz had worked out how to give herself an orgasm when she was three or four, for her the main enjoyment of sex, and thus that which she missed most during her years of celibacy before Molly, was the touching, the kissing, the wet smiling laughing giggling grunting and licking of the before and after. She desperately missed the touch, the interplay of passive and active interchangeable action, the soft electric friction of skin on skin.

Saz knelt across Molly so that the sheet held her down. Molly opened her eyes in surprise and then smiled with pleasure almost immediately. She started to lift her arms but Saz's knees pushed them down tighter.

"Stay there. I want to look at you first."

"Just look?"

"I'm looking with my hands."

Saz closed her eyes and ran her fingers gently over Molly's face. The heavy eyes, the small nose, her fine lips, slightly dry from sleep and the tiny scar on her lower lip from a baby years' accident. The lips kissed Saz's fingers and then spoke.

"I missed you, Saz."

Saz nodded, her eyes still closed, "Sshh. I'm looking."

She slid down the hard futon until she was lying beside Molly, pulled the sheet over herself and reached out one hand to touch Molly's shoulder, feeling through the rip in the thin soft nightshirt material, along the sharp collarbone to the cavity at the bottom of her throat. Saz kept her fingers there for a moment, feeling Molly's breath rise in and out, the gentle double tremor of her pulse, checking the rhythm until they were breathing in unison. In and out breaths falling together, she took her hand down to Molly's small, tall woman's breasts, her eyes still closed, she felt the skin darken at the nipple. Her touch was very soft, very still, very deliberate. Her hand pushed through the rip in the shirt, easily tearing threads, widening the opening even more and crossed to the long appendix scar left on Molly at thirteen, puckered in the centre and silky with age. She pushed a little against it and ran her fingers along the fine, irregular seam, hard scar tissue running right down to the edge where Molly's nearly flat stomach tipped over into the thick, very dense pubic hair that had horribly embarrassed the twelve-year-old girl and now delighted the love of that girl's woman self. Saz ran her hand just over the top of the hair, slowly, backwards and forwards, almost not there, almost there. Molly's breath quickened in time with Saz's and she turned to Saz, ripping the nightshirt down the centre and pushing Saz's hand into her, with her free hand she pulled Saz's head to her mouth and kissed her, forcing her tongue between her lips, across the teeth, tasting the woman who had slept all night on a plane, tasting the sour mouth of her lover who had come so fast to find her she hadn't bothered with the niceties of kissing protocol.

"Hang on Molly, I've got morning breath."

"I don't care. I want you. Do it. Now."

Saz did, her hands on Molly, seeing, feeling who she was loving, her eyes still closed she let the fingertip, tongue-tip, sense memory identify her lover. Saz felt Molly tensing, her thigh muscles growing taut as she prepared to come, she kept kissing and with her free arm held Molly tight, breast to breast, tensed and swayed, Molly's back arcing upwards, her shoulders stiffening, her mouth fiercer, more insistent, their teeth clashed against each other and Saz pulled her head away, opening her eyes. Molly lay in her arms, in the circle of her body, eyes closed, eyelids fluttering fast, face drawn in the tight smile/grimace of close to perfect anticipation. Saz bent her head to kiss Molly's breast and just as she started to leave a soft breath there, Molly grabbed her in a crushing hold and came in a deep, fast contraction, fitting their bodies tight to each other.

They lay quiet for a while, Saz's head on Molly's heaving stomach. Molly was drifting back to sleep when she felt wet by Saz's head, she reached down her hand to touch her.

"Babe? Are you crying?"

Saz looked up.

"Sort of."

Molly pulled Saz up to her.

"Why? Is it me? I'm sorry, I've been working all night, I know you probably want me to . . . "

"No. No, I don't actually. I just wanted to touch you. Wanted your skin, your smell. It's not that. Not sex. Not you."

"The job?"

"Maybe. I don't know. I'm just tired I think. I've had so little sleep in the past week and it's all so confusing and I don't even know what I'm supposed to be doing any more and . . . I've missed you so much."

"Good. I'm glad you missed me. I thought you might be liking the travelling and being busy so much you wouldn't need me. I think maybe I'm not exciting enough for you."

"No. You are. You are exactly exciting and exactly safe enough for me. Quite frankly I could do without any more bloody excitement."

"OK, then listen. We'll sleep now, and then when we wake up . . . "

"But . . . "

"Just for a couple of hours. I'll set the alarm, we'll get up by three I promise. We can wash, eat something – you can clean your teeth – and then you get on with whatever you have to do. I can't say it's cool, because it's not. I'm really unhappy about having to leave my place but I want it sorted out soon. So, while I'd much rather spend the next few days canoodling with you, the sooner you get on to the case, the sooner we'll have our normal lives back again."

"Thanks."

"Yeah, well it's not just me who wants it all fixed up you know. Judith and Helen aren't exactly unaware that there's something happening. You can't have friends who are cops and then not expect them to notice when something fishy's going on. Now kiss me goodnight and go to sleep. I want you to finish this job so we can go back to being a nice normal suburban couple."

"Yes darling, I love you when you're masterful."

"Mistressful and shut up."

Saz closed her eyes and kissed Molly easily, finding her lips with blind eyes, no ordinary perception needed.

But even as she folded herself into Molly's arms and settled into the sleep that had been waiting for days, Saz couldn't rid herself of the feeling that there was something wrong, something she'd missed, something bad just waiting to happen. Even in Molly's arms, still warm from the sex, she felt an uneasy cold as she fell into sleep.

CHAPTER 35

Max lay in the room trying to work out why he hadn't recognized her sooner. Maybe it was her voice. She had a strange accent – part English, part American. Or rather, the English of an American trying to sound English. Like she'd been trying a little too hard to round out the vowels, clip the consonants. Actually he remembered wondering once if she was a South African trying to hide her long, flattened vowels from the other Process workers. He thought for a while and then dismissed the sound of her voice. It was a useless line of enquiry and not likely to do him any good anyway. He had seen her though, this girl had come to work for him for a while, calling herself Janet, she'd helped out on a couple of courses and then disappeared. He'd met her through his work, she was just another, just like all the rest. She'd tell him what she needed soon enough, he'd give it to her, heal her wounds if he could and then she'd let him go. Like everyone else, she'd listen to him and do as she was told. Max assured himself that this was so and then went on to his next thought – himself.

He was very uncomfortable. His feet and hands were cold and the bonds around them a little too tight. Again, he tried to roll over but couldn't, she'd tied him face down on the ground, his hands and feet were tied up and then stretched, hardly racked, but stretched painfully anyway – attached to something at either end of the small room. The floor was wood, clean, like it had been newly scrubbed. Like it had been prepared for him. Max shivered, partly cold, partly – not fear exactly, but in a way there was almost a sense of exhilaration, the chase, the hunt – for the first time in years he didn't know what was coming next, he had no plan. Max was wise enough to know that panicking, giving in to his fear would be pointless. The situation was almost interesting – if extremely inconvenient. The girl who said she was his daughter was certainly clever. Waking him in the middle of the night, physically hurting him a little – had he been completely awake he had no doubt he'd have been able to overcome her with basic force, but as it was . . . he would just have to wait. He had no choice and Maxwell North was certainly not going to waste energy or time trying to get some mad little bitch to explain herself to him. In his experience, the slightly mad, the very insane and the terminally stupid always wanted the same thing. They wanted to tell you all about it. Once they had, and you'd said "there, there", tucked them in, kissed them better, then they were happy. Max assured himself she'd tell him all about it later and lay his cheek down on the floor to get some sleep.

When he woke, it was dark. It had been light and now it was dark. The light had gone – but surely he couldn't have slept for a whole day? She'd taken him away in the middle of the night, tied his hands together as he lay in bed, one hand to twist the knots, the other holding the knife to his throat. She'd gagged him, pulled a jacket over his shoulders, put shoes on his feet and walked him out to a car parked by his front door. He climbed into the back seat and lay down, astonished at the passivity the sharp knife induced in him. In the car she tied his feet together and blindfolded him, covering him with an old rug. The rug smelt of dogs. When she finally stopped driving she helped him out, undid his feet, and walked him just a few steps, the knife at his kidneys this time.

Prodding and occasionally piercing. By the time they were inside the building, Max had ten or eleven sharp cuts on his torso, each one bleeding just a little. She'd opened a large door and pushed him through into a big space, very likely empty by the sound the slamming door made behind them. She'd taken him in a lift up to this room, tied him up and removed his shoes and the blind-fold just before she left.

But it had been dark then and, as he'd thought over his situation, the sun had come up. In the dark he hadn't noticed but as the day opened the room got lighter and lighter from above. He assumed there was a skylight, it was white, sunshine kind of light. He could twist his head around enough to see the rectangle of concave translucent glass above him. Other than that – and the hooks in the walls that held his bindings – he was alone in the white room. Only now, having slept, it was com-pletely dark again. It had to be night – eight, nine o'clock or even later. So he'd slept all day? Max couldn't take the confusion and he did what he'd always done when faced with a problem he couldn't solve – he blocked it out and hurried on to his next thought. There was no confusion about this one. He was dreadfully uncomfort-able. Physically uncomfortable. His silk pyjama bottoms and the jacket she'd thrust on him in the bedroom were hardly padding enough to lie on a floor for two hours let alone what must have been at least half a day. He couldn't move anything other than his head – and that only from one side to the other, and he was cold. But worse than that, his bladder was on fire and his mouth was parched. The irony of desperately needing to piss and desperately needing to drink simultaneously did not escape him. A way to alleviate the problem however, did.

He called a few times – "Excuse me!", "Girl", "Janet!"

– and when that brought no response he waited and tried again a few minutes later.

"Please?" Still no response. He tried again, but less polite this time. "You!" "I'm thirsty." "Can you hear me? I must drink!" and finally – "Jasmine!"

Only quiet came back at him. Max shrugged his shoulders as best he could and lay his head down again. He wasn't used to shouting – he hardly ever had need of it, except when it was for show, to prompt a reaction from a recalcitrant patient or group. But that wasn't real shouting, that was just for the work. That was controlled. Projected, from the diaphragm, just like he'd been taught at the elocution lessons his mother had taken him to as a boy. And that kind of shouting didn't hurt his already parched throat, make him dizzy. That kind of shouting didn't come from a small, tight knot of fear in his stomach. And that kind of shouting produced a result.

An hour later Max wet himself. There was nothing for it, he thought about his options and took the best route available, twisting his body a little so he could piss to one side. It almost worked. He wasn't as wet as he would have been had he just done it where he lay. But he was still wet. At first the physical relief and the warmth were soothing, almost pleasurable, but after a while, lying in his pyjamas, soaking in his own urine, the delicate skin of his penis and balls itching and tender from the ammonia, the physical pain brought about a change in him. He was able to recognize it as a change, but not to do anything about it. Max started to become unhappy. He knew it was irrational, he knew it was foolish but, against his will and in a horribly embarrassed way, Maxwell North began to cry. About half an hour after the first couple of tears, Max cried again. More tears this time, big tears, hot and salty down his face and on to the hard wood floor. He was frustrated and he was angry –

he was also completely helpless. Max knew he was crying the tears of an infant, of a small, dirty, helpless baby. Only he was also crying them as an adult trapped in the helplessness of a child. Doubly frustrated. Aware and yet still caught. His tears turned to sobs, arms and legs straining against their ropes as his body rocked inwards from the stomach. The sobs became retching and, a tiny part of his adult self still there to see it, Max watched himself vomit. Sharp, strong smelling bile from an empty and dry stomach. Throwing up, Max finally recognized that he was about a fifth of the way into the Process.

He recognized it with a yelp of shock and fear. He'd never done the Process himself, how could he have acknowledged the initial stages? He was normally off reading a book or listening to music when people were going through that – anything so he didn't have to hear their screams for help, for water, for the toilet. Anyway, everyone's Process was different, that was why it was so unique, so special. The tiny part of his rational self that remained laughed a bitter ironic chuckle and then Max was gone. Completely sublimated in the Process that would start with his reversion to mewling infant and end with his rebirth. At least it would as long as there was someone at the other end to guide him back. Someone who knew what they were doing. Someone as skilled as Max North himself.

Each Processee was like a newborn. Each one needed a lifeline, a willing midwife at the other end. Just as he'd been there at Jasmine's birth. Soft, quiet baby that she was. Her needs fulfilled each day and smiling in the casual constant love of the whole House. But the skill for birthing a baby was nothing compared to that needed to birth new adults. They needed the debriefing, the light at the end of the tunnel, the soothing father to take the mess and help them recreate the whole person, the one they now saw in truth. The open self, the honest self, the whole self who now knew what he or she had been, who saw what their past was and knew exactly what had made them what they were today. The Process had worked for thousands and thousands of people, each one carefully guided through the pain and sweat and shit to the promise of glory at the other end. And the harder the case, the harder the leader had to work, the harder it was to facilitate the Process. When Jake had wanted to go through it again a couple of years ago, Max had insisted he wait until he himself could be there to see Jake through. The Process of a forty-five-year-old man has a lot more depth than that of a boy of eighteen.

And even Max had failed on a couple of occasions. Sent people off to their deaths rather than bring them back from the place they had ventured too far. Even Max had failed. And in his last moment of self-awareness before he became the self with no division for "awareness" he knew he was going there. That in an hour or so he would be there. Where Michael had been, where he'd guided Anna Johnson to and then back just long enough so she could remove herself for him. Even Dr Maxwell North had failed – or chosen to fail – sometimes. Everyone needed help back. Everyone needed a guide, a rescuer, someone trained and aware enough to know exactly how to save them from their own self.

This sobbing, retching creature, tied between two walls, thrashing around in his own bile and piss was no more capable of rescuing himself than any of the others had been. And he had far further to go than most.

This has been so easy.
Far easier than I expected.

I will cure him.
I am the child of my healer parents and I am curing
him.

He will be whole and well and ready.
He will say it, make confession and then give the assent.
And I will do it.
As she wishes.

We are one, the mother/child and, through his labour,
have given birth to the pure father.
We three will be unit and united.
Clear, clean and in the cold running fire will become
whole.
Consumed. Consummation.

My breathing is excited and shallow.
I can barely hold it back.
I await only his word.
His voice is quiet.
But I will hear it.

CHAPTER 36

Saz paused outside Molly's flat and looked up at the big French windows that opened on to the balcony. The curtains were half-drawn and the flat looked late afternoon quiet. She got off the bike and walked it round to the back of the house. As usual she had to negotiate the basement tenants' collection of recycling and rubbish bins and by the time she'd moved the bins and bike she knew that the flat had to be empty – any intruders would have heard her coming a mile off and still had a good few minutes to get away. At least she hoped they would.

She'd woken with Molly at three, they'd showered together – purely perfunctory and more for the sake of cleanliness than sex, though that had been there too, and then Molly had broken the news. In the couple of days Saz had lost to travelling, Maxwell North had gone missing. Biting back a furious urge to scream at Molly for not telling her when she first arrived, Saz took off and headed north. She borrowed Judith's three-year-old but almost completely unused mountain bike to get to their home. The extravagant present from Helen had always appealed to Judith more in theory than in practice, but it was ideal for Saz's purposes. Molly had offered the car but, even with the urgency created by Max's disappearance, Saz was still desperate for some exercise and knew that the mostly uphill ride to Hampstead would at least dissipate some of the jetlag that hung rock solid to the

back of her head. The jetlag that was making it impossible for her to concentrate on anything other than just
how much she really wanted to crawl into bed. The bike
ride was ideal. It cleared her head and got her back in
touch with her body – knee joints in particular. It also
got her out of the house before Judith and Helen got
back with any awkward questions. She arrived home hot,
sweaty and very much awake.

Molly had told her the flat was well secured and that
everything should be in perfect order, but Saz was not at
all surprised to find broken glass by the back door as she
wheeled the bike round to chain it up. She looked for the
origin of the thin shards of pale blue glass and saw that
the bathroom window three feet above her head had been
smashed in, leaving a few chunks of glass outside but
probably even more decorating the bath inside.

   Leaving the bike against the garden wall, she went up
the few steps to the solid wood back door. The door was
still double-locked and she quietly turned her keys in
each lock. She pushed the door back and the evening
sunlight fell into the hallway, casting her shadow along
its length. After checking the bathroom and finding it
perfectly normal except for the shattered chunks of glass
in the bath, she walked slowly and deliberately through
the flat, opening each door in turn, going through cupboards, looking under the bed, in the wardrobes, behind
doors. When she had satisfied herself that the flat was
empty she then started to look for the reason behind the
smashed window. Nothing obvious had been stolen, the
TV, video and sound system were all still in place, no
drawers appeared to have been touched, everything
looked perfectly clean and tidy, exactly as she would
have expected Molly to leave it, although Molly would
have been quick to remove the fine layer of two days'

accumulated dust. Saz retraced her steps to the back
door and closed it, locking herself into the flat. She left
all the lights on, pulled back the curtains to let in the
last of the setting light and went through the flat again,
this time looking not for things missing, but for things
added. It took her a while, but once she saw it she was
surprised she hadn't noticed it in the first place.

A fire had been made up in the open grate. It was an old
Victorian fireplace that Molly kept under protest, loath-
ing all the mess and dirt left after the romance associated
with a roaring open fire. She was threatening to have it
ripped out and a gas version put in as a replacement but
Saz had almost persuaded her to give it a reprieve, at
least until after their first winter together. Usually, Molly
just left the fireguard in front of the hearth and had a
few flowering potplants on the grate to set off the warm
tones of the old tiles. The plants and guard were still
there but, in the usually empty grate, there was a layer
of kindling and rolled newspaper and placed on top of
that was a box. Saz lifted it out and carefully set it down
on Molly's grandmother's oak coffee table. It was a gold-
painted box, about two foot square and six or seven
inches deep, covered all over in small plaster stars and
moons. Saz thought she recognized it as one of the many
similar articles piled up in Midas's Daughter, although
it could just as easily have been picked up down the road
at Camden Market. A brief panic about letter bombs and
underground terrorists went through her head and then
she carefully lifted the lid off, placing it on the floor
beside her. Inside there was a thin sheet of purple tissue
paper over more boxes, these were numbered one to six
and, though they were irregular shapes – circles, tri-
angles, hexagons – they all fitted perfectly into the larger
box. Saz lifted each one out and lined them all up in

order. Box One was slightly bigger than the others, inside there was more of the tissue paper and then a photo. The photo was of Anita, a copy of the one Julia had shown Saz, the one she kept in her purse. Taped to the back of the photo was a match. The next box held more paper and a photo of a man, Saz didn't recognize him but she felt fairly certain she was looking at a picture of John, this photo too had a match taped to it. She put her hand into the next box and pulled back quickly as a drop of blood spurted from one of her fingers. She'd cut her hand on something and sucking the small wound, turned the box upside down to let whatever was in there fall out safely. She'd half-expected a piece of glass from the bathroom but it was a razor blade attached to a picture of a young man. Saz had seen this photo before too. This was Michael and the picture was one Rose had of him, only in Rose's photo Michael was in the centre with his outstretched arms around Max and Anita, here Michael was smiling out at the photographer, his arms stretched out holding no one, Anita and Max cut out so he looked like a smiling seventies Christ. In the fourth box there was a photo of Deb, a copy of the one in Caron's bedroom and another razor blade, this one didn't cut her as she'd guessed what was coming and had handled the contents very carefully. The fifth box held a clipping of a woman Saz didn't recognize, the photo obviously cut from the same sort of magazine as the ones Saz had initially been sent about Max and a tiny vial of what looked like water along with a service station sachet of salt. Saz paused before opening the sixth box. It was the smallest of all and she realized she was scared of what she might find. She took the lid off and removed the usual piece of purple tissue, only this time the tissue had writing on it – in thin silver pen. It was a letter addressed to her.

Dear Ms Martin,

I do hope your return journey was pleasant and that you aren't suffering too much from jetlag – I know what a killer that trip can be.

I guess you'd like to know what's been going on, but to tell you the truth, that isn't really much of your business. You can keep whatever's left of the money, you've done your job now.

All I want from you is that you tell them the truth. That's what you've been paid for. I know they won't believe me, but I don't think they'll call you mad.

I'm sorry about the window, I wanted you to have this as soon as you got back.

I really want everyone to know the truth and I think you'll have to tell it.

That's all.

Jasmine.

Saz picked up the box and turned out a photo. It was a polaroid of a man tied by the hands and feet, stretched out on the floor, widthways across a small empty room and he appeared to be screaming, his head was arched back, his mouth wide open, his eyes shut tight against whatever pain was hurting him. The photo was so shocking, so ugly in the naked simplicity of the man's pain that it took Saz at least five seconds to recognize him. The dirty, screaming man was Max.

She was jolted from her shock by a hammering on the back door. Saz jumped up and pulled all the boxes together, shoving them behind the sofa. She opened the door without thinking, half-expecting to see Jasmine standing there and not at all expecting to see Grant. He thrust a bunch of flowers into her hand and smiled. Not a charming smile like the ones she'd seen in San

Francisco, but forced and angry. He jumped up the three steps until he was six inches from her face.

"We had a date remember? You didn't make it, so I thought I ought to come to you."

CHAPTER 37

When Max woke a while later he lay soft in Anita's arms. She was smiling down at him and they were in the white room he had rented for them in Mexico. He could hear the trees outside, scraping branches against the cool whitewashed walls of their building, the building that was little more than an extended collection of huts strung together by trees and tiny gardens. He lay with his head in her lap and opened his eyes to look up at her, she was smiling down at him, white blonde hair falling over her face. He looked at her soft lips, they were speaking, she was talking to him but he couldn't quite hear what she was saying. He moved a little away from her, to clear his ears, tell her he couldn't hear, but he couldn't. He tried to sit up with stiff legs and arms, his limbs distant for some reason, he lay down again, unable to move. It was all slow, terribly slow, yet with the rushing sound in his ears getting louder and louder. Then her face came into focus again and it wasn't Anita, but like Anita, not quite Anita and not quite himself.

Max looked up into his daughter's face, recognizing her just as she reached over for a cup and began pouring water down his mouth. He was so thirsty, so dry, his swollen throat could barely take the water in and she was still talking to him, talking at him, but he couldn't hear what she was saying. The water kept coming, pouring out of his mouth, down his face, into his ears, making her words even more muddied, he struggled for breath against the stream of water and began to choke. He choked, fighting to take in air, his lungs straining against his chest, he saw now she wasn't pouring from a cup but a jug, a big metal jug of water which she kept on pouring, throwing cold water at him, he couldn't breathe, couldn't swallow, couldn't take it in, and the sound was still roaring in his ears, still making no sense until she opened her mouth again, this time in a laugh, her mouth wide so he could see all her teeth and she held the jug back from his face, and the noise stopped.

It was quiet. He wasn't in Mexico, this girl wasn't Anita, she was his daughter and she hated him. She was telling him she hated him, spittle on her lips and fury in her eyes, yet she held his head in her hand, tenderly, like a lover, she bent her head to his, her lips to his, he thought she was going to kiss him, his face wet from the water, raw and chapped from the drying of his salt tears, she bent so close he felt her soft lips against his, dry and cracked. He opened his mouth, he had no idea what to say, how to speak, he had no words left and, just as he did so, she kissed him, kissed him soft on the lips then, drawing back and laughing at the shock in his eyes, she spat full in his face.

"What Daddy? Surprised? Is it so shocking to have your little girl kiss you? Is it?"

The tender touch on his head was rough now, she'd grabbed a handful of his hair, pulling at him, shaking his head.

"Answer me Max, surely these aren't the manners of a good Bostonian? Your father would never approve, I know. He'd never be rude to a lady. Tell me, do I disgust you? Is it really possible that I could offend even you?"

Max shook his head, the words weren't there, he didn't know what she wanted him to say and he didn't know how to speak any more anyway. He had no thoughts that made sense. He closed his eyes and she let his head bump hard on the floor. She emptied the rest of the water over his face, this time he didn't choke, this time he tried to swallow as much as he could. She walked to the door and turned.

"A little longer perhaps? You've barely begun. As I've heard you say so often, the Process lasts as long as it lasts. I think we'll both know when you're done. Oh, and don't worry about the water. I wouldn't let you drown. That's the last thing that's going to kill you."

Later, it really was Anita that came to him, and this time she did kiss him, kiss him long and hard and he felt ready for her, wanted her, wanted to fuck her like in the beginning, the best times, those new times when he'd completely given himself to her, the passion of sex he could never get back no matter how hard he tried, how many women he fucked. And he kissed her again and he was ready now and he opened his eyes to look into her face before he entered her and it was Michael, Michael waiting for him, Michael wanting him, wanting Max to make love to him, wanting Max to love him. But Michael was the wrong body, the man's body and too young, too easily broken. Max wanted Anita's strength, wanted to hold her and pierce her so she flowed into him, so he could be strong too. Not this boy, not this vulnerable, wanting child. And so Max held Michael in his arms, kissed him softly on the forehead and told him what to do, told him this way he would be free, talked and talked until Michael believed the story, talked until Max believed the story himself. Talked until the telling became the story. Max held the manchild, held him and kissed him and, terrified by the giving, left him alone, in the dark, to bleed himself to death. Max climbed into bed with Anita and rested against her strength as Michael curled himself, small whimpering puppy, in the chair at the foot of their bed.

And then he was older, wiser, stronger. Now he was strong too. Anita was gone and he had the strength of both of them. And the blood was the same with Deb, but this time he hadn't trusted her to do it herself, hadn't dared leave her in case her own strength asserted itself, freed her. This time he held her and she didn't much struggle, she was tired, sleepy with the wine he'd been feeding her all night. He sat on the landing floor with her and, one hand around her mouth, he cut deep into her. True, vertical cut, fast and sure like the surgeon his father had wanted him to be. His fingerprints on his own blade and who to check? Who to care? The blood on his clothes purely from the discovery, the quilt there to protect him from the worst of it. His strength there to protect him from the worst of it.

And Anita and John, so involved, such a plan, an endeavour. A trial of purpose. And successful. When Anita had whispered her last breath to him, he'd kissed her strength out of her, taken it from her, made himself whole. Healed himself as every good physician should. Only he wasn't whole, couldn't have been whole, without his ghosts. He knew that, he'd invented that, created the Process that found them, confronted the ghosts, made them part of the Now so they could be owned and filed and then finally left for really dead not just nearly dead. And here they all were. Anita and John and Deb and that stupid Anna woman and Michael. Poor little bird-thin Michael. Max screamed out to him, vocal chords ripping in the effort to find words that would convey meaning, bring him back from where he was all sense and feeling and no boundaries. The shock of the pain in his throat cleared his vision a little and Max watched Anita bringing Michael forward and Max took him, sat up to hold him in his arms and rocked the sobbing boy to sleep, kissed his eyes gently, held him as he slept and so softly, so quietly kissed him, loved him. And the boy smiled and Max smiled and Anita touched them both, on the head, like a blessing.

Then they were all gone and Max lay awake. His throat was swollen from the lack of water and the tears, his dry lips were bleeding and his wrists and ankles were rubbed raw from their bindings. He lay in the white room, daylight flooding in from the skylight and he breathed deeply. Each breath bringing him back to himself, more to himself than he'd been in years. He knew what he'd been through and what he had to do. Max looked at the five people he had killed and put them away. He was exhausted but easy. He smiled to himself, a big open smile and winced as the smile tore another shred of the skin on his bloody lower lip.

A key turned in the door lock and she came in.

"Is that it? Are you finished?"

Max turned his head stiffly and looked up at her. He spoke quietly in even, measured tones.

"Yes. I'm done. I think I've come back. I think it's all over."

"Good. Do you want to say anything?"

Max thought, then waited, then spoke.

"Yes. I'm grateful. Grateful to you. The enforced Process is not something I'd ever recommend," he smiled at her, wincing again in pain as his speech cracked his lips and dribbled more blood into his mouth. "Not even for me. But ... well, my past is confronted and put away now. I feel calm. I believe it worked. How long did I take?"

"Almost three days."

"Christ! That's incredible. Ah ... I don't really know what to say ... thank you."

She smiled, a genuine smile.

"You're very welcome."

"And now?"

"Now? Well, now it's all done. Finished. Your Process is over Max. You are whole."

"Will you let me go?"

She looked startled.

"What? Oh God no! I'm sorry. How silly of me, guess I'm not as good a Process leader as I thought I was. It's my fault, I obviously didn't make myself clear. I don't mean this is finished. Not you and me, not all this stuff. Not that. I mean you're finished."

Max frowned, stiffly twisting his head up from the floor to see her better.

"But I don't understand. I've completed the Process. I've acknowledged my culpability and I'm ready to go forward. What else is there?"

Jasmine reached around the side of the door and held up a can of petrol.

"Ever seen one of these before?"

CHAPTER 38

Saz looked at Grant.

"What the fuck are you doing here?"

Grant answered her, pushing her backwards into the flat.

"Hey Sarah, that's not a very English greeting is it? Where's the tea? The crumpets? The sympathy?"

Saz stumbled backwards, looking at him blankly.

"Huh?"

"I've come to help."

"Help what?"

"You're not very quick today are you Sarah? I know, jetlag can be a killer like that, still, it is all just a state of mind – you can talk yourself out of it if you want."

"For God's sake Grant, I don't know what you're talking about!"

"I'm here to help you find Max. That is what you're doing isn't it?"

"How did you ... ?"

"Know he was gone? He's the boss, it's not difficult to notice when your head honcho goes missing."

"No – I mean, me. How did you find me?"

"Oh, that? Well, when you didn't turn up for our meeting I was initially a little put out by your lack of commitment, then I figured you must have had a problem – real or self-created – and called the hotel. They told me you'd checked out and so I did a little checking of my own. San Francisco desk clerks are notoriously easily bribed. I 'obtained' your London address, which wasn't listed as this one by the way, this I got from your incredibly efficient British Post Office, and I also found out who booked you into the hotel. So, now we know you only told me half the story, perhaps you'd like to tell me how long you've been working for Jasmine?"

"You'd better come in Grant. Things have got a little out of hand."

"Yeah. Looks like it."

Saz took Grant through to the kitchen while she made them both coffee, stalling for time while she figured out what to do next. She told him what she'd found out about Max, warning him that he wasn't going to like what she had to say. By the time she'd finished, Grant's coffee was stone cold and his face was white, his huge brown eyes standing out in relief against the sharp, drawn cheekbones. She then took a deep breath before moving on to the next part of the story.

"The thing is, Grant, it's gone further than that. I think Jasmine has kidnapped him or something. Have a look at this."

Saz went into the lounge to get the boxes Jasmine had left her. She brought them back and showed them to him in order, then handed him the sixth box keeping a close eye on his face. Grant read the letter and then looked at the photo, it took him a few seconds to register that he was looking at a photo of Max, but when he did, his lower lip began to tremble and he started to cry. He threw the photo down and stood up, knocking the cold coffee over as he did so, pacing the tiny narrow kitchen and shaking.

"Jesus, bitch. Jesus fucking bitch, I'll fucking kill her if she's hurt him, damn her, I will fucking kill her. I mean it."

Grant grabbed Saz who had reached into the sink for a cloth to mop up the coffee.

"Where is she? Where is this? Where the fuck is this?"

"I don't know. Calm down. This won't help. Stop it Grant, you're hurting me."

Grant was holding Saz by the upper arms, digging his fingers into her, she pushed out against him, her hands against his chest, both to calm him and to move him away and he slowly backed off. He crouched down against the wall breathing heavily, obviously going through a great deal of effort to regain control. After a few minutes he looked up again at Saz, calm now.

"I'm not sure you realize how important Max is. It's not just me who thinks he matters. They're about to approve the Process for Federal funding – in the States I mean, and whatever is the same thing here. The medical thing. It's huge. This is going to change the mental health of both nations. Probably within our lifetimes. In centuries to come they'll say he was bigger than Freud. If she hurts him . . . "

Saz rinsed the coffee-stained cloth out in the sink.

"Come on Grant, no one is indispensable. I'm sure your mother or father could take over, even you soon enough. And what if he did kill those people? Won't the work be compromised then too? What if Jasmine's right?"

Grant glared at Saz.

"I think you're supposed to believe in innocent until proven guilty here too, aren't you? Or is that just another of those American concepts you English think is too wacky and Californian to take seriously?"

Saz turned to face him.

"No. We believe in it too. It just seems to me you're very ready to believe Jasmine is the only baddie here."

Grant rubbed his hands over his face, seemed in an

effort to control himself. He looked at Saz and smiled wearily.

"Not so. But she's certainly the only kidnapper here. I believe in the work, maybe even more than I believe in Max, I'm just not willing to let it all go without a fight. If he's guilty, then of course, he'll pay. But for now, can we just try to find him? Please?"

Saz left Grant going through the boxes again while she went to call Carrie. She managed to give as little away as possible and not get overly involved in the discussion Carrie really wanted to have – the one about her latest sexual conquest, a five-foot-nothing red-headed Irish beauty with a delightfully Catholic sense of guilt and play. Having listened to a few of the more sensational details and "oohed" and "aahed" in most of the right places, Saz obtained Caron McKenna's new address and then abruptly ended her conversation with Carrie so she could call a cab to take them there.

A little under an hour later, Saz had boarded up the bathroom window, triple-locked Molly's flat and she and Grant were sitting opposite Caron in a converted warehouse flat in Soho. Caron was dressed in white silk and was pale to the point of translucence, very thin and quite drunk. Saz had politely refused her offer of a "slightly warm but very drinkable Sauvignon blanc". Caron was explaining about her brief meeting with Jasmine while Saz asked the questions and Grant sat silent on the floor, his white knuckled hands clasped tight together.

"She said she needed to be alone with Max, so I gave her the keys to my old studio."

"When?"

"Three days ago."

"And what did she say she was going to do?"

"Oh, I don't know – make him confess I suppose. I hope."

"To what?"

"Everything."

"What's everything?"

"All the killings of course. The deaths. Deb, Anna Johnson, the other woman – her mother."

"Anita?"

Caron slopped some more wine into her glass and took a long mouthful.

"Mmm, her. Jasmine wants him to tell the truth."

"Why didn't you just go to the police with it?"

"To the police?"

Caron laughed at Saz.

"You are joking aren't you? Even if they did listen to me it wouldn't get very far. Max hasn't chosen to treat half of the wives of the cabinet just for the money you know. He knows more juicy secrets than the Chief Whip. Anyway, even if they did decide to take me seriously, what would I tell them? 'Excuse me, Mr Detective Inspector, but I think my husband has made my girlfriend kill herself. Almost ten years ago. I just forgot to tell you earlier'. Oh yes, that'll go down wonderfully well with the tabloids. How do you think the newspapers get half of their sleazy stories? Do you think all those police papers are leaked by nosy cleaners who just happen to stumble on the right document?"

Caron paused for breath and took another gulp of wine, this time some stayed dribbling down her chin, she looked wildly up at Saz and Grant and added,

"I mean, do you really think my family want 'society dyke' slammed all over the front pages of every trashy tabloid in the country?"

Saz was just about to launch into one of her "well you

should have come out in the first place" tirades when Grant stood up.

"OK, I've had enough. Your self-pity is boring me and we have much more important things to deal with. Where's this studio?"

Caron looked up at him startled, he'd been so quiet she'd almost forgotten he was there.

"Wonderful. Just what I need in my life. Another pushy bloody American."

"Yeah fine, we can deal with your insults later, where's this studio?"

"Why?"

Grant leant over Caron and snarled into her face.

"Because you've very stupidly given the keys to Jasmine who, just by chance, wants to kill Max and what's more, you gave her those keys three days ago, so there is now every chance that she has kidnapped Max and probably killed him yesterday and perhaps it might be a nice idea to get there before the body starts decomposing. After all, that won't look so nice on your famous front pages either, will it?"

Caron perceptibly sobered up a few notches and sat up straighter, whispering, as much to herself as to the others,

"I'm sorry, my lover died, my Deb. I haven't, I mean . . . "

Grant turned away from her in disgust.

"Oh for Christ's sake, don't start again. She's dead, she died years ago and you're behaving like you did too. Get over it."

"I don't want to."

"Obviously not. But if you don't . . . "

Saz interrupted him then.

"Grant, I hardly think this is the time to start a grief therapy session."

Grant walked to the door, as far away from Caron as he could get.

"You're right. So, Mrs North, where is this studio?"

Caron was draining the last of the bottle, tears falling down her cheeks and into the glass she held to her lips. Saz put out her arm to steady her.

"I'm sure it's not that bad, Grant's a little distressed himself. I'm sure Jasmine just wants to scare Max. Why don't you just tell us where the studio is and at least then we'll be able to see if they're there or not, OK?"

Caron began to cry again then stopped herself, her blubbering turning into a tiny hysterical laugh.

"It's just round the corner, sort of. It's a warehouse – was, they're renovating the building again. Still can't sell the flats. My father bought it for me as an investment – and a safety valve. My luxury hideaway apartment. A nice safe place to bring my not so safe friends. Or 'lady friends' as he charmingly puts it. Since Deb I've just used it as a studio and a storage place. It's really close. Only a few streets away, you'll be there in ten minutes."

w a v e w a l k e r

So this is what it feels like. Strange. I am not god or
devil but feel mortal, shaking. I feel very flesh.
Perhaps that is right.
Perhaps it is right that I feel my flesh just as he feels
his, railing against it.
He will not believe me if I tell him he should slip into
it gently, he cannot believe me now, I am his midwife
and he hates me for the pain of the birthing.

Mother, I am your daughter who will give birth to my
father into the true waters.
Is this what you want? Are you content?
Will you sleep now?

Let me go, I am tired of this and want it over.
I expected exhilaration and feel only exhaustion.

I want it done.

CHAPTER 39

Saz and Grant made it to the warehouse in about seven minutes flat, Grant running ahead to Saz's shouted instructions. It was just after eleven o'clock at night and Oxford Street was filled with summer revellers, tipping out of the pubs and down into the tube. Saz lost Grant briefly around the Tottenham Court Road end of the street and then found him again waiting breathlessly for her outside the Dominion. They slowed now to a less conspicuous fast walk and followed a couple of back streets, startlingly empty in contrast, to the old building covered in signs detailing the "luxury conversions" going on in the floors beneath Caron's studio. It was tall for the area, seven storeys high and old, though it had obviously been renovated once before in the boom eighties, the excesses of chrome and glass gleaming dully in the orange night glow.

Caron had given them her spare set of keys and they let themselves in through the metal door in the side alley. After listening to the silence for a few minutes they began to climb, both panting with the effort of climbing seven sets of stairs with held breath. They let themselves into the back room of Caron's studio, Saz gritting her teeth as each knotch of the key sounded like another thunderous metal clang in the lock. The long, narrow back room was lit by the skylight from above, cloud reflected streetlight throwing pale orange across the floor and walls. They could clearly see the small table, with electric kettle and coffee-making materials, a few old newspapers and magazines, a coffee mug sitting on them. Other than the littered table, the room contained a sink and a bench running the length of the other wall, laden with lumps of clay covered with wet cloths and chunks of discarded wood and stone. On the wall above the bench was a range of about twenty different types of chisels, hammers and a variety of stone-cutting drill bits, from a tiny one no bigger than a sewing needle to a couple the size of a fist. Grant crossed the room and helped himself to one of the larger chisels, Saz was right behind him.

"What the fuck's that for?" she hissed.

"You're English, I assume you don't have a gun, right?"

"Right."

"Well I don't intend to deal with her with nothing to protect me."

"It isn't necessarily Jasmine we need protecting from."

"Whoever, there's something about sharp, cold steel that's very comforting."

Grant slipped the chisel inside the front of his zipped up jacket, patting it into place. They turned to go out of the room and into the main hallway leading to the studio. As they did so, Saz ran her hand along the edge of the table and felt the heat from the kettle, she lifted the coffee cup to her lips and tasted it, the liquid was very strong and still quite warm.

"She can't have gone far, the coffee's still hot."

Grant turned from the door where he was listening intently to the silence outside the room.

"Is it sweet?"

"What?"

"Is it sweet? Jasmine drinks coffee with two sugars. My mom tried real hard to get her to give up but she wouldn't even think about it."

"I don't think so, I'd have noticed."

Saz tried the coffee again and made a face, it was strong and bitter, not a hint of sugar.

"No. Tastes like shit anyway, but no sugar."

"Good, then she must have made it for Max."

"Unless she has given up sugar after all."

Grant wheeled around and snarled at Saz.

"I'd like to maintain my own illusions, futile though they may be, if you don't mind. Just for a few moments, OK?"

Saz glared at Grant, standing a good six inches above her and looming down with his controlled fury. She thought back to the last week in San Francisco and how charming he'd seemed then, and the huge gulf between that intelligent, affable Californian boy and this angry, violent man pushed her a little further than she really meant to go. She spat back at him.

"That's fine with me, just as long as your illusions don't put me in any danger, you feel free to go on dreaming as long as you want. Now can we just get on with this please? You may be attached to Maxwell North by some sort of warped umbilical cord, but I've got a lover I've hardly seen for a week, a family, my work and a life to lead out there and I'd actually like to get on with it as soon as possible. Preferably both sane and alive, in that order."

She crept out into the hall and Grant followed her silently. Saz almost immediately regretted her outburst, locating Grant as yet another mixed-up kid in her mental classification system and, finding herself feeling sorry for his wounded feelings, she turned to apologize to him.

"I'm sorry Grant, I'm just on edge. I don't make a habit of trawling through warehouses looking for murderers and madwomen in the middle of the night. I apologize."

Grant looked at her, his face impassive and set.

"Apology accepted Saz, you can't be expected to be able to completely control yourself in moments of stress, you haven't had the training I have. When this is over, I'll take you through the Control Process Patterns if you like."

Saz bit her tongue and whispered back to him.

"Let's talk about it when we've found Max, all right?"

Max had tried placating Jasmine, reasoning with her, cajoling her. It was all no good, his words held no value in her mind. Jasmine was determined that her plan – her Process as she kept calling it – was to be put into operation. Indeed, that it had been put into operation the moment Max allowed Michael to kill himself. As she centred him in the big studio – tied up on the floor, hands and feet together in a foetal imitation – and placed the various objects around him, she explained what he had done and what she now had to do.

"Look, you took his life, right?"

"No. I allowed him to kill himself. He was very unhappy. In some countries it's almost legal you know. Holland, for example . . . "

"When people are extremely physically ill. I know. I do know about the Netherlands."

"Naturally."

"Only Michael wasn't extremely physically ill."

"He was emotionally."

"What are these excuses? You know you helped him kill himself, you said that during your Process."

"Yes."

"And my mother and John?"

Max looked up at her.

"They were endangering the Process, they were threatening to blackmail me."

"So you killed them."

"They died too, yes."

"That other woman, the Australian woman?"

Max sighed, "Yes, yes. We both know all this, I've said so. I'll tell anyone you like, but you must realize that it won't do any good. You'll still be charged with kidnap and grievous bodily harm after what you've put me through and you'll still have no proof, you can't do anything to me, I'm too important to the system. You're the one they'll say is mad."

Jasmine ignored him, continuing to place the small boxed items all around him.

"And that English woman? The rich one – your client?"

"What about her?"

"Her too? You killed her too, right?"

"She drowned herself."

"Because of you. And in the Process you say we have to acknowledge our past deeds."

"Yes, and then put them away, not carry on prolonging the agony like this."

Jasmine smiled, opening the lid on the last box.

"Don't worry, it's not going to last much longer."

She went to sit beside Max, taking his head in her hands she turned him to face her, he could smell the spilt petrol on her clothes as she stroked his forehead gently and explained.

"This is my Process Max. This is my Process to free you, and me; both of us will be free after this. She wants us back, wants her family back, the one you stole from her, the one you stole her from. I've wanted this for so long, wanted our family. She is close now, can you feel her? She is so happy with me, I am her baby and I have done very well. We are all together now."

Max started to speak but she held her hand tight over his mouth, he could taste the strong petrol alcohol, making him gag. Jasmine kept her hand on him until he was still again.

"You know they never took me to the house, the burnt house? I wanted them to, but they would never walk me through it because I was only a little girl. But everyone wants the truth, wants to know what really happened. Were there screams? Did they scream when they died? When you burnt my mother to death, what did she say?"

Max shook his head.

"It wasn't like that. They didn't feel a thing. I didn't want to cause them actual pain."

Jasmine smiled.

"Lucky them."

Jasmine got up and went to the circle of boxes. Around each she had spilt just a little petrol, running in a thin trickle to where Max lay. The boxes were small and wooden, about six inches square and each one contained a single candle, curled honeycomb wax made into a short fat candle the size of a child's fist. She took a long taper from her bag and lit each candle, very carefully, taking her time. As she lit the fourth candle they both heard a door slam far downstairs, Max started to shout and Jasmine ran over to him, screamed at him to shut up, holding the taper close enough to his face to sear the rough, dry skin on his cheek.

"Be quiet! She's not here for you. I need a witness. She'll come up soon enough. Just wait, we can't rush this, everything must be perfect."

Five minutes later, all the candles were lit and Jasmine waited by the studio door, a box of matches in her hand, ready to let in her audience.

Saz was trying to locate the right key when the door was pulled open for them. Jasmine stood in the doorway, her clothes stinking of some sort of petrol or alcohol and a box of matches in her hand.

"Hi! Welcome to my show."

Jasmine's face fell when she realized Saz wasn't alone. "What the fuck is he doing here?"

But Grant had looked past Jasmine to Max, lying on the floor in the semi-darkness, lit only by the faint city light from the skylight and the six candles placed in a circle and was already moving towards him.

"Max? Is that you?"

Jasmine ran in front of him, jumping inside the candle circle.

"Back off Grant. You shouldn't be here. This is between Max and me."

Saz moved forward more slowly, very aware that the liquid she was walking through, which was no doubt ruining her favourite pair of DMs, was probably the same flammable liquid that Jasmine smelt so strongly of.

"I'm sorry Jasmine. Grant was worried about Max. He wanted to help."

Jasmine looked up witheringly at Saz from where she was crouching above Max.

"I'm not mad, Ms Martin, so you don't need to humour me. And I know exactly what Grant wants. Looks like he's charmed you just like he tried to charm me back at the House. I'm very well aware that Grant has been jealous of me from the day he met me, wanting himself to be Max's child. He thought that fucking me would be a way to get to Max, but he was wrong there, weren't you Grant?"

"It was sex Jasmine, just sex. I tried to tell you that. But you never listened, you've always been too obsessed with yourself to see what anyone else was doing."

"I saw you. You cheated me. You're as bad as him."

Grant started to walk towards Jasmine.

"No. I'm better than him."

Max watched from the floor as Grant moved slowly towards them. He looked momentarily back at Saz, a flicker of recognition across his face. He started to speak to her but then stopped to watch Grant. Grant was bending down until he was level with Jasmine, just an arm's reach from the hand where she still held the box of matches. He carried on talking, and Max willed himself to stay awake, the caged fear instinct having started to shut down his body's natural flight reactions. He concentrated on Grant's voice and felt himself becoming proud of this boy's technique, his mellifluous voice soft and even, his tone sensible and firm but also ever so slightly pleading.

"I didn't cheat you Jasmine. You're talking crazy. I don't want to be Max's son or anything else. That's not why I tried to get close to you, to be honest, you were just a fuck, OK? But now I do think you should let Max go and then we'll all just take off. You, me, Sarah and Max. We'll go away, we'll talk this through and we'll make it all better. I can sort this out. Max has fucked up too badly, but I haven't. I can fix this. I'm sure you're hurt Jasmine, I know you've had a lot of pain, but this won't solve things."

Saz watched Grant, he was level with Jasmine and Max, just an arm's reach from the hand where she still held the matches. He carried on talking, his voice soft and even. Jasmine stared at him in the candlelight, smiling.

"You can't Process me Grant. I know all the tricks. I know what you're doing. You can't talk me out of this. This is my Process. Mine. I made it. Look – one candle for each of the dead, one extra for Max, and fire for the fire that cremated my mother. This is the cleansing. This

will save us all from him. You can't change it, you can't
talk me better."

Grant laughed, placing his hand on his chest in a
gesture of innocence.

"Jasmine, sweetheart, I have no intention of talking
you better. None whatsoever."

Saz stared, shocked that she hadn't realized sooner what
would happen, what Grant meant to do. She looked on
as, in what seemed like slow motion, Grant moved his
hand into his jacket and pulled out the chisel, its sharpened blade catching a little dull light from the candles,
briefly reflecting before he dug it into her, her chest heaving and then caving in under the blaze. Saz heard a soft
thud and the sound of a gentle slap as the metal made
contact with the flesh. She lunged forward to stop Grant
but the four slow motion steps she made to get to him
took too long, Jasmine was already dying, blood gushing
from the deep wound in her face where he'd stabbed her
the second time and pouring more slowly from the first
jagged hole in her chest. Her blood was on the ground,
mingling with the petrol and she fell, crumpled into the
same shape her father made beside her. Saz grabbed
Grant's hand, knocking the bloody chisel flying, she was
screaming now, they all were. Max's screams barely audible through his dry, swollen mouth. Saz saw Jasmine
fall, her hands clutching at her head and chest, feeling
and motion in her lower limbs already gone. The chisel
flew against one of the candles, knocking it over and
almost instantly the floor around them was swimming in
flames. Grant scrabbled over Jasmine's body, her left
hand still flailing, and reached for Max. He picked Max
up and, stumbling, Max's pyjama bottoms on fire, he
tried to carry him to the door. As he did so he kicked
Jasmine's legs out of the way and her petrol wet clothes

caught the flames around them. Saz watched Jasmine's hand saw the air and then crumple beside her, she pulled at Jasmine's head, clumps of hair coming away in her hands and then retreated as the flames took over the whole of Jasmine's body, streaming up from her legs, covering the torso and the already closed eyes.

Saz stumbled away from the circle, smoke-blind, the room pitch black, she could hear Grant making his way to the door with Max but she couldn't see either of them. Max was moaning in pain from the burns on his legs and Grant was trying to untie his hands and feet so they could move faster. Saz followed the sounds, finding the door and letting herself out just as the flames swallowed up the surrounding wall and forced her out into the hallway. Grant was dragging Max down the stairs trying to get away from the flames that followed them in the trail of petrol Jasmine had set. By the time she reached them Max and Grant had again been caught in another wave of fire, pinned up against the long staircase window, trying to get away as it lapped around their feet. Maxwell North had stopped his hoarse howling and Grant had given up trying to untie the bonds on the feet, the bonds that had been burnt off along with much of the flesh on his calves and ankles.

Max was calm, the dryness in his throat had taken over again and he was no longer able to cry out, but now he didn't want to, the pain in his feet and legs had been taken over by another sensation. He was there and not there. He was watching as Saz called to Grant from the other side of the flames and he found he was interested but didn't care. He watched her shouting at Grant through the smoke. She stood on one side of the flames and called through the noise, the smoke and heat and fumes catching in her throat and making her retch as she did so.

"Jump to me, I'll catch you."

"I can't, he's too heavy."

"Then throw him first, this is getting worse, I can hardly see you. Grant, you have to come this way, you can't break that glass."

"I can't leave him."

"Then throw him."

Max felt himself thrown and closed his eyes as he fell into the flames, their heat surrounding him and he opened his mouth, not to scream this time but to drink in the fire. Max smiled, opened his eyes, bathed them in soothing flames and then closed his eyes again.

Saz fell under the heavy weight of the burnt man. The heavy weight of the dead man. Max's legs caught in the flames again and Saz was caught under him as what was left of his jacket started to burn. The smell of searing flesh brought back incongruous thoughts of summer barbecues, picnics by the river with Cassie and their parents and Saz was floating close to them, close to her childhood pictures. Then Grant was beside her again, he pulled Max's body to himself, freeing Saz who dragged herself to her knees, the pain of her own burns clearing her head. Grant crouched down beside her, trying to hold life into Max.

"It's too late Grant. Leave him."

But the more Saz pulled at Grant, the more he clung to Max. Finally the flames beat him off, a few seconds later when his own hands and arms were too burnt to hit out the flames on Max's body any longer and the fire coming at them was level with his face, Grant turned and, with Saz supporting most of his weight, they stumbled and fell and crawled down the back staircase, out into the street and the strangers who had gathered for the viewing.

CHAPTER 40

The two charred bodies were removed for examining later when the ashes were cold. Very little was made of the chisel cut found in Jasmine's cheekbone, the coroner was an old friend of Max and assumed it was his doing. Both dead, he decided there was really no need to mention it in his report.

Caron McKenna sold the London house and almost immediately moved to New York where she opened a gallery of her own, stunning the city within six months with a shocking and hugely successful exhibition based on the revitalizing nature of fire. A year later she met a new woman and once again shocked the establishment by coming out. Her father maintained he never got over the shame, but her mother made visits to New York every three months and liked nothing better than to stay with Caron and Glenda whenever she could.

Grant went back to the States for rest and reconstructive plastic surgery to his hands and face and within three years was running the European Process Centre in the Hague which was taking the Process into eight other European nations and would soon be working on an international basis. When he regained the use of his hands he sent Saz a shakily printed get well card. She didn't bother to reply.

The burns Saz had incurred – mostly to her legs, stomach

and hands – healed very slowly, the healing partly held up by the depression that accompanied them. A depression to do with Saz's feeling of failure as much as the pain she had gone through. She did however, have her own private doctor in attendance and the weeks of enforced bed rest gave her the sleep she was desperate for and gave Molly the time she'd been longing to spend with Saz.

"Not that I'd wish this pain on anyone Saz, but I do love coming home and knowing you'll be here."

It also gave Saz enough time in Molly's flat to learn to call it home.

She chose not to tell the police about Grant. She didn't have a clear reason for this but she knew it was something to do with her own guilt at having let him be in a position to hurt Jasmine in the first place. Her own guilt at enlisting the help of someone she'd chosen to trust, not because she knew him and knew his value, but because of his persuasive manner, his words, his charm. She felt as culpable in the deaths of Maxwell North and Jasmine as she assumed Grant did. Or should.

Saz did tell the police all she knew about Maxwell North but, with no supporting evidence and a marked lack of interest from those whose job it should have been to care, Max's record remained unblemished. Certain people firmly believed that no good would come from raking through the ashes of Max's life. As one of the civil servants responsible for allocating funds to mental health research told both the coroner and the investigating officer at a damage limitation meeting,

"It's a man's work that counts once his life is over, and we know the girl was completely mad anyway. She must have been. Max was a good chap."

The three men laughed and closed their folders. Funding for the initial stages of the nationwide implementation of the Process was approved.

Five months later Saz finally took her long-awaited holiday with Molly, not to the sun, but to Molly's parents in Scotland.

As Molly explained,

"Saz, believe me, the last thing you need when you're trying to grow new skin is winter sunburn. We'll go and stay with my parents. It's cheap, the food's wonderful and you certainly won't be tempted to rush out and strip off for a swim when it's snowing outside."

Saz turned over in bed and looked at Molly.

"Is that a polite way of saying you don't like the look of my scars?"

Molly pulled the sheets back gently. She kissed the puckered, dark red skin on Saz's naked stomach, then the thick long grafts on her lower legs, finally taking both of Saz's burnt hands in her own.

"Saz, I loved you before these scars and I still do now. You're my girl, the same girl. Lightly toasted or fried to a crisp. It's all right. OK?"

Saz nodded and closed her eyes, but as she fell asleep under Molly's watchful gaze she saw Jasmine's hand flailing around in the petrol and the flames, she felt the weight of Maxwell North's dead and burning body as it fell against her and she knew she wasn't really the same girl. Not yet. She hoped Molly would wait around until she was.

Serpent's Tail

1986 to 1996

TEN YEARS WITH ATTITUDE!

"If you've got hold of a book that doesn't fit the categories
and doesn't miss them either,
the chances are that you've got a serpent by the tail."

ADAM MARS-JONES

"The Serpent's Tail boldly goes
where no reptile has gone before ... More power to it!"

MARGARET ATWOOD

If you would like to receive a catalogue of our current publications please write to:

FREEPOST, Serpent's Tail,
4 Blackstock Mews, LONDON N4 2BR

(No stamp necessary if your letter is posted in the United Kingdom.)